THE
LOCAL

THE
LOCAL

A LEGAL THRILLER

Joey Hartstone

DOUBLEDAY · NEW YORK

Copyright © 2022 by Joey Hartstone

www.doubleday.com

DOUBLEDAY and the portrayal of an anchor with a dolphin are registered trademarks of Penguin Random House LLC.

Book design by Cassandra J. Pappas
Front-of-jacket photographs: building © Joe Sohm/
Visions of America/Getty Images; man © Roger Wright/
The Image Bank/Getty Images; truck © Tami Ruble/Alamy
Jacket design by Michael J. Windsor

Library of Congress Cataloging-in-Publication Data
Names: Hartstone, Joey, author.
Title: The local : a legal thriller / Joey Hartstone.
Description: First edition | New York : Doubleday, [2022]
Identifiers: LCCN 2021056776 (print) | LCCN 2021056777 (ebook) |
ISBN 9780385547819 (hardcover) | ISBN 9780385547826 (ebook)
Subjects: LCSH: Murder—Investigation—Fiction. |
LCGFT: Detective and mystery fiction. | Novels.
Classification: LCC PS3608.A787566 L63 2022 (print) |
LCC PS3608.A787566 (ebook) | DDC 813/.6—dc23/eng/20211203
LC record available at https://lccn.loc.gov/2021056776
LC ebook record available at https://lccn.loc.gov/2021056777

MANUFACTURED IN THE UNITED STATES OF AMERICA

1st Printing

To Abby,
my collaborator for a lifetime.

To Teddy,
our collaboration of a lifetime.

PART I

—◆—

IN LOCO PARENTIS

In the Place of a Parent

· ONE ·

Small towns are defined by their secrets. Some are even haunted by them. There is a communal consciousness that remembers everything no matter how hard people may try to forget. You can't keep a secret in a place like this, at least not forever.

Marshall is only forty miles from the state's eastern border but still deep in the heart of Texas. Folks live and die with the Mavericks on Friday nights and seek salvation in church on Sundays. Since World War II, the population has remained unchanged at twenty-three thousand souls. It's almost as if there's no incentive to come here, but people can't find a good reason to leave either.

We have an equal number of white and Black citizens, but the scars of inequality run deep. The ghosts of slavery and segregation still roam our streets. To this day, a statue of a Confederate soldier casts a shadow over the town square.

Behind the bronzed effigy of Johnny Reb stands the old Harrison County Courthouse. Its bright yellow facade, marble columns, and domed top make it our unofficial capitol building. Lawyers love a good courthouse the way players love a good ballpark. It makes us believe that our lot in life is more important than it probably is. The best lawyers in these parts, however, don't work in this building.

Just beyond the hand-laid redbrick parking lot of the old county courthouse stands another building, another courthouse. It's a simple beige-and-brown rectangle, thirty feet high, with small columns in front. Its demeanor suggests you need not notice it at all. This is the Sam B. Hall Jr. Federal Building, home to the US District Court. For the past twenty years, the Eastern District of Texas has been the epicenter of intellectual property law in the United States. It is Marshall's best-kept secret.

For some reason that morning, as I sat at the plaintiff's table with my client and a team of lawyers from the Chicago law firm of Rosewood & Barkman, I was overcome with a feeling of awe. It was the final day of my final trial for the calendar year, and I found myself in a moment of reflection. As I looked up at Judge Gardner's wrinkled face, I couldn't shake the idea that the kingdom he had built was as impressive as it was improbable, and that we all owed him a debt of gratitude.

There had been whispers around the courthouse for months that the judge was contemplating stepping down. People were even speculating that he would announce his retirement that night at the annual Christmas party. I dismissed these rumors as baseless because I believed he would have told me privately if that were his plan. Still, I'd had a sense lately that he was trying to savor certain moments as if they were passing by, never to return. As he glanced in my direction, I wondered if he felt a sense of pride. I was, after all, his protégé. He had crafted me in his image.

"Mr. Euchre?" Judge Gardner drew the court's attention my way without revealing any affection for me. After I'd spent five days sitting quietly beside my client with nothing to do but ponder the wonders of our universe, the time had come for me to do what I'd been hired to do. I was going to deliver a closing argument.

"Thank you, Your Honor." I rose to my feet but didn't button my jacket. I walked toward the eight members of the jury in complete silence. It was the first time they would be hearing from me since they were selected, and I wanted to give them a few more beats. I found my mark and then hesitated, as if unsure of how to begin. Truthfully, I knew every word that was about to come out of my mouth. I was going to deliver my patented "Ford pickup" closing. As a matter of legal fact, a collection of words, such as a speech, cannot be patented but rather copyrighted. Suffice it to say, it was my favorite summation.

"When I was fifteen years old, the widow who lived next door to me decided to sell her late husband's truck. It was a 1964 Ford F100 with a cracked windshield, missing fender, and dented grill. Its original Rangoon Red paint job, which perfectly matched the high school's colors, was peeling and had faded under the sun. It was the most beautiful vehicle I'd ever seen.

"I struck a deal with the widow. In one year, I would buy that truck for twenty-four hundred dollars. Bagging groceries at the Kroger for three thirty-five an hour wasn't going to cut it, so I got a paper route and started mowing lawns on the weekends. I took any odd job I could find, and for one year, I didn't spend a penny unless I absolutely had to. Where most boys would keep a picture of their girlfriends in their wallets, I had a photo of this old truck, a reminder of what all the hard work was for. The best day of my young life was when I emptied out my savings account, handed my neighbor all twenty-four hundred dollars to my name, and became the proud owner of a Ford pickup. When I got behind the wheel, a feeling of achievement washed over me. I'd never felt that way before.

"Two weeks later, I stepped outside my home with the keys in my hand and discovered that the driveway was empty." I paused here, as if overcome by the memory.

"I'm embarrassed to admit how many minutes passed before I accepted the reality. I'd never owned anything, and now my one possession in the world had been stolen. For weeks, I kept my eyes peeled, hoping I'd spot my Ford abandoned somewhere, just waiting for me to rescue it. Then one day I get a call from Detective Elliot.

He says they think they may have found it up in Marion County, but before they go and accuse someone of grand theft auto, they want me to confirm that it is indeed mine.

"So Detective Elliot drives me to Marion, and we pull up to this ratty old house with weeds for a yard, and there, parked right in front for all the world to see, is a 1964 F100 with a cracked windshield, missing fender, and dented grill. I jump out of the cruiser and run up the driveway. Just then, a man in his twenties comes out of the house and hollers at me to get off his porch. I move right to him, fish my wallet out of my pocket, hold the photo of the Ford up in his face like it's a police badge, and declare, 'My name is James Euchre, and that is my truck!'

"The man looks at the photo and then back at me and says, 'That can't be your truck. Your truck is red. That truck right there is black.'" I paused again, allowing the audacity of this comment to infect my listeners.

"Not only had this man taken my vehicle, but now, caught dead to rights with my property in his possession, he had the nerve to deny everything because, after he had stolen my beloved truck, he had covered that original Rangoon Red body with a cheap coat of black paint."

For all of the flaws in our legal system, the one thing that we got right was entrusting ordinary people to dispense justice. Even in a field as complicated as intellectual property law, we put our faith in common citizens. Patents can be incredibly complex. It often takes an advanced degree in electrical engineering or microbiology to understand how something works, let alone whether or not the idea behind it was taken from someone else's design. The lawyers from the firms on both sides of this case had spent the past five days asking these jurors to think. In my first five minutes, I had asked them to feel.

Every one of us has a different capacity to understand information based on who we are, what the subject matter is, and how our education and intellect relate to the issue at hand. What makes us alike, what makes us human, is that we all experience the same range of emotions—the same fear, the same love, the same rage. My job was to distance the jurors from the complicated facts of the case and remind them how it feels when someone takes what is rightfully theirs.

I loved my Ford closing for a lot of reasons, but principal among them was that it genuinely enraged me. By the time I was done talking about the bastard who stole my truck, my own blood was boiling. And emotions are transferable. Of course, I would ultimately bring my discussion back to the issues at hand, but not until every one of those jurors was thinking about their own experience of being wronged—that time someone hit their car and didn't leave a note, the day their boss took credit for their hard work, that moment when they were victimized by a faceless thief, never to be made whole again. Once that courtroom was overflowing with rage, I turned our collective attention to my client, the plaintiff who was wronged in this case, and I gave the jurors the power to make it right.

I stepped toward the plaintiff's table. Typically, I represented corporations, but in this case, my client was a home economics teacher with arthritis from Skokie, Illinois. Over the years, as Marta Sexton's condition had worsened, her doctors had prescribed her more and more medication. One day, her hands were in so much pain that she could no longer open her childproofed pill bottle. Frustrated but not defeated, she conceived of a new design for a medicine container that didn't take much force or a strong grip to open but was still impenetrable to a young person's inquisitive paws. Inspired by a combination lock on a high school locker, she sketched a design that required a person to line up three designated spots on the pill bottle with three corresponding points on its twisting cap. Once all three arrows on both components were aligned, the top would lift off easily. It was something that any patient could use and no child could hack. Thankfully, Mrs. Sexton filed for a patent.

The United States Patent and Trademark Office is located in Alexandria, Virginia, and is an agency within the Department of Commerce. If you have an invention, or if you have a design for an invention, or if you have an idea for a design for an invention, you can apply for a patent. If someone or some company infringes on that patent, you can sue them in federal court. Which federal court? That's the billion-dollar question.

One day, Mrs. Sexton was walking through the Hartsfield-Jackson airport in Atlanta when she stopped at a kiosk that sold phone chargers, candy bars, and other travel accessories. On one of the shelves was a variety of medicines. She thought it would be a good idea to take an aspirin before flying. So she bought a bottle of pills and some water and went to her gate. As she prepared to board, she removed the pill bottle, and lo and behold, it was childproofed. To the untrained eye, it may have looked like any other medicine container. But my client saw something different. She understood the specs, the modifications, and every working component of this little plastic contraption right down to the familiar three-part locking mechanism. Her blood, sweat, and tears had gone into inventing this design that someone, or rather some company, had stolen. When her plane landed at O'Hare, her first call was to Rosewood & Barkman.

The company that created the medicine was headquartered in upstate New York, while the pill bottle itself had been manufactured in a factory in Seattle. It was well within Mrs. Sexton's rights to file her patent infringement suit in either the Northern District of New York or the Western District of Washington, but that was the opposition's home turf. She also could have filed suit in the Northern District of Illinois, her own backyard. All of these options would have made a lot of sense since these were the venues where the item was invented, where it was stolen, and where the company that profited was based. But what about the Atlanta airport? When an employee at that kiosk put one of those products on their shelves, a product that contained my client's intellectual property, that was an act of patent infringement. Of course, she wasn't going to sue the owners of a little kiosk because they don't have deep pockets, but that didn't matter. What mattered was this: a lawsuit can be filed anywhere in the country that a single act of patent infringement has occurred. Since Mrs. Sexton was the wronged party, it was her choice where to file suit. With all the kiosks in all the airports in all the country, the options were almost limitless. The best option though, at least for the past twenty years, has been the Eastern District of Texas. The reason is Judge Gardner.

Gerald Gardner was born on March 24, 1944, down the road toward Kilgore, next to the old ghost town of Danville, Texas. He grew up playing baseball and football like most boys, but his true passion was acting. He enrolled at Southern Methodist University in 1962 and found his home in the theater department. His favorite professor encouraged him to pursue his craft professionally, but Gardner replied, "I have no interest in going to Hollywood or Broadway and I doubt either has any interest in coming to Texas." Not wanting his theatrical training to go to waste, Gardner chose to stay at SMU and earn his law degree.

Good lawyers are performers. It's not an act, which is to say that it's not fake, but there is an element of show to it. Gardner turned examining a witness into a mystery. Every closing argument was a soliloquy. People would travel from neighboring counties just to watch him in a big trial. One time, a court even handed out popcorn. True story.

Every law firm from Houston to El Paso tried to recruit him, but he didn't want to work for anyone else. He was content taking whatever clients happened to come his way in East Texas. He was also adept at creating opportunities seemingly out of thin air.

One such job involved an oil and gas company from Lubbock that needed to resolve a land rights issue. It didn't bring in significant business, but Gardner secured the deal and managed to impress the executives, one of whom was a young man by the name of George

Walker Bush. Decades later, when a federal judgeship in East Texas became available, one of our US senators recommended Gerald Gardner. President Bush nominated him the following Monday.

To say that Gardner was inheriting an unimportant venue would have been an understatement. The Eastern District wasn't exactly a hotbed of criminal activity or major litigation. But Gardner wasn't the type of person to rest on his laurels. The dearth of cases was a blessing because it gave him the freedom to reinvent his court how he saw fit. In his entire career as an attorney, Gardner had only had one patent case. It was, as patent trials tended to be, a clusterfuck. But where there was chaos, he believed he could create order.

Judge Gardner overhauled the whole trial process. First, he allowed for broad discovery of materials so that lawyers couldn't drag things out indefinitely with pretrial motions. Second, he set trial dates in stone. There would be no delays, no excuses. More than a few attorneys had to miss the births of their children so that they could appear in Gardner's courtroom as scheduled. And third, he limited the lengths of the trials themselves. In most jurisdictions, a typical patent case could last weeks, sometimes months. But Gardner believed, "If God can create the universe in six days, surely we can finish a patent trial in less time." Five days was his limit.

With these changes, EDTX had the capacity to become one of the most efficient and effective courts in the entire country. It took a little time, but eventually the legal world realized that the new judge had designed the perfect place to sue for patent infringement.

So where did I come in? Lawyers are licensed to practice law in specific jurisdictions, namely in the state or states where they have passed the bar exam and where their law firms are based. When a case takes lawyers out of their jurisdictions, they need to add someone within the new state to the team. That someone is called local counsel.

A local can do as much or as little as the rest of the team demands. Often, a local counsel does nothing more than advise the team on any unique quirks of that particular venue and serve as a signatory on any documents that need a regional John Hancock. All of this can be done for a nominal fee. Clients may never even realize that a local is on their team. That's how it used to be in Marshall. After all, intellectual property law is complex, and no one in East Texas had ever tried a patent case. Lawyers here, though, had other skills that aren't taught at top ten law schools. It didn't take long for white-shoe law firms to discover that something was missing, something essential that local counsels could provide.

Here's a scenario that happened too many times to count. A twin-engine Cessna Citation with the inevitable moniker "Law Firm One" touches down at the quiet Harrison County Airport. Six attorneys step off their firm's jet, all wearing bespoke suits purchased on Madison Avenue. A private car, probably from Dallas, picks them up and drives them five miles, past broken fences and run-down trailers, into town. They march into the courthouse with Italian leather briefcases and polished expert witnesses. A casual observer may understand that this doesn't go over too well with our juries, but rich and powerful people often lack self-awareness. There was a major disconnect between our humble citizens of Marshall and these corporate attorneys from big cities. To make matters worse, some of these people thought they could fake their way into the good graces of the jurors. I've seen out-of-town lawyers go straight from the airport to the Boot Barn on Pinecrest Drive, buy a pair of shiny new Buckaroos, and then walk their blistered feet into court as if they've just come from the ranch. Mistakes like this have cost clients millions.

The top patent law firms around the country began to realize that what was missing from their teams was someone who spoke the language, someone who could connect with the eight citizens on the jury. The more we locals were asked to speak, the more the jurors seemed to listen. Locals, who for so long had been undervalued and underused, were finally being called upon to perform an indispensable service. Like strong pinch hitters and clutch relief pitchers, our roles were small but vital. And we began to be paid accordingly.

So it came to pass that the best trial lawyers were not in Houston, Austin, or Dallas but rather in a small corner of the state, practicing an area of law that none of us had ever studied, working on cases worth tens or even hundreds of millions of dollars. We were the final component to a billion-dollar industry, a magnificent legal universe created by one visionary judge in Marshall, Texas.

· TWO ·

I concluded my summation and returned to my seat, where I would spend the rest of the morning watching an attorney for the defense deliver his closing argument. My work was done, and I felt it had gone well. I'd made the desired connection with the jurors and hoped I'd left them with the feeling of rage. If all went according to plan, they'd deliberate swiftly, return a verdict in favor of my client, and award her a nice chunk of change.

Once this case was completed, I would have five weeks of nothingness in front of me, as December faded into January. After remaining relatively sharp and clear-eyed for the trial, my plan was to drink my way into the darkness and emerge in the new year rejuvenated, even if I would be a little worse for the wear. If the verdict was good, my night would inevitably begin with a champagne celebration. If it was bad, I'd crack a beer and begin my descent alone on a barstool. Either way, I'd end the night with a solitary bottle of whiskey that was waiting for me at home. I had a feeling I'd be tasting the bubbly before the night was through.

During my closing, I had noticed a familiar face in the rear of the courtroom. I spun around in my chair to take a second look. Abraham Rabinowitz, a top lawyer from New York, was sitting in the last row. He was dressed sharply and his silver locks, despite being wet and combed back, were beginning to break free into their natural state, which resembled a lion's mane. On either side of him were a man and a woman whom I did not recognize, though I assumed were his clients. They were both considerably younger than he was. I gave Abe the slightest wink, and he nodded back. Whatever he wanted would have to wait until the next recess.

The defense gave a ninety-minute closing argument, during which I saw two jurors nod off. It was an unceremonious conclusion to a case they hadn't presented particularly well. The court reporter distributed Gardner's written instructions to the jury. Someone along the way had screwed up because there were seven copies instead of eight.

"Don't worry about mine, Judge," said Juror Number Three. "I can't read none anyway."

The Chicago lawyers couldn't hide their contempt. A complicated patent design and a verdict worth millions were about to be in the hands of eight people with six high school degrees between them, one of whom was apparently illiterate. It was classic EDTX, and I loved it.

"Well, you'd better listen extra close then, sir," said Judge Gardner. His Honor read the instructions aloud, and then the jury retired to the deliberation room. There was nothing left to do but wait.

As I expected, Rabinowitz motioned for me, and I held up my index finger to let him know I'd be there in one minute. Abraham Rabinowitz, or "Honest Abe" as I liked to call him, was a top litigator at the Manhattan-based firm of Gordon & Greene. He couldn't have looked less like Abraham Lincoln if he tried. He was a short man whose midsection was shaped remarkably similarly to the matzo balls his mother used to make. Originally from the Brownsville neighborhood in Brooklyn, Abe was, to me, the quintessential New Yorker. I called him "honest," but more accurately he was blunt. He simply didn't have time for bullshit. I admired him for this, and our juries often embraced him because he didn't pretend to be anyone other than his authentic self.

Abe's firm specialized in intellectual property law, so it handled a lot of cases in Marshall, and while he used the services of a few locals, I was Abe's favorite. We shared a similar perspective on how the game should be played and an appreciation for the other's roles in it. We also won a lot more than we lost.

As I approached him, he stepped away from the man and the woman with whom he'd been sitting so that we could speak alone.

"Jimmy! You looked good out there today."

"Thanks, Abe."

"I give it a nine-point-three. You started out strong, but you didn't stick the landing."

"Everybody's a critic."

"I grade you on a steep curve."

"I didn't know you were in town," I said, putting an end to my performance review.

"Just for the day. We have an eligibility hearing this afternoon."

"In front of Gardner?"

"It was supposed to be downstairs with the magistrate judge, but since you guys have this wrapped up early, maybe Gardner will hear it after all."

"Those are your clients?" I asked, motioning to the couple in the back, who looked uneasy in their unfamiliar surroundings.

"He's the client. She's new to our firm."

At second glance, she did dress the part of an attorney. I should have pegged her as a lawyer. Despite the fact that half of the prospective jurors in Marshall were Black, it was still rare to see a Black attorney in EDTX. Aside from general racism in hiring, the prevailing "wisdom" was that a Black attorney was more likely to alienate our white jurors than gain the support of our Black ones. It had taken an embarrassingly long time for firms to finally begin to reject this theory. In addition, the firms that had expanded their hiring practices were discovering not only the benefits of diversity but also a great deal of untapped talent.

"Any chance you can join us for lunch?" Abe asked.

I looked back at the plaintiff's table with Mrs. Sexton and the

Chicago lawyers. I'd been eating with them all week and was getting tired of hearing about how much better the food was in the Windy City.

"I'll see if I can sneak away."

Abe leaned in toward me. "This client's going to be spending a lot of time in Marshall." That was music to my ears. I preferred representing plaintiffs, but a defendant who gets sued repeatedly can bring in a lot of business. I nodded, letting Abe know I'd make it to lunch one way or another.

"Hey, Jimmy, let me ask you something." I stopped and waited for his question. "Did you ever actually own a Ford pickup?"

I grinned. Not a lot of people would have had the balls to ask me that outright. "Come on, Abe. All the best stories are true."

I broke off from the Chicago lawyers and exited the federal courthouse. As I walked across the brick parking lot, I spotted the district attorney, D. Calvin Lucas, and two of his underlings heading toward the old Harrison County Courthouse. "This must be where the real lawyers are at," I said as our paths crossed.

"It's not patent law, but we can't all do God's work," replied D-Cal, as those of us who'd known him since grade school called him. He was a special breed of asshole. He was a born politician, and everyone expected that the DA's job was just a stepping-stone to his higher aspirations. I figured he was a good enough attorney, but he suffered from big-fish-in-a-small-pond syndrome. He was a prosecutor in a town with no crime. In another universe, Lucas and I could have been good friends. In this universe, though, we'd been competitive for far too long to be anything but adversaries.

"Best of luck taking down the shoplifters and jaywalkers, D-Cal," I said as I continued on my way.

I made a quick stop at the little tobacco shop just off the square. A box of Dominicans was on display next to the cash register. By the smell of it, I suspected a customer had extinguished one only a few minutes earlier. The smoke was gone, but the sweet scent lingered. I asked the clerk for a pack of Marlboro Reds and a plastic lighter. I'd retired from being a full-time smoker years ago, but I treated myself to one pack at the end of every trial. I was overpaying by buying them there, but I liked the atmosphere. The clerk handed me my cigarettes and a pink lighter.

"Sorry, that's the only color we got left," he said.

I rolled my thumb down the spark wheel and watched the flame come to life. "The fire's still orange," I replied.

As I walked the side streets, I kept thinking about the deliberation room. Juries are the great enigma of the trial process. Anyone who says they can confidently predict which way a verdict will go is full of shit. Juries are as varied as the people that comprise them. Still, there are patterns that can emerge. About two years into Gardner's tenure, the new judge had overhauled his court, but no one had really noticed yet. Then a big piece of the puzzle fell into place, one that would solidify EDTX as the ideal venue in which to sue for patent infringement. That piece happened to be the juries.

Out in Fort Worth, around the turn of the twenty-first century, lived an eccentric inventor named Neil Sampson Carlyle. Carlyle worked in his shed, sketching elaborate designs for new devices and thinking up ways to improve upon old ones. One cloudy April day, inspiration rained down on him, literally. A monsoon tore into town, and Carlyle's ratty old roof was no match for the torrential downpour. He ran around placing buckets and bowls under every leak in the ceiling. When the storm broke, he climbed up on top of his house and discovered that the wood-shingled roof looked like Swiss cheese. He'd been doing some sculpting work with lightweight concrete and decided to repurpose the material for roofing. He covered his house with new shingles he'd made in his shed. The next time it rained, his house remained bone dry.

Carlyle set a meeting with a major building supply chain based out of Dallas. He showed some samples to the executives, did a demonstration with a garden hose, and assured them that this composite concrete could be the future of roofing technology. They were interested and said they'd think about it, but a month later they passed on the product. Carlyle forgot all about it and moved on to whatever else popped into his mad-scientist brain next. Two years later, Carlyle was out walking his Australian shepherd, Elroy, when what did he see? A neighbor's house had a brand-new roof made of lightweight composite concrete. He had a hunch about which company had manufactured the materials. Turned out, he was right.

Carlyle hired a lawyer, and they went to file their suit in Dallas but were told there was a backlog of cases and they should expect to wait at least eighteen months just to get into a courtroom. The lawyer did some digging and came up with a list of about twenty cities and towns where the company had sold this roofing product. One of them was Marshall, Texas.

Carlyle's suit was filed in the Eastern District. Judge Gardner granted broad discovery of the company's documentation, R&D work, and financial records, and then set a trial date. One look at a side-by-side comparison of Carlyle's patent and the company's new product, and you didn't have to be an expert in carpentry to conclude they were identical. Moreover, not only did Carlyle clearly own the patent, but he had made detailed contemporaneous notes about his meeting with the company's executives, right down to the many questions they asked him about how the product was made.

After a four-day trial, the jury retired to deliberate, and the building supply company sensed impending doom. Carlyle's lawyer was asking for $4 million in damages. The attorneys for the company met in the hallway and convinced their client to offer $1 million to settle the case and another $1 million to buy Carlyle's patent outright. Carlyle decided to roll the dice and take his chances with the jury.

It took the eight jurors a little over an hour to reach their decision. As the foreman would later recount, "We knew the verdict right away. The real discussion was about the amount." The jury found that the company had infringed on Carlyle's patent, and then, in what became the shot heard round the patent litigation world, they awarded Carlyle damages in the amount of $70.2 million. Where the .2 million came from, we'll never know. If you ask me, it was just an added "fuck you" to the man.

Word of this massive award spread throughout the intellectual property law community, and Gardner's docket was quickly flooded with patent cases. Everyone watched closely to see if Carlyle's verdict was an outlier. Turned out, it was the norm. One by one, plaintiffs in EDTX were not only winning their patent cases, but they were also being awarded ungodly sums of money. This created a gold rush.

Lawyers, politicians, hell, even sociologists would spend the next decade trying to explain what was going on with these juries in East Texas—they were not only unusually sympathetic to plaintiffs in patent cases but were also prone to delivering verdicts with huge dollar amounts. Thousands of legal articles and dissertations were written on the subject, but it all boiled down to this: when people who are overlooked for their entire lives are given a modicum of power, they will wield it with great force.

There was a stampede to EDTX. Nearly every plaintiff in the country wanted to file suit in the Eastern District. Most courts wouldn't have been able to handle the influx of new lawsuits, but thanks to the way Judge Gardner had rewritten the rules, his venue was designed with efficiency in mind. The speed with which Gardner's court burned through patent trials became legendary, and it earned his court's calendar the nickname the "Rocket Docket."

· THREE ·

I spotted Honest Abe seated along the near wall of Central Perks. It was a short walk back to the federal courthouse if the jury reached a quick verdict. I had hoped this meeting would be a short one. Ordinarily, Abe would have simply asked me to join him on a case, but apparently this particular client had insisted on vetting me first.

Abe embraced me with the warmth of an old friend. "Jimmy, allow me to introduce you to Mr. Amir Zawar. Amir, this is James Euchre, the best lawyer in Marshall."

"Nice to meet you, Mr. Zawar." I shook his hand. He was at least a few years younger than I was and, I suspected, tens or even hundreds of millions of dollars richer. At about five feet ten inches, he looked to be very physically fit though not overly muscular. I pegged him as the type to be more fixated on his core strength than the size of his biceps, a lesson he surely learned from his personal trainer.

"And this is Layla Stills," Abe said as she rose from her seat with determination and shook my hand firmly. She also seemed to be in great shape, though given her line of work, her exercise regimen was probably limited to running on a treadmill while reading legal briefs, or some other activity that allowed for multitasking.

"A pleasure, Ms. Stills."

"Layla joined us at Gordon & Greene last month."

"It's always nice to meet a new associate," I said.

"I'm counsel, as a matter of fact."

The difference meant something, and I liked that she felt compelled to highlight it. She, too, was probably a couple years younger than I was. If she had joined Gordon & Greene on the partner track, she must have had an impressive résumé.

"Is your background in IP?" I asked.

"Criminal law," she answered.

Abe jumped in. "Layla was an AUSA in DC for seven years. She's got more time in court than you and I combined." I admired the way he always looked out for his people.

I took a seat across from Amir. Layla sat beside him while Abe positioned himself at the head of the table, between me and his client.

"So what brings you to Marshall, Mr. Zawar?" I needed to get the meeting started.

"It's not your Southern hospitality," he said with more than a hint of indignation. This didn't faze me. No one likes being sued, and most clients despised being sued in EDTX.

"Jimmy, Amir created a company called Medallion. There was a big profile last month in *The New Yorker;* maybe you saw it?" I shook my head. I didn't want to insult the man by admitting I hadn't heard of him, but it was better not to begin with a lie. "Why don't you tell him about it, Amir?"

"My father came to this country from Karachi, Pakistan, when he was nineteen years old. He drove a taxi in New York City for almost four decades. He worked every day of his life to earn his piece of the American dream." As Amir described his background and highlighted the pertinent details that would become ingredients for his future business ventures, I figured he'd told this story before. But it didn't feel overly rehearsed. His occupation was more than a job; it was a calling. I was also struck by Amir's sincere admiration for his old man. It was a feeling so foreign to me that I had to remind myself that his was authentic.

Over the next ten minutes, Amir told me all about his father's life. He had arrived in New York in the early eighties and found work driving a cab. For a quarter of a century, he saved every dollar he could with two goals in mind. The first was sending his son to college. The second was one day becoming his own boss. For a driver in the Big Apple, that meant owning a taxi medallion.

The city of New York issued a limited number of medallions and you couldn't drive a cab without one. As the years passed and the population grew, medallions became more and more valuable. By the twenty-first century, a taxi medallion was seen not just as a license to own a cab but as a piece of equity that would appreciate over time. Most medallions were controlled by a handful of companies, but if an individual driver could scrape together enough money to buy one himself, it could be his ticket to financial independence.

"In 2006, my father took out a loan and purchased a medallion, using all of his meager savings for the down payment," Amir continued. "He was, in his mind, working for himself now. He had to make loan payments every month, but this was just like paying the mortgage on a house. Eventually, he would own it outright, or so he thought."

Wherever there is honest money being made there are dishonest people scamming for their unfair share. The predatory loans in the medallion industry put the housing loans of that era to shame. Amir's father, like so many, was an easy mark for those unregulated companies awarding loans to mostly immigrant drivers, some of whom couldn't read the English in which the loans were written.

"For the next eight years, my father took in $6,000 per month, $4,500 of which went to paying off his loan. It was steep, but at least the value of the medallion was going up. He had purchased the medallion for $650,000. Eight years later, they were going at auctions for $1.1 million. So my dad's net worth rested not on his income but rather on what percentage of his medallion he owned. Tragically, he would discover that he didn't own it at all."

Amir's father had unwittingly been put on an interest-only loan payment plan. In eight years, he hadn't paid off a single dollar of the principal. To make matters exponentially worse, right around the time he and scores of other drivers like him were discovering the truth behind the shady loans they'd signed, the bubble burst. Medallion prices that had skyrocketed for decades began to plummet. The lucky drivers were the ones who got out just in time, defaulting on their loans and simply walking away with nothing. The unlucky ones were on the hook for million-dollar loans while their medallions were suddenly worth less than a third of that. They were underwater with no hope of resurfacing. Savings vanished, and families were ruined. More than a few drivers took their own lives. Others, like Amir's father, were simply broken. His health declined rapidly as the bills piled up and threats of foreclosure weighed heavily on his mind. By the time he passed away, he had become a shell of his former self.

"Predatory lending I understand, but what caused the bubble to burst?" I asked.

"Uber," said Abe, who hadn't spoken for several minutes.

"Rideshare apps," Amir clarified, "did massive damage to the taxi industry. Men like my father had been the lifeblood of cities like New York. Then, almost overnight, they were kneecapped, undercut by Silicon Valley."

If I had read the profile in *The New Yorker,* I would have known the rest of the story. Amir had three semesters at Caltech under his belt when his dad's financial problems began. Unable to cover tuition, Amir was forced to drop out. He managed to find work as a programmer in California, though. Then, after he buried his father, Amir had an idea.

"I created Medallion because I believe that the gig economy must embrace the people it generally displaces. My mission is to build an organization that welcomes in workers like my father." As a general rule, I didn't like Silicon Valley bros, but I had to admit that Amir was a compelling figure.

"I saw that Uber and Lyft were decimating the taxicab industry in cities all across America," he continued. "So I developed an app that would give customers the convenience of a rideshare service with the reliability of a professional taxi company."

"Doesn't New York City already require a special license for ride-share drivers?" I asked, failing to see the novelty of the idea.

"That's merely a way to limit the number of cars on the streets," Amir responded, "but to the customer, there's no difference at all. You're still likely to end up in the back of a college student's beat-up Hyundai Sonata. There are passengers who want a truly professional experience, from the driver behind the wheel to the vehicle itself. The problem is that it's more convenient to order a car from your phone than to stand on the street and hail a cab. What Medallion does is take licensed taxi drivers and their cabs and transform them into a rideshare service. Operators can drive as they usually would, picking up random passengers on the street, or when they want assistance finding customers, they can turn on the app and be paired with riders. Rather than displacing an entire sector that helped build this country, we made taxi drivers an essential component of our service."

It was an ingenious twist on a popular idea. It was also the kind of alteration to protected intellectual property that so often found itself on the wrong end of a lawsuit in Marshall.

"So what can I do for you, Mr. Zawar?" I asked, hoping to get down to brass tacks before I had to return to court. Instead of answering me, he looked at Abe to respond.

"Several suits have been brought against Medallion. Today's hearing involves the first of many. The claimant is a software company called Astral that designed a navigation program that, it claims, Medallion's software infringed on. We've got an eligibility hearing this afternoon, and trial is set for April."

"If there is a trial," added Amir.

My eyes met Abe's. This client was hopeful. Someone needed to administer a dose of reality. Abe ran his hand through his long hair, an unconscious gesture intended to lower his blood pressure. "That is one thing we wanted to discuss with you," Abe started. "Amir is insistent that if the case is not dismissed today we should ask for a change of venue."

A motion for a change of venue can be brought for a variety of reasons, but typically lawyers do this when they believe that a case either belongs in a different jurisdiction or that the jurisdiction in question cannot render impartial justice because of some inherent bias. Patent defendants have been complaining about being sued in EDTX for twenty years, but changes of venue were never granted. They also irritated Judge Gardner.

"You don't want to do that," I said. "It'll be denied, and you'll insult the judge."

"So if the case isn't dropped today, we just accept that we're going to trial?" Amir asked.

"The case won't be dropped, Mr. Zawar." It wasn't what he wanted to hear, but it was better to be honest with a client, especially when he was only hours away from discovering that I was right.

"A lot of good it does having the best lawyer in town." Amir's tone changed, no longer attempting to conceal his contempt. "What does that title get you, anyway? A blue ribbon at the county fair?"

"Amir," Abe said, "let's keep going."

"Medallion has no affiliation with this town," he continued. "I'd never even heard of this place until I got sued. My company doesn't do business in this shithole. So can we at least stop pretending that my presence here is in any way appropriate?"

Amir's grievances were nothing new. Medallion was joining a club of frustrated defendants from companies like Apple and Boeing to Xerox and Zappos. None wanted to belong to this group, but most had accepted that there wasn't much they could do about it. It was the cost of doing business in America.

"I understand that no one likes being party to a lawsuit, and it compounds your resentment when it takes you away from home. But patent litigation is our specialty," I said, referring to the collection of lawyers at the table, "so you should take some comfort in knowing that you're in good hands."

"Medallion has a pilot program in eight cities right now. By Q3 of next year, we will have doubled that. I should be tending to the demands of my business, not wasting away here in Mayberry getting sued by every rideshare company and navigation software developer from Silicon Valley," Amir said. "My father busted his ass to try to get ahead. He did everything that was ever asked of him, and then the system screwed him over. I won't allow that to happen to me."

There were two sides to Amir Zawar. The first was the creator, the visionary who had founded a burgeoning empire that would have made his father proud. The second was the defendant, the man who resented being accused of theft and whose business was under attack. Amir seemed to switch from one to the other as easily as a faucet turns from hot to cold. There was a chip on his shoulder, and it clearly motivated him to succeed. It also told him to fight when his back was up against the wall. I found myself drawn to him, though the fact remained that my least favorite part of practicing law was the clients.

"Look, Amir, I hear what you're saying. Your frustration is understandable. But you've got to let Abe do what he does best. Start with the eligibility hearing. It almost certainly won't go your way, but then you'll have a Markman hearing. That will determine the meaning of the terms in the patent itself and, if that goes well, might even dissuade others from filing similar suits against you. There are several battles along the way before we ever get to trial. So my advice is to keep your head about you and to let your legal team do what it was designed to do."

"And I should make you part of this team?" he asked.

"Well, you're going to need a local counsel—"

"Because Abe doesn't speak hillbilly?" Amir asked.

I let out a little smile. "Actually, Amir, here in Marshall we speak redneck. Hillbilly is a dialect you'd find farther east. But to answer your question, yes, it will benefit you to have someone with my skill set at your disposal."

"And how much is it going to cost me to have you persuade your ignorant neighbors by making a little speech about your missing truck?"

Amir wasn't the first person to call into question my value as local counsel. As he would find out either the easy way or the hard way, though, a local was absolutely essential to his defense.

"Everyone seems to forget that simple people know the rest of the world thinks they're simple," I said. "Consider this for a moment, Amir. Any time we have an election in this country that breaks in a way no one expected, experts from LA to New York are baffled by these unpredictable swing voters. It always makes me wonder, if you're all so fucking smart out there on the coasts, and we're all so fucking simple down here, why can't you figure us out?" This wasn't my normal sales pitch, but Amir didn't strike me as a typical client.

"Jurors are human lie detectors," I continued. "They instinctually sift through all the jargon and all the bullshit to get to the core of a case. They'll never fully understand how your software crowdsources users' geotracking to provide optimal real-time navigational routing. It will never be clear to them whether the interface of your app is novel or if it was built by replicating entire blocks of code pilfered from other rideshare programs. But you're right about one thing, Amir. The fate of your company will ultimately be in the hands of ordinary citizens from Marshall, Texas. They won't trust you one bit, and you shouldn't trust them either. This has been my home since I was a kid. Marshall is in my blood. I will be your advocate. It will be my job to make sure that they see you as a man who built his own company from the ground up rather than as a thief who took something that didn't belong to him in the first place. They will trust me, Amir, because they are me, and I am them."

My phone buzzed, but I held Amir's gaze for an extra beat just to make sure he'd heard me. Then I checked my text. "I've got to get back," I said. "They've reached a verdict."

· FOUR ·

There's nothing quite like the feeling in a courtroom right before a jury delivers its decision. My client fidgeted with her fingers, a nervous habit that likely didn't help her arthritis. Even the Chicago lawyers seemed jittery. As we waited for Judge Gardner, I heard the rear door of the courtroom close. Abe, Layla, and Amir entered and returned to their seats. I figured this was promising news for me. Amir hadn't agreed to add me to his team, but he was intrigued and wanted to see for himself if I could deliver the goods.

Judge Gardner took his seat and then had the bailiff bring in the jury. For some reason, jurors instinctively put on their best poker faces right before a verdict is read. Maybe it's because they've seen enough legal shows on TV to know they should milk the suspense of the moment.

I've always been competitive by nature, so my desire to win was independent of any windfall that might come my way, though I can't say that money wasn't also on my mind at that moment. My fee arrangements varied depending on the case. Sometimes, I simply made my fixed hourly rate and left it at that. Other times, depending on a variety of factors, I worked on contingency, meaning I only got paid if we won. My workload had been particularly busy that year and I had been in high demand. The Chicago lawyers had lobbied aggressively to get me, and so, in exchange for my services, we worked out an alternate fee arrangement in which I would get 3 percent of the total damages, should we prevail.

The foreman was an older man, and I'd fought hard to keep him on the jury. He had done backbreaking construction work his whole life, and I'd had a hunch he'd be sympathetic to anyone who was getting screwed over by a corporation. Judge Gardner asked if they'd reached a verdict, and the foreman stood up and declared, "We have, Your Honor." The courtroom clerk approached him, took the paper with the verdict from his hands, and walked it over to the judge. The verdict form had three pages. The first two pages included my client's claims and the jury's findings. The third page was for the award, assuming there was one. If the jury found that the claims were invalid, that my client's patent had not been violated, then the third page would be blank. As Judge Gardner flipped from the second page to the third, I zeroed in on his eyes. He read the words closely and then read them again. Something was written on that last page. That was good news for us.

Gardner handed the verdict back to the courtroom clerk, and she turned to face us as she read. "'We the jury, in the matter of *Marta Sexton versus Syracuse Pharmaceuticals, et al.,* find in favor of the plaintiff.'" I clenched my fist in private celebration, and my client let out a joyous cry. After reading through the claims and the guilty verdicts attached, the clerk turned to the third page. "'We hereby award the defendant to pay damages in the amount of $23.5 million.'"

Math was never my strong suit, but I did the calculation as quickly as possible. I would clear three-quarters of a million dollars for the law firm of Me, Myself & I. Somewhere in my near future there were champagne corks popping.

Judge Gardner thanked the jurors for their service and dismissed them. I gave a grateful nod in their direction as well. Not only had they just handed me a victory, but I had a feeling that this verdict was going to pay dividends almost immediately with my private audience in the back of the courtroom.

Mrs. Sexton took my hand in both of hers. As she squeezed my palm to show her appreciation, I thought of her arthritis and how joy can help all of us overcome pain. Money doesn't hurt either. I congratulated my colleagues and agreed to meet them for dinner to celebrate. As I headed for the door, Amir Zawar stopped me.

"Mr. Euchre, I'm trying to build something with Medallion, something that proves there's a better way for this world to treat people. If all it takes is a couple of lawsuits to completely destroy a man's work, then something is rotten in the state of Texas."

"Don't give up on Marshall just yet," I said.

"I'd like you to join my team," he concluded. I glanced at Abe and Layla behind him and then back to Amir.

"It'll be my pleasure to represent you," I said as I extended my hand. I'd work out the payment structure with Abe later. For the moment, a handshake would be good enough.

I could feel the outline of the pack of Marlboros in my pocket. Hearing the verdict read had spiked my craving to light one up. Despite my late addition to Amir Zawar's team, Abe had asked me to join them for the eligibility hearing that afternoon. I didn't want the odor of cigarette smoke in court, so I would have to wait just a little while longer.

A patent trial ultimately poses the question: Did Entity B violate a patent held by Entity A? Before a trial even happens, though, a more fundamental question must be asked: Should Entity A have been awarded a patent in the first place? There's a mysticism surrounding patents, a belief that if you hold one you belong in the archives of history with Thomas Edison and Benjamin Franklin. But the truth is, all it means is that a couple of nerds in the patent office looked over your application, spent an hour or two doing a half-assed job reviewing it, and then rubber-stamped their approval. A lawsuit tests the true merit of the patent.

In the case of *Astral Navigational Systems v. Medallion, Inc.,* Astral's claim was that the Medallion app had infringed on its patented navigational software. Amir's company hadn't done anything as audacious as steal programming from its competitor. But Astral's patent was broad, and its claim largely rested on the definition of the term "mapless."

Whereas other navigational software relied partially or entirely on existing digital maps, Astral's software used no preexisting map technology at all. Instead, its software relied on a combination of original programming and real-time user information. Medallion hadn't replicated Astral's software or even used the same approach. But what Medallion had done was create a navigational system that issued turn-by-turn instructions based on current traffic patterns and the history of its own drivers' optimized routes rather than simply relying on preexisting maps. In doing this, Medallion had opened the door to the lawsuit in question.

Astral was suing Amir's company, and Amir was, in essence, here to make the argument that the patent Astral held shouldn't have been awarded in the first place. According to federal statute 35 USC § 101, a patent must be novel, nonobvious, and useful. If a judge deems that the patent in question fails to satisfy these requirements, he or she can dismiss the claim at an eligibility hearing. Despite the ability to wield enormous power over the outcome of a case, Judge Gardner had great reverence for the Seventh Amendment to the Constitution. He believed that, in almost every single instance, a civil case belonged in front of a jury.

Judge Gardner didn't bang his gavel often. His was a quiet power, understated though universally understood to be intimidating. I didn't know if it was because this was his last piece of business for the year and he was tired or if he found this pairing of boisterous attorneys particularly irritating, but the old man's patience had run out.

"Cross talk will not be tolerated in my courtroom. Mr. Rabinowitz, plead your case and do so succinctly."

Abe straightened his jacket and obeyed the command. "Your Honor, the other side does not allege any infringement based on the software itself or even how it works, with the sole exception that it works without relying on existing maps. It goes without saying that one can patent an idea, but what the claimant is attempting to do here is declare ownership of the absence of an idea."

"Thank you, Mr. Rabinowitz." I don't believe Abe had intended to yield the floor, but he knew better than to overstay his welcome. "Ms. Naruko, your response?" The lead attorney for Astral stood up. I'd never faced her before but knew of her reputation as a formidable opponent.

"Your Honor, I commend Mr. Rabinowitz on his clever turn of phrase, but patenting the absence of an idea is not a new concept. Headphones without wires are patentable. Locks without keys are patentable. When my client conceived of the first navigational soft-ware design that did not use existing map information, it was not only a groundbreaking approach to the field but a patentable design concept as well. To gloss over the word 'mapless' in this suit, or to define it as narrowly as the defendant requests, would be to excise the heart of the matter from the case at hand."

She took her seat before Judge Gardner could cut her off. It was a smart move. She knew she'd effectively argued her point.

"I'm inclined to agree with Ms. Naruko," said Gardner. "The meaning of the term 'mapless' carries considerable weight here. Moreover, I see no need for expert witnesses to complicate the mat-ter when the term speaks for itself. The motion to dismiss is denied. We will proceed to trial as scheduled."

"This is fucking bullshit."

Though he and I were seated three chairs apart, with Layla and Abe between us, I knew Amir had said it. If he'd intended to whisper, he had failed.

"I beg your pardon?" Judge Gardner glared through his glasses at my client.

"I said—"

"Do not address this court from your seat."

Abe rose in his client's stead. "Your Honor, allow me to apologize on behalf—"

"When I want you to weigh in, Mr. Rabinowitz, I will call on you. Mr. Zawar, stand up."

As Abe's ass returned to its seat, his eyes met Amir's and made a silent plea not to make matters worse. Amir rose to his feet.

"If you've got something to say, the floor is yours." Gardner was giving Amir just enough rope. I feared my new client was impulsive enough to hang himself with it.

"I am an innovator. I have spent every day for the past five years building a company. I should be devoting every waking hour to making the best possible product. But instead I'm out here in Nowhere, Texas, defending myself against unfounded claims of patent infringement by hacks from companies that lack the ingenuity to design anything of real value. And what's worse is that they will probably be successful because you welcome parasites into your community with the promise of easy lawsuits and enormous cash prizes. And then you have the audacity to expect someone in my shoes to stand here quietly while these trolls run their scam? I should genuflect before this corrupt institution? If you think I'm going to display even the slightest amount of deference to this court while it threatens to destroy everything I've built, then, respectfully, Your Honor, you are out of your fucking mind."

The judge's face was like stone. "Mr. Zawar, I assure you that you will enjoy the same fair administration of justice that all parties receive in our town. I would also like to remind you that while your corporation is compelled to face accusations of patent infringement in the Eastern District of Texas, your presence here is entirely optional. So you are to conduct yourself in accordance with our high standards of decorum, or you will no longer be welcome in my courtroom. And finally, let me say that for the sake of your company I hope that the ideas on which it was created were far more innovative and original than were the complaints you have raised here today."

The rage seemed to burst through Amir's eyes. "Go to hell."

"Mr. Zawar, you are held in contempt of this court. I am fining you one thousand dollars, and until the clerk has received payment, you are banned from this courtroom." Judge Gardner shifted his attention to some paperwork in front of him, letting Amir know that he was moving on.

"A thousand dollars? I made a thousand dollars in the five seconds it took you to utter that sentence." Amir dug into his pocket and removed a wad of hundreds thicker than the pack of smokes I so desperately wanted to open. He peeled off ten bills and threw them in Gardner's direction as if the judge had just given Amir a private lap dance.

"Is that enough? What's another grand buy me?" He carefully set ten more hundred-dollar bills on the podium in the middle of the court. "How about this?" Amir raised both middle fingers. "Five hundred for each sound about right?"

For the first time since this exchange began, Gardner looked in my direction. It was a look reserved exclusively for me because I was the only person who ever enjoyed leniency from the otherwise rigid judge. Gardner was giving me one chance to protect my client from himself. I jumped out of my chair and moved to Amir, putting my body between him and the judge. Our noses were only inches apart. I wanted him to focus entirely on what I was about to tell him.

"You are doing real damage to yourself. As your lawyer, when I give you advice, I'm going to need you to take it. Starting right now. Sit down and shut up." I put my hands on his shoulders, just to give him a nudge in the right direction toward his chair.

"Fuck you, too!" Amir's hands simultaneously struck my shoulder and face, knocking me backward. I landed hard at the base of the judge's bench. I lifted my head just in time to see the other lawyers scatter and the bailiff tackle Amir to the ground. Amir's reaction was to do the worst thing he could—he fought back. He resisted, writhing his lean frame, trying to escape the bailiff's grasp. The bailiff jammed his knee into Amir's sternum, pinning him to the floor. As Amir struggled to break free, I saw the bailiff remove his firearm.

"No!" I shouted, as I dove toward them, throwing my body on top of Amir's shoulders and face. He was strong, but between me and the 220-pound officer of the court, we were able to roll Amir onto his stomach long enough for the bailiff to fasten the handcuffs around his wrists.

The last clear sentence out of Amir's mouth was "I'll fucking kill you!" Then he wailed in pain as the bailiff forced him to his feet so that he was standing face-to-face with Judge Gardner.

"Lock him up."

· FIVE ·

I sat on the steps of the federal courthouse and dug into my pocket to retrieve the pack of cigarettes and pink lighter. I lit up and removed my necktie. There was a spot of blood about the size of a dime on it. There was even more blood on my favorite shirt. I realized it originated from my split bottom lip. As I exhaled, I tried to let go of the stress from the day. I wondered how much money I stood to make representing Amir. I tried to settle on a dollar amount that would be worth all of the headaches that would surely come.

The door behind me swung open. I turned around and saw Layla emerge from the building, alone. She descended the steps and sat down next to me. "Is that pretty typical for an eligibility hearing?"

I laughed, inadvertently letting out smoke before I'd had a chance to properly inhale it. She set her bag down as if it contained all of her troubles. She breathed a sigh of exhaustion. I held up the pack of Reds, offering her one.

"I don't smoke," she said.

"There are no nonsmokers in a foxhole."

"I'm not sure that's how the saying goes."

We looked out at the town square just as businesses began to vacate for the evening. Some of the shops were fully decorated for the Wonderland of Lights display that was held every winter. Even though the holiday season was upon us, there was a touch of sorrow in the air. It was the feeling that descended upon us every year when Marshall High School's state championship run came to an end. That past Friday, the Mavericks had lost a quarterfinal game to Austin's Lake Travis High, 42 to 6. It would take the town several weeks to get over it. The players never would.

I felt a dull pain in my left shoulder, so I stretched my arm above my head.

"Are you hurt?" Layla asked with genuine concern.

"Just an old football injury. It comes back from time to time."

"Like when a client throws you to the ground?"

"You want to know the crazy thing about that? This was the second time this year someone hit me in court."

"I guess you bring out the best in people."

"It would seem so."

The door to the courthouse slammed open, and Honest Abe stormed out.

"Where the fuck is Texarkana?" Abe said as he jogged down the steps.

"Seventy miles north of here. Is that where Gardner sent him?" I asked.

"Apparently that was the closest federal correctional institution." Abe looked at Layla. "We've got to go bail him out."

Layla stood and gave me a little wave. I waved back, happy to say goodbye to my work for the day.

I hadn't planned on going home before my night of festivities, but thanks to my swollen lip and propensity to bleed, I needed to get cleaned up. I walked into my closet and decided to eschew the suit-and-tie for a shirt and blazer. As I got dressed, I threw my bloodied clothes into a pile in the back of the closet, and I ran through the night's agenda in my head. My first stop would be dinner with the

Chicago lawyers and then on to the Christmas party. It was barely mid-December, but we had to gather before people scattered for the holidays. Knowing that I had a long night of drinking ahead of me, I figured the smart move was to catch a ride back into town. I finished my third cigarette of the evening just as my phone alerted me that my driver would be arriving in one minute.

I climbed into the passenger seat of a four-year-old Nissan. I still felt weird sitting in the back of someone else's car, so I always opted to ride shotgun instead. The Nissan's owner was a guy in his early twenties. He wore a baseball cap and shorts and never exceeded the speed limit.

"You been doing this for a while?" I asked.

"A couple months. Lets me keep my own hours, which is nice because I'm in a band."

Thank God for amateur artists, I thought.

"You drive exclusively for this company?"

"I have a couple apps on my phone, but this is the one most riders use. Sucks, too, because the popular ones don't pay the drivers as much."

"Ever hear of Medallion?"

"Nah, but a new rideshare company pops up every so often. We're always last to get them here, and we miss out on the small ones. If it's legit, it'll eventually make its way to these parts."

I had no idea if this driver knew what he was talking about, but he said it with confidence, and that seemed to persuade me.

We don't have fancy restaurants in Marshall, so there are only two dinner spots that out-of-town lawyers patronize. One is an Italian restaurant that has never seen a tablecloth, and the other is a sushi joint that's at least two thousand miles away from the ocean where its fish were caught. Sometimes opposing legal teams will communicate with one another to avoid going to the same place. This night, however, they had failed to do that. So the only sushi restaurant in

Marshall was jam-packed with lawyers from opposing firms, one celebrating its victory, the other lamenting its defeat.

Given the awkward atmosphere, my objective was to get in and out as quickly as possible. We got the obligatory champagne toast out of the way first. Everyone was in good spirits though I found champagne to be an odd pairing with raw fish. I ordered a Sapporo to wash down my salmon roll. Once the Chicagoans started doing sake bombs, I took that as my cue to leave. I bid them all adieu and trusted that we'd be in touch as soon as they found themselves representing another client in the Eastern District.

I smoked my fourth cigarette while waiting for my next ride. The buzz from the beer was beginning to creep through my veins, and the nicotine gave it a jolt. Part of me regretted not taking my own truck that night. My Billet Silver Dodge Ram 3500 was only a few months old, and I was still enjoying the hell out of driving it. I bought a brand-new truck every two years. It was the one financial indulgence I allowed myself. To me, the point of success was making money, not spending it. Also, part of my job was to relate to my fellow Marshall resident. I couldn't do that if I appeared to forget where I'd come from.

The annual Christmas party, which was never to be referred to as the "holiday party," was held in the old Harrison County Courthouse. The inside of the building matched the awe-inspiring outside. Every floor had a circular hole in the center, twenty feet in diameter, so if you stood in the middle of the main level and looked up, you could see all the way through to the dome's ceiling. During the party, the offices around the perimeter of each floor were closed, but lawyers, judges, clerks, and other employees were free to roam.

By the time I arrived, the place was crowded. My colleagues from the federal court made up only a small fraction of the partygoers. The majority in attendance were employees of the county, many whose departments were in that building. I spotted D-Cal holding court with his staff in front of the DA's office on the second floor. He tipped his drink in my direction when he caught me looking at him.

I could never quite figure out if people enjoyed these events or if they simply felt compelled to attend. I counted myself somewhere in the middle. As a solo practitioner, it was nice to be reminded that I was part of a larger community. Though most of them would never set foot in the federal court, I still recognized that we were a clan of sorts.

I made my way to the makeshift bar on the first floor. There were four beer options, as well as one label of red wine and one of white. I selected what seemed like the most palatable of the domestic beers and started to mingle. I took the opportunity to say hello to as many of the clerks and office workers as I could find. Not only did they keep their respective courts running, but I found them easier to talk to than other lawyers. There was also less chance of my saying something that would come back to bite me in the ass, which was becoming more and more likely as I exchanged my empty bottle for my fifth drink of the night.

"Euchre, I need to talk to you a minute."

I recognized the voice as I turned around to see one of my least favorite people on the planet. Samuel Earl Whelan was 145 pounds and stood five feet six inches on his best day yet was always preening with his chest puffed out as if he were the heavyweight champion of the world. Thanks to a perfect blend of nepotism and dumb luck, he managed to become a successful patent attorney, another local in EDTX. He was the physical manifestation of the Dunning-Kruger effect, the principle that unbridled self-confidence is often found in those who are utterly incompetent.

"What do you want, Sam?"

I hadn't spoken to him in a couple of months, not since he'd cold-cocked me in open court. We'd been opposing locals on a weeklong trial. In my opening statement, I had mocked Sam's entire understanding, or misunderstanding, of the case. He had cited bad precedent, forgotten key facts, and even referred to his client using the wrong company's name. It was clear that he was the weakest part of his side's case, and I used every opportunity to exploit that. I also made passing comments to Sam under my breath, little jabs at his expense that a fragile ego like his wasn't built to withstand. My needling had taken its toll, because Sam delivered a particularly terrible performance at the end of the trial. Even the jurors seemed embarrassed for him as he struggled to recall the most basic arguments his side had put forth. After he'd completed his closing argument but before he'd reached his seat, I had stood up and begun my summation by saying, "Now that the court's jester has spoken, it's time to hear from the actual lawyers." Sam whirled that little body of his in my direction and punched me, nearly rendering me unconscious. I'd generally considered myself a tough person, but I was developing a habit for getting knocked down, and it was concerning. Ultimately, Sam was removed from the courtroom, while I managed to deliver my closing in the same amount of time it took for my left eye to swell shut.

"The evidentiary panel set a date for my hearing," Sam said, as if I was supposed to know what the hell he was talking about. "Before the chief disciplinary counsel . . . my conduct hearing."

"Oh, that. I guess the state bar doesn't take too kindly to lawyers committing assault and battery in court."

"You insulted me."

"Is that an apology?"

"When the old man retires, you're done getting special treatment. So maybe it's time you start playing nice."

"Maybe," I replied. "Or maybe we just cross that bridge when we come to it."

"Stop being an asshole, Euchre. I could lose my license."

"It's honestly a miracle you even had one in the first place."

I could see his fuse shortening. Even as he sought my help, all he wanted to do was commit another act of violence. Watching him swallow his animosity was rather enjoyable.

"All you need to do is write a letter to the disciplinary counsel on my behalf."

"You forgot to say 'please.'"

I was ready for him to take another swing at me.

"Fuck you, Euchre."

Our stare-down was interrupted by the clinking of silverware on glass, the unmistakable call for a toast. Sam and I separated as people turned their attention to Tammy Lamb, whom everyone referred to as "Tammy Tex." She stood in the center of the main floor so partygoers on higher levels could look down and see her. Tammy was the court clerk for Judge Jay Knox, the magistrate judge for EDTX. Judge Knox handled all of the work Judge Gardner was too busy to deal with. He was a dignified man in his early fifties, handsome and quiet, projecting an air of professionalism with everything he did. His court clerk was a perfect counter to his reserved demeanor. Tammy had become the de facto leader of all of the legal assistants in town basically by steamrolling anyone who got in her way with her unrelenting kindness. There wasn't a prouder Texan anywhere. She always wore the Lone Star State's flag pin on her lapel, and her office looked like it belonged to the reigning Miss Texas.

"I want to thank y'all for being here tonight, celebrating the birth of our Lord and Savior. To kick off the spirit of Christmas, all of the clerks and assistants from the various courts are passing out a little gift to our beloved judges."

As if following orders, about a dozen women, each of whom served a different judge, presented their bosses with a small present. There were judges from the district and county courts, as well as four justices of the peace. Each received a gift-wrapped box about the size of a book but longer and not nearly as wide. They were wrapped in Texas flag wrapping paper.

It had become an annual tradition for the judges to give their assistants a Christmas bonus and for the assistants, in turn, to give them a small token of their appreciation. Apparently not wanting the gifts to be opened in the moment, Tammy reclaimed the floor. "While we are paying tribute to our esteemed judges, I want to highlight one in particular. We have a notable milestone upon us. Judge Gerald Gardner has just completed his twentieth year as a federal judge!" Tammy looked toward a side wall where Judge Gardner was standing. He acknowledged the applause, and Tammy motioned him to take center stage.

Tammy slinked off to the side and stood next to Judge Knox while a hush fell under the domed ceiling. I noticed more than a handful of my fellow locals paying particularly close attention. We braced ourselves for the revelation we'd been dreading. If Gardner had, as expected, reached a decision to end his tenure as the judge of EDTX, this felt like the appropriate time to announce his retirement.

"It's good to be with all of you tonight. As I get older, I've learned to embrace moments that allow for reflection. The first time I set foot in this very courthouse was to represent a client who needed help with a building permit. It wasn't exciting work, and I'm not sure I ever collected my forty-dollar fee, but I'll never forget walking through those doors and being struck by the realization that I was finally a real lawyer. So much has changed, so much has been built in our town and in our profession. I am honored to have played my small part in that. I am grateful to have worked alongside all of you, my colleagues, for so long. It has been the greatest privilege of my life to have served for twenty years as federal judge for the Eastern District of Texas." He paused and held a thought all to himself. He ran his forefinger along his brow and then scanned the faces of his audience, as if searching for an answer. His eyes met mine. I could tell something was weighing heavy on him, but as soon as he realized I was trying to get a read on him, he smiled, allowing whatever was plaguing him to seemingly evaporate into thin air. "And the good Lord willing, I look forward to serving here for another twenty years."

A sincere applause echoed all the way up to the dome and back down to the marble floor. For the patent lawyers in the building, we were the beneficiaries of the gold rush that Gardner had contrived. None of us was eager to see him leave. But it was more than just self-interest. Gardner's tireless devotion to the world that he had created earned him genuine affection. I couldn't imagine the Eastern District without him.

· SIX ·

I stood in front of the old courthouse, contemplating whether or not I should go back inside when I finished my cigarette. I had been at the party for over an hour and managed to slip outside without anyone noticing. It seemed I had flawlessly executed the Irish goodbye without even trying. All I had left to do was leave.

I looked up at the Confederate statue that stood in the middle of the walkway. The concrete path split into two as it passed the monument, only to rejoin like a river whose flow was temporarily divided. The statue had been placed on the east side of the courthouse in 1905 by the local chapter of the United Daughters of the Confederacy, an organization that had aligned itself very closely with the Ku Klux Klan. The official dedication ceremony for the statue took place the following January, on Robert E. Lee's birthday. Not too long ago, a petition was drafted and delivered to the city council calling for the statue's removal, in part because: "[It] was erected to promote and justify Jim Crow laws in the South and assert white supremacy." But this part of the country had a reputation for fighting hard to defend the indefensible. I wondered if one day soon the Confederate statue might disappear into the night. The town would wake up to discover that the bronze soldier had executed his own Irish goodbye, never to be heard from again.

As I stepped on my cigarette butt, I decided I was done with the party. I took out my phone to call for a car when I heard someone yell out to me, "James, my boy, I was afraid you had left." Judge Gardner worked his arms into his coat as he joined me outside. "Hell of day for you, young man."

"It was one for the books," I replied.

"I see you've already begun your celebration," he said, referencing my freshly extinguished cigarette.

"I earned it."

"Walk with me," he said, motioning to the far side of the parking lot where his granite-colored Chrysler 300 was parked. In his hand, he held the gift that was still wrapped in Texas flag paper. "Take this for me, would you?"

"You haven't even opened it?"

"It's a fountain pen with a Texas flag on it. Tammy Tex has given us the same thing for the past three years. The woman's got a heart of gold and the memory of a goldfish."

I chuckled and took the gift. The truth was Gardner was as uncomfortable accepting gifts as he was praise. He was a stubborn old judge, and I loved him for it.

"Do you have plans for the holidays?" he asked, more out of concern than curiosity.

"I intend to catch up on some bad habits and then see what the new year has in store for me."

"I worry about you, kid."

"I'm fine, Judge."

"Law and liquor do not a full life make."

I grew quiet, not liking where the conversation was heading. He stopped walking and faced me.

"James, I've remained silent out of respect for what you've been through—"

"I have everything I want."

"Then you don't want enough." He squinted, trying to determine if his comments were hitting their mark. "Sometimes a life can become so small that you can hardly see it at all."

"Life is supposed to be small in a small town," I shot back.

I'd been having a relatively enjoyable night up until that point. I couldn't believe that the last person I was going to interact with, my favorite person in the world, was hell-bent on ruining it.

"I'm not really sure where you get off telling someone else to change their life," I said, "especially when you just declared to a room full of people that you intend to spend the final chapter of yours doing the exact same thing you've always been doing. Why don't you make some changes, you fucking hypocrite? All you have is the Eastern District."

Even as I said it, I regretted it. Gardner never married, never had any children. But he'd been more of a father to me than the man who had given me life. In fact, when I was in law school, and abandoned by my old man for the last time, it was Gerald Gardner who stepped in. My dad's name had opened doors for me because he was something of a celebrity in the Texas legal community. So when I got caught cheating on an exam, the dean of the law school called him up. My father, the famous defense attorney, advocate for people who were in the worst kinds of trouble, told the dean to throw the book at me. I would have been expelled, too, except Judge Gardner intervened on my behalf. He'd already hired me to clerk for him the upcoming year, and I told myself he didn't want to go through the hassle of finding my replacement. The truth was that he was looking out for me. His own father had died when he was a boy, and I think he sympathized with the pseudo-orphan in me. He knew that, in many ways, I had always been fatherless, so he stepped into the role. In loco parentis, as we say in the law. Judge Gardner served in place of the parent.

As we stood by his car, I felt sick. A night's worth of booze was meant to dim my world, but in an instant, Gardner had shined a sun's worth of light on my existence.

"Why are you coming at me like this, Judge?"

"Who else is going to do it?"

I had no answer and he knew it. He let the conversation end, telling me he needed to swing by his office. We said goodbye, and I watched him walk away and disappear into his courthouse.

I didn't know what woke me. It was still dark outside. I had stopped at a bar on my way home and downed another couple beers before ultimately landing on my couch with a bottle of Jack. That's where I'd passed out only a few hours earlier when my ringing phone disturbed my drunken slumber. I opened one eye and saw that the number was unknown.

"Hello," I said, barely audibly. My voice was nearly gone thanks to the Marlboros.

"James Euchre?"

"Yeah," I said with more force and a little irritation.

"This is Sergeant Moffard. We've arrested a client of yours, and he asked that we call you."

"My clients don't get arrested," I replied, now fully aware that it was still the dead of night, and I did not want to be awake. I got this call once or twice a year. Usually, some high school pal of mine would get popped for a DWI, and in his inebriated stupor, he'd remember me, the only lawyer he'd ever known. I'd have to explain that I'm a patent attorney and unable to do anything for him. It wouldn't have bothered me except people tend to get arrested while everyone else is in bed. "Tell him to sleep it off and talk to the public defender in the morning."

"Mr. Euchre, he's not drunk. And he says he won't talk to anyone but you."

"Who is it?"

"His name is Amir Zawar."

I drove myself to the Marshall police station even though my blood alcohol content was probably still above the legal limit. The adrenaline had cleared my mind, and I felt my synapses firing as I approached the north end of town. I ran through all the reasons Amir might have landed himself in jail for the second time in one day, but nothing jumped out at me.

I parked near several patrol cars and tried to weave my way through on foot. I discovered that my balance wasn't perfect as my knee banged the fender of the one closest to the entrance. I limped inside and was met by a uniformed officer and the smell of fresh coffee. I'd expected the graveyard shift to be quiet, but the hum of the fluorescent lighting was drowned out by a burst of activity. There were cops in blue and detectives in suits hustling through the halls. I felt as if everyone were here for the same reason, and without knowing what that reason was, I sensed I might be a part of it.

"I'm James Euchre. You've got my client in custody."

"He's in holding," said the officer, who didn't look old enough to drive a car, let alone have a badge and a gun. He escorted me past the break room and a row of desks. He unlocked the door to a windowless room, and a group of cops watched as I followed the officer inside.

Amir was alone, handcuffed with his arms behind his back. He jumped up when he saw me. "This is racist, small-town bullshit—"

"Don't say a fucking word!" I nearly shouted at him. I had already witnessed Amir's loose lips get the better of him in court. By no means an expert in criminal law, I knew that rule number one was to keep your mouth shut. Technically, I was Amir's lawyer, so our attorney-client privilege extended to matters beyond patent law, but there was no privilege if an officer was in the room with us.

I turned to the young cop. "Any chance Detective Elliot is around?" I asked, hoping I could find a familiar face.

"He's out on an investigation."

"At this hour?"

The young cop shrugged.

"Who's the watch commander?"

"Sergeant Moffard."

"I need to speak with him. In the meantime, you want to get those handcuffs off my client?"

"That's not my call, sir."

I looked back at Amir. "Have you spoken to anyone else?"

"No."

"All right. Abe just texted me. He's on his way. So hang tight and stay silent."

Amir nodded. I followed the officer out.

A crowd of police had formed near the holding room during my brief meeting with Amir. It was clear that whatever he had been arrested for had gotten the attention of the entire Marshall Police Department. Suddenly, I felt completely out of my element. It wasn't a feeling I was accustomed to, and it made my stomach turn.

I sat at the watch commander's desk, across from his empty seat, when he entered without shaking my hand.

"I'm Sergeant Moffard. We spoke on the phone."

"James Euchre."

"This is one hell of a mess, Mr. Euchre."

"What's he been charged with?"

"We haven't charged him with anything. Yet."

I felt stupid for having asked that particular question. They had seventy-two hours to hold him without charging him with anything. I hadn't thought about criminal procedure since my second year of law school though. I was rusty and it showed.

"Why has he been arrested?" I asked, choosing my words more carefully.

"Suspicion of murder."

I had started to suspect something serious, but I hadn't entertained anything close to murder. My mind raced through options for my next move, but I quickly decided it was best to wait for Abe. I had a duty to my client, and given that I was not a criminal defense attorney, the best way to serve him was for me to remain as quiet as I'd admonished Amir to be until the cavalry arrived.

I stood up and told the watch commander that I needed to step outside. I stopped at his door and turned around. I could hold off on knowing most of the information, but I couldn't help but ask what seemed like the most obvious follow-up question.

"Who was killed?"

"Judge Gerald Gardner."

· SEVEN ·

As I stood outside the police station, I saw things I hadn't noticed on my way in. There were at least fifteen squad cars, haphazardly parked. A few were on the lawn right out front, as if their drivers hadn't had the time to put them in an appropriate spot. There were a dozen officers standing around, and nearly all of them were on their phones. The sun hadn't even come up yet, so I had to assume they were talking to other law enforcement or emergency personnel, people who would need to be called in to work a homicide.

I didn't know if the police knew who I was, but this was a moment for high alert, and I could feel their eyes on me. I walked toward the edge of the lawn, away from the building, and sat at the base of a large oak tree. I'd left my house in such a hurry that I'd forgotten my smokes. I didn't really want a cigarette anyway.

My brain was flooded with questions, wanting to know what had happened to my mentor, my friend with whom I had been speaking only hours before. But I didn't want all those answers, not yet anyway. I wanted to remain in that fragile state after you learn something terrible has happened but before you accept that it's true. I guess I just wanted to sit with the memory of Judge Gardner for another moment.

A nondescript sedan, which could only have been a rental car, peeled into the parking lot. Abe and Layla jumped out and hurried toward me. "What happened? Where is he?" Abe demanded. I couldn't find the words, so I simply pointed toward the police station, and they ran inside. I wasn't ready to join them.

I came into this world quietly on November 22, 1977, in a cramped delivery room in Parkland Memorial Hospital. It was fourteen years to the day that President John F. Kennedy had been pronounced dead in the very same building. And so it was that at the time of my birth, even in a nursery room full of new life, an air of sorrow cast a chill. Every year, on the anniversary of his assassination, a crowd would gather outside of Parkland to honor the fallen president. My own father stepped out for a few minutes to pay his respects. It would mark the first time he left me and my mother.

One day, after years of being underappreciated and overlooked, Mom finally had enough. She told her sister it was his sneaking around with other women that forced her hand. I think it was the daily reminder that his work was more important to him than we were. Whatever her reasons, she woke me up that September morning, fixed me a bowl of Honey Nut Cheerios, and told me to eat quickly while she loaded the last of our belongings into the station wagon. There weren't a lot of options for a woman whose last place of employment had been an all-night diner outside of Fort Worth a decade earlier. So with Dallas in our rearview mirror, we headed east on I-20, a mother and her eight-year-old son, bound for the hometown to which she had vowed never to return. It would become my adopted hometown as well.

Marshall was the kind of place where people looked out for one another. Folks knew a single mother could use a helping hand every now and then, so they pitched in. I had my fair share of surrogate fathers. Detective Elliot, the man who would later drive me to Marion County to identify my stolen Ford pickup, would come by during his night shifts when he knew my mom was working and make sure I'd had my supper. It wasn't uncommon for coaches and teachers to send a little extra attention my way. But the most important guardian angel I had entered my life the summer before my senior year. Football practice wouldn't start for another couple of weeks, so a few of us on the team got the bright idea that we should break into the school, cover our bare asses with every color of paint in the rainbow, and press our rear ends up against the wall that led out to the main entrance. With perfectly stenciled letters, we painted the words: "Class of '96: Shoot for the Moon!"

The paint was removable, but since we didn't have a key, we broke a fairly expensive door to get inside. Our buddy Mikey sat outside listening to a police scanner, and as soon as he heard the call for a break-in at Marshall High, he laid on his horn and then took off. Two police cars pulled up just as the rest of us were rushing out of the exit. We knew we could outrun the cops on foot, but even varsity athletes aren't faster than squad cars.

It's hard to look a woman in the eye when she's been called away from her second job to bail you out of jail. We didn't even make it into the parking lot before my mom started hollering at me, telling me she couldn't afford a lawyer, let alone the money she'd just forfeited by leaving her shift. As fate would have it, an attorney overheard my mom's reprimands and asked if he could lend a hand. Gerald Gardner offered his services pro bono, but that didn't sit right with Mom. She insisted I work off my debt. Gardner managed to get the charges dropped, and I got my first unpaid internship. By the end of that summer, I wanted to be a lawyer just like him.

With Abe and Layla inside the station, I approached two cops whose name tags identified them as Sergeant Jefferson and Sergeant Ramirez.

"Can I ask you officers a couple of questions?"

Jefferson, who was at least fifteen years older than his colleague, looked me up and down for an exaggerated beat. "Got nothing to say to no lawyers." He spit near my foot, which was something I didn't realize people actually did. Then he went inside the station.

"Sergeant Ramirez, I'm just looking to understand what happened."

The younger officer seemed torn. "I'm not authorized to speak with an attorney."

"The victim was a friend of mine. I was with him at the end of the night," I offered. This eased Ramirez's reluctance to speak. Once he realized I could help them narrow the time-of-death window, he agreed to return the favor with some minimal information of his own.

Judge Gardner was found dead in the redbrick parking lot, near his car. He'd been stabbed and, by the looks of it, had bled out quickly. Other officers had sealed off the crime scene while Ramirez and Jefferson arrested Amir at a nearby house and transported him to the station. As far as Ramirez knew, no one had found the knife or anything else that could link a murderer to the killing. Ramirez said he didn't know much more than that.

"When did you last see the victim?" he asked me.

"In the parking lot of the old Harrison County Courthouse. At about 10:35 last night."

I headed toward the building.

"I'm going to need to take your statement," the young officer insisted.

"Did Detective Elliot get assigned this investigation?"

"I believe so."

I suspected Elliot hadn't handled a murder investigation in years, but he was generally understood to be a solid detective.

"I'll give my statement to him. He knows where to find me."

I went back inside and found Layla sitting on a bench usually reserved for arrestees. Before she could speak to me, Abe's booming voice echoed through the building. "Then wake him up! I need to speak with someone who's got some goddamn authority here!" Abe stormed out of the watch commander's office and slammed the door behind him.

Layla and I were silent as Abe approached. "Amir wants to talk to us. All of us."

"I'm not going back in there," I said matter-of-factly.

"He's insisting you join."

"If you put me in a room with him, I can't guarantee we'll both come out of it."

Abe wisely shifted gears.

"I know how much Gardner meant to you."

"Then you know why I can't go in there."

"He says he's innocent."

"Isn't that what they always say?"

"He's a stranger in a strange land, and the only representation he's going to get right now is what the three of us can cobble together. I'm not asking you to do anything except come in and listen to what your client has to say."

· EIGHT ·

The teenage-looking cop took me, Abe, and Layla to a different room at the end of a short hallway. The walls were made of large cement bricks and had been painted bright white, almost matching the floor and the ceiling. It felt antiseptic, though I suspected that the metal table bolted to the ground hadn't been cleaned in months. There were two chairs on one side of the table and a third on the other.

"I'll try to find another seat for you," offered the officer.

"I'll stand," I said curtly.

The officer stepped out. As the three of us waited for Amir, we swapped what little information we had managed to acquire. I told Abe and Layla how the cop outside had described the crime scene and said they hadn't found a murder weapon. Abe and Layla filled me in on what had happened earlier in the day, after the eligibility hearing had concluded. The original plan had been for Abe, Layla, and Amir to drive the 172 miles back to the Dallas/Fort Worth airport, drop off the rental car, and fly back to their respective cities that night. However, after Amir's outburst in Gardner's court, he was taken to the nearest federal lockup in Texarkana, 73 miles in the wrong direction, and processed. It took a few hours for his lawyers to secure his release. By the time he was freed, they had missed their

flights and decided to spend the night in Marshall and drive to Dallas early the next morning.

Typically, out-of-towners who come to Marshall on patent business stay at the Fairfield Inn & Suites out by the interstate, about
four miles from the courthouse. The rooms are clean enough, but it's
what you'd expect to find in a hotel on the side of a highway. Since the
firm of Gordon & Greene argued a high volume of cases in Marshall,
a few years back they purchased a four-bedroom house on the 200
block of South Franklin Street, a stone's throw away from the courthouse. Abe affectionally referred to this house as "the Compound."

Gordon & Greene bought the property for $189,000 and their
lawyers used it for both lodging and as a base of operations when
they had a trial in Marshall. Due to the unplanned nature of their
extended stay that night, Abe thought it best to let their new client
have the Compound all to himself so he'd be more comfortable. My
guess was, after the way the eligibility hearing unfolded, Abe was
concerned about losing Amir's business and worried that stashing
him in a dumpy room at the Fairfield would have been the final straw.
Abe, Layla, and Amir ordered takeout and ate dinner at the Compound at around eight o'clock. The lawyers departed shortly after
and checked in at the Fairfield. Their plan was to get up early, swing
by the house to get Amir, and drive to Dallas for midday flights back
to New York and San Francisco. What Amir had done after Abe and
Layla departed the Compound was unknown to them.

Two uniformed officers brought Amir in. They didn't speak as they
sat him in his seat, leaving his handcuffs securely fastened to his
wrists. Amir wore the pants he'd had on in court and an undershirt.
He was hunched over a little. The officers left us alone to confer
with our client. The heavy door slammed shut behind them. I stood
against the wall and never took my eyes off of Amir.

"I didn't kill anyone." His voice shook.

"Tell us what happened last night, after we left the Compound." Abe was calm enough to coax Amir into talking.

"Nothing happened. You left, and I caught up on emails, read the news. I was a little tired, but I couldn't fall asleep. I stepped outside of the house—"

"What time?" Layla interjected. She still had a prosecutor's fixation for details.

"I don't know. After two o'clock."

"What were you doing outside?" Abe asked.

Amir paused. I tried to read his face.

"I smoked some weed."

"Where'd you get it?" Abe continued.

"I brought it with me. It calms me down. And I wanted to go to sleep. So I smoked half a joint on the porch, and then, when I was done, I realized that the door had locked behind me. I walked around the house and tried the back door, but it was also locked. The windows, too."

"Why didn't you call us?" asked Layla.

"I'd left my phone inside the house. And the code to the door was on my phone."

Abe had installed a keypad-locking mechanism to the front door so lawyers at the firm didn't need to worry about physical keys when they stayed at the Compound. Amir hadn't memorized the six-digit code.

"So you broke a window?" Abe said with a hint of incredulity.

"It was the middle of the night. What was I supposed to do, walk around looking for a locksmith? I couldn't think of a better solution and I was freezing. So yeah, I found a rock and broke the small window next to the back door. I was able to get my hand through and unlock it, but the alarm was already going off."

"You armed the alarm before you stepped out to smoke?" Layla was voicing my own skepticism.

"No," Amir said. "I didn't even realize there was one."

"It must have been the glass-break alarm," Abe said. "It's not like the alarms on the doors. The glass-break is always armed."

"Yeah, and apparently it works," Amir added.

"And then what happened, Amir?" Abe was growing impatient.

"Like three minutes later, the cops break down the door, guns drawn. I put my hands up and kept screaming, 'Don't shoot! Don't shoot!' One was shouting at me to turn around while the other kept ordering me to lie down. Fuckers looked trigger-happy, so I just froze. Then they threw me to the ground, jammed a knee into my back even though I wasn't resisting, and finally handcuffed me. I told them who I was. I told them to call you, but they wouldn't listen to me."

Amir was livid as he recounted being held for nearly half an hour on scene. The responding officers continued to interrogate him, demanding to know why he'd broken a window in a house where he was supposedly a guest. He tried to convince them to call the hotel though he couldn't remember the name of the place where Abe and Layla were staying. Then, about fifteen minutes into the questioning, additional officers arrived, and everything got more tense. Four officers searched the Compound, while Amir continued to repeat his story to no avail. Finally, they stood him up and told him he was being placed under arrest. He demanded to know why and that's when they told him he was being booked on suspicion of murder. That was, he claimed, the first he'd heard that someone had died. It wasn't until he arrived at the station that he overheard the officers say it was Judge Gardner who had been killed.

"So a local hero is murdered and racist cops arrest the only person who looks like me in this whole fucking town. Case closed," Amir said, apparently feeling he needed to make a closing argument. His arrogance was beginning to wear on me.

"You were held in contempt of court for an angry outburst at a federal judge who had you arrested and hauled away to jail," I said, making sure not to blink. I wanted Amir to see every thought, every emotion on my face. "Then, only hours later, that same judge is murdered in a parking lot a couple hundred yards from where you are staying. Officers respond to a breaking and entering and find you, the only person awake in town, high and agitated. And, as it turns out, the person you despise the most in Marshall just happened to have gotten himself killed right around the time you stepped outside to smoke a joint. Either you're the unluckiest son of a bitch on the whole fucking planet . . ."

Abe turned around and looked at me, wanting me to stop. I didn't need to finish my thought. I'd made it clear I wasn't about to pretend Amir's story might be true.

Abe decided we'd done enough interrogating for the moment. "All right, Amir, in a few hours we should have more information. In the meantime, they're going to keep you here. Is there anyone else you'd like us to contact?"

"Yeah, call Haq."

"OK," Abe said. "Is that all?"

"I'm cold."

I'm not sure why, but this comment almost sent me over the edge. I couldn't imagine what kind of a man, accused of murder, manages to concern himself with his body temperature. I wanted to ask the officers to crank up the A/C in his cell just to make it more frigid, but then I understood that Amir wasn't asking for a change in temperature. He wanted something else to wear. Abe was in his suit jacket, but he had about a hundred pounds on the client. As Amir looked at me, I realized he and I were roughly the same size and that my denim jacket with flannel lining must have looked pretty warm to him right about then. There was no chance in hell I was going to give him the coat off of my back.

We three lawyers exited the police station. Abe seemed unaffected by the cold air, even though he'd surrendered his jacket to Amir. "Layla and I will make some calls back at the hotel and see what other information we can get our hands on. Let's touch base in a few hours." I nodded and looked at Layla, who tightened her lips down and to one side, as if she knew words would fail in that moment. I could sense her sympathy though.

I climbed into my truck, unsure of where to go or what to do. I stopped at the first gas station I saw for a pack of Marlboros. I'd found the pink lighter in my pocket, though I couldn't remember when I'd put it there. As I drove with the window down, I realized I was instinctively heading toward the courthouse.

The redbrick parking lot was sealed off with yellow police tape. Black-and-white cruisers were parked at each entrance. There were several unmarked cars as well. I assumed some belonged to the people whose navy windbreakers bore the letters "FBI." I could see several small placards placed throughout the lot, markers for potential pieces of evidence. I wondered what more they'd found and if any of it could be linked to Amir.

A makeshift shrine of flowers and cards had already sprung up at the front of the federal courthouse. I could see several attorneys as well as clerks and assistants huddled together in somber reflection. I wanted no part of that. I looked at the keys dangling from the ignition and knew where I should go.

Gardner had given me a key to his house years ago, though I'd never used it. He rarely traveled, and even when he did, he didn't have a pet or anything that needed tending to. I think he felt better knowing that someone had access, just in case.

I drove down the long driveway that led to his house, which looked more like a cabin. It was dark brown and blended in with the various trees that surrounded it. He had neighbors, but his property was expansive enough that you couldn't see any of their houses from his front door.

I was slightly relieved when the key worked. I'd only sat on Gardner's porch with him a couple of times, drinking and sharing stories, but it felt like I was invading his privacy as I stepped inside. I discovered the real reason Gardner had never invited me in. The old man was a slob.

There were no empty surfaces. Everything was covered with books and papers. A new microwave sat atop his old one. In his living room, there was a television that wasn't plugged in and a DVD player still in its box. The couch was unusable, buried underneath clothes, packs of paper towels, rolls of toilet paper, and other items that belonged in a closet. A recliner on the near wall was the only clean piece of furniture, evidence of isolation.

What struck me more than what I found was what I didn't. There were no photos of Gardner or anyone else. There was no proof that he had gone to a university or traveled the world. There was no evidence of a life well lived. Perhaps his existence had become, as he had warned me, so small that he had trouble finding it at all. I had only known the king in his kingdom, on his throne. There was a private man who was a stranger to me. The house seemed empty, and it made me sad.

Someone opened the front door, knocking over a stack of unopened mail.

"You in here, Euchre?"

"Living room," I shouted, not knowing to whom I was speaking.

My old friend Detective Elliot rounded the corner. Thirty years on the job had taken its toll on him, but he looked particularly tired that morning and a little on edge.

"What the hell are you doing in a dead man's house?"

"Gardner gave me a key."

"You're lucky I made your Dodge out front. I didn't expect to find anyone here."

"I didn't know where else to go."

"Until I inform you otherwise, this property is sealed off as part of our investigation."

"You having trouble cracking this case, Detective?"

"Just making sure no lawyer can claim I didn't do my job."

Elliot always rode me hard. He thought it was for my benefit, and I'm sure for a time it was. But I wasn't in the mood that day. "See you around," I said as I headed for the door.

"When one of my guys asks you for your statement, you give it to him."

"I'm likely the last person who saw the judge alive. And I saw him in the very place where he was killed. I'm not giving my statement to a rookie."

"What were you doing in the parking lot with Gardner?"

"We were leaving the Christmas party."

"Together?"

"He found me out there, smoking a cigarette."

"How long were you with him?"

"Five minutes."

"What'd you talk about?"

I paused, realizing that we'd had the kind of conversation you wouldn't have if you knew it was going to be your last.

"Nothing," I said. "Holiday plans."

"What time was this?"

"About 10:35. He said he was going back to the office. I took a car to the East End Pub. Had two drinks and then I split."

"Will anyone be able to verify that you were there last night?"

"The same seven people who will be there tonight."

"All right, Jimmy. Go get some sleep."

While in Gardner's home, I'd received a text message from a 269 area code. It was Layla. She said Abe was busy, but he wanted her to give me an update. I texted back and suggested a little Mexican restaurant that was a short walk from the Fairfield Inn. Layla was already waiting when I walked in. She had a margarita in front of her, on the rocks with salt. She nursed the drink slowly but had eaten most of the lime. I was envious of whatever tequila was already coursing through her veins, so I stopped the waitress before I got to the table and ordered a shot of Patrón with a Pacífico behind it. Then I sat down.

I didn't really know what time it was, but since we were the only customers in there, I had to guess lunchtime was still at least an hour away. The mariachi music played through the speakers loud enough to give us some sense of privacy from the employees. The waitress brought chips and salsa with my beverages and asked if we were ready to order. Layla said she wasn't hungry. I was perfectly content to drink my calories, so the waitress took our menus and left us alone.

"Where's 269?" I asked.

"Michigan. Kalamazoo."

"Small-town girl, huh?"

"Not for a long time. I should probably get a new number, become a proper New Yorker."

Her phone buzzed, and she checked her message. A smile came over her face as she read it. She texted something briefly and then flipped her phone over and forced her smile to disappear. "Sorry, that was my dad."

"Do you need to call him?"

"No. He just heard a song on the radio—" She paused, as if considering whether the story was worth telling. "This happens every year around this time. You know the song 'Santa Baby'?"

"Sure."

"Well, my dad always says I look like Eartha Kitt."

"I know the voice, but I don't think I know what she looks like," I said.

Layla seemed resistant, but I was genuinely curious, so she pulled up a photo on her phone. The image was from the 1960s, the subject looking directly into the camera. There was a remarkable resemblance, but the first thing that caught my attention was the difference in their eyes. Ms. Kitt's were hauntingly revealing, windows into a pained soul. Layla's were guarded, protecting whatever was behind them.

"Abe wanted me to give you an update," she said, switching topics.

"I'm not comfortable being considered part of this legal team," I said.

"Neither am I. But this is temporary, and I'm just the messenger." I nodded and she continued. "Abe spoke with the managing partner at Gordon & Greene, and the firm is adamant that we stay with Amir until we've secured him appropriate representation."

"We have to babysit him now so that if he somehow doesn't spend the rest of his life in prison, your firm can continue to represent him in patent cases?"

"Again, just the messenger," she said.

I took a sip of beer and looked around for the waitress, hoping to get a refill on the Patrón.

"Abe's making calls to the top criminal defense attorneys in the country. In the meantime, he's trying to stay ahead of this and make sure Amir is taken care of."

"Fantastic," I said with a tinge of sarcasm that she ignored.

"I also called my old boss, and he put me in touch with someone at the US attorney's office here in the Eastern District. Apparently, there are so few federal crimes committed in these parts that they don't even have an office in Marshall."

"Yeah, I think the AUSAs from Tyler and Texarkana moonlight out here."

"Well, this case won't be handled by an assistant US attorney. Their boss is coming in tomorrow from Dallas. My guess is he's going to want this case for himself. We have a meeting with him at 10:00 a.m. Will you be able attend?" She knew I didn't want to go, and I knew she didn't want to ask.

"Sure," I managed.

"Thank you," she said.

I finished my beer and wondered if our waitress had forgotten about us since we weren't ordering food. I saw that Layla's glass was empty, too.

"You want another one?"

"I should get back to work."

She stood up to leave, so I stood as well, though I didn't grab my jacket from the chair. "I think I'll stay and have one for the road," I said.

"OK. Well, I'll see you tomorrow morning."

"Ten o'clock."

She took two steps toward the door and then stopped. She came right back to me, standing closer than we had been before. "I'm sorry about your friend. He seemed like he was a good man."

I was caught off guard. All I could do was nod. She put her hand on my shoulder, expressing genuine sympathy. She didn't know it, but she was the first person who had offered me condolences. The moment she exited the restaurant, I made for the men's room, thankfully found it empty, and for the first time all day I wept.

· NINE ·

I had my last cigarette of the night a few minutes after 1:00 a.m. I'd fallen asleep on the couch with a half-drunk bottle of beer next to me and the TV on for distraction. When I woke up, it was still dark outside. I traded the warm beer for hot coffee and was on my third cup when my futile alarm told me it was time to start the day.

Layla had texted to let me know our meeting was to be held at the district attorney's office in the old Harrison County Courthouse. As I strode in that morning, I thought about the party thrown in that very place only two nights earlier. Though it was a county building, I wasn't surprised the US attorney wanted to meet there, and I knew damn well our publicity-seeking DA would be thrilled to host the event.

I found Abe and Layla on the main floor, standing directly under the dome. Abe was dressed in his favorite pinstripe suit. Layla wore a charcoal skirt suit with three-inch heels. I had only seen her wear flats before. Something told me she had developed an alter ego, the tough cop, when she worked as an AUSA, and while she'd attempted to shed it as she transitioned into patent law, she thought it best to dust it off for today's meeting.

We entered the DA's office, and his assistant took us right inside. I don't know what I was expecting, but it certainly wasn't the law-and-order convention that awaited us. The room was filled with police officers and lawyers. I was sure we had passed maximum occupancy.

The US attorney for the Eastern District was a man named Keith Otis. He'd worked in DC for the bulk of his career, first with the Department of Justice and later at the FBI. But he was still a Texas boy through and through. He wore a slick pair of cowboy boots with a buckle that you should only wear if you can hang on to a bull for eight seconds.

Otis was talking to D. Calvin Lucas when we arrived. D-Cal took it upon himself to make the introductions. Otis had come with three AUSAs, who said their names and then never spoke again. Detective Elliot sat in a chair against the wall. He wore his shirt tucked into his jeans. I assumed he'd dug his blazer out of the trunk of his car and had every intention of stuffing it right back in there when this meeting was over. Neither he nor the two detectives with him looked like they'd slept much.

And finally there was a slim, sturdy man with a cowboy hat and a gun. Agent Hull was the special agent in charge of this case. He looked like he'd ridden in on horseback from the FBI's field office in Dallas. His steely eyes were the perfect complement to his permanent five o'clock shadow.

"I want to welcome you all to Marshall. Thank you for making the trip," said Lucas. It must have been killing D-Cal to be this close to a major case and have to observe from the sidelines. He milked the introductions and then turned it over to Otis. I expected we wouldn't hear another peep out of D-Cal, and that was fine by me.

"As some of you know, I was born in Plano," Otis began. "I had the opportunity to cross paths with Judge Gardner on a number of occasions. He was a Texas lawyer of the highest order. He was a giant among men and won't soon be forgotten. How about a little prayer for his soul?" Otis didn't wait for a response. He closed his eyes and bowed his head. "Dear Heavenly Father . . ."

I couldn't tell if Otis's piety was sincere or performative. Either way, I didn't make it a habit of talking to God in public and wasn't interested in talking to Him now. When Otis mentioned that God sent us His only son, Jesus Christ, to die for our sins, I glanced at

Rabinowitz to see how he was reacting to the decidedly denominational prayer. Honest Abe had his hands folded in front of him, head down, the model of respect. Then I realized Detective Elliot had been watching me the whole time. He smiled, and I felt like a kid who'd been caught fooling around in church.

A chorus of "amens" brought us all back to life.

Layla spoke up without anyone yielding her the floor. "Gentlemen, our client has been in custody for thirty-one hours. Does anyone intend to charge him with a crime, or should we be preparing for his imminent release?"

Otis looked to his AUSAs, then to Agent Hull, and finally to D-Cal. It was clear these men hadn't expected the only woman in the room to take the lead or for that matter to speak at all.

"I'm sorry, Ms.—?"

"Stills."

"Ms. Stills," continued Otis with a smile, "are you the lead attorney for Mr. Zawar?"

"I'm *an* attorney for Mr. Zawar."

"Well, I'd like to talk to whoever is representing him in *this* matter," Otis said as he shifted his focus to Abe.

"Mr. Otis, all three of us represent Mr. Zawar, and unless the rules are different in Texas, it's none of your goddamn business who the lead attorney is," Abe replied. "Ms. Stills asked you a question, and we'd all like an answer. Do you intend to charge him with a crime?"

The US attorney flashed a politician's smile, but I thought Abe's demeanor had rattled him a little. "As I'm sure you noticed when you entered the building, there is still an active crime scene outside. The investigation is ongoing."

"Then," said Layla, "release our client until such time as your investigation bears fruit."

Otis laughed. He certainly wasn't going to let her push him around in front of all of these men. But he was discovering that she wasn't going to let him push her around either. Otis looked to D-Cal, who I'd already written off as mere window dressing for this meeting.

Apparently, though, Otis wanted D-Cal to speak. He'd been leaning against his desk but now stood up straight.

"Charges will be brought before Mr. Zawar's seventy-two hours have expired," said D-Cal. "And while the issue of discovery can wait until his first appearance, I'll give you a head's up on something right now. The arresting officers found what they ascertained to be blood on the accused's hands and jacket cuffs. Agent Hull has been kind enough to send it to the bureau's lab in Dallas, where tests are being expedited. It is our expectation that the blood found on your client was Judge Gardner's."

I had no idea if what D-Cal said was true. Maybe he was posturing; maybe the officers couldn't tell the difference between dried blood and ketchup. In any event, I wasn't in the habit of giving opposing counsel the benefit of the doubt, and I wasn't about to change that approach with him.

"Perhaps we should discuss jurisdictional matters before we get ahead of ourselves," Otis suggested to Abe.

Layla was not thrilled with the way Otis repeatedly spoke past her, but unflustered, she switched seamlessly from one legal topic to the next. "Obviously, a change of venue is appropriate here," she said. "We are happy to file the motion if you prefer, but I suspect you may have some thoughts about potential settings."

"It's a bit presumptuous of you to assume the trial can't be held right here," replied Otis, finally speaking to Layla.

"I'm sure you would love nothing more than to try him in your own backyard, but that's simply not going to happen," she responded. "The last time a federal judge was murdered was in 2011 in Tucson."

I remembered that case. That was the shooting that wounded Congresswoman Gabby Giffords and claimed the life of US District Judge John Roll.

"That case was moved by the Ninth Circuit out of Arizona to the Southern District of California," Layla explained.

"So you'd like to see this case transferred out of state?" Otis asked with even more condescension.

"Given the precedent, somewhere else in the Fifth Circuit would make sense. Shreveport or New Orleans, perhaps," she said.

"We do things a bit different in Texas. You're too young to remember this, but the first federal judge ever assassinated was killed out in San Antonio."

"I am familiar with the assassination of Judge Wood," Layla said.

"Then you know that his murder trial took place right there in the Western District of Texas."

"First, that was over forty years ago. Second, it took fifteen months for authorities to apprehend a suspect and another two years before his case was brought to trial. You've already arrested our client, and if you do in fact charge him, we will call for, and expect, a speedy trial."

"We can do speedy in Texas, Ms. Stills," promised Otis.

"Not without a judge you can't," Layla shot back. "I don't mean to sound insensitive, but the judge who would have overseen this case also happens to be the victim in this case. There is no chief judge in the Eastern District of Texas."

Layla's performance made me wonder why someone with her talents had changed career paths and given up on criminal prosecution when she seemed so at home there.

"You've raised some compelling points, Ms. Stills." Otis's statement was clearly criticism laced with a compliment. "However, everything you just said was based on the supposition that your client will be charged with a federal crime."

"The crime in question is the murder of a federal judge. That is a federal crime," she noted.

"It can be," said D-Cal, who had been lying in wait. Everything about his demeanor suggested he was ready to strike. "USA Otis and I had a long discussion about how justice would be best served, and after some serious soul-searching, and a prayer, we agreed that this case ought to be tried in state court."

It didn't make sense. This was a high-profile case and prosecutors are notorious publicity whores. I understood why D-Cal wanted the case; I just didn't understand why the US attorney would let it go. But Layla had already figured it out.

"You want the death penalty," she said matter-of-factly.

In 1972, the Supreme Court of the United States placed a moratorium on the death penalty. Four years later, the moratorium was lifted. Since that decision in 1976, the federal government had executed a grand total of 16 people. The state of Texas, on the other hand, had executed 573. There were years in which the Lone Star State was executing people at a rate of nearly one per week. There are other states that condemn people to death in similar numbers but none that carry out those sentences like we do in Texas.

Otis wanted this case, probably as much as D-Cal did. But he was a red-blooded Texan first and someone had killed one of our own. If these prosecutors wanted Texas justice, if they wanted the accused to pay the ultimate price, then Amir would have to stand trial in a Texas state court.

"We'll be making a joint statement at a press conference this afternoon," D-Cal said. "USA Otis has graciously offered to help in any way he can. Agent Hull has likewise agreed to lend the FBI's support to assist Detective Elliot and the Marshall PD in its investigation. But it will be my office that charges Mr. Amir Zawar with the first-degree murder of Judge Gerald Gardner, and he will stand trial right here in Marshall."

I sat with Abe and Layla in the holding room at the Marshall police station. We all had our reasons to feel dejected. None of us wanted Amir's case to remain in the local jurisdiction. The notion of a fair trial would be out of the question. Abe surely would have preferred to move it as far away from EDTX as possible to keep the stench off the rest of his business. And I had hoped to mourn the loss of Judge Gardner in quiet solitude. That wouldn't be possible with Marshall hosting the murder trial of the slain federal judge.

A guard brought Amir into the room. His hands remained cuffed in front of him as the officer left us alone. I watched him intently as Abe explained the developments from the morning's meeting at the DA's office. Abe made reference to the supposed bloodstains on Amir's jacket. He hadn't mentioned them during our first meeting, though now it was clear why he had been shivering with only his T-shirt to keep him warm. They'd taken his jacket as potential evidence. Honest Abe, true to form, didn't present the scenario to Amir as anything less than the dire situation that it was.

"Do you have any idea how blood may have gotten on your jacket?" Abe asked.

"I think I cut my hand when I broke the window trying to get back into the house," Amir responded. I looked at his hand but didn't see any visible wounds, though I supposed a very minor injury could produce enough blood to warrant suspicion under the circumstances.

"The next order of business is to find you the best criminal defense lawyer to handle your case," Abe said, moving on. "I've spoken with firms all over the country, some as far as the coasts and some as close as Dallas." Abe paused, but Amir didn't seem ready to speak. "What I'd like to do is put together a short list with my top recommendations, let you meet with them, and you can decide who you want to go with."

Amir was silent for a long time. Finally, he spoke.

"I want Euchre."

Abe and Layla looked at me and must have seen the shock on my face.

"Jimmy's not a criminal defense attorney," Abe replied.

"I'm going to stand trial here in Marshall. My fate will ultimately be in the hands of ordinary citizens from this town. These citizens, I've been told, will never trust me. And I shouldn't trust them." He locked eyes with me. "But Marshall is in your blood. So why would I want someone from a city, even a Texas city, when I could have a lawyer from right here? They will trust you, because they are you, and you are them. Or was that all bullshit?"

It had taken all of my strength to provide even the most basic level of representation for Amir over the past day and a half. I had agreed to hold his hand and escort him out of the city limits, where I'd turn him over to whomever he hired to mount a defense. But that was as far as I was prepared to go.

"Murder trials are a different animal," Layla interjected. "This is in no way a comment about James's abilities, but you wouldn't want to be a passenger on a plane the first time a pilot attempts to land. There's no substitute for experience, particularly in a capital case."

"But murder trials are also in his blood," Amir said cryptically. Layla was confused. I was not. "It's the family business, isn't it?"

I never liked it when people attributed my chosen profession to my father. The more I insisted he had nothing to do with my decision to become a lawyer, the more people seemed to believe the opposite was true. So I'd stopped protesting long ago. Still, it really pissed me off.

"I am not offering to represent you," I said.

"What did they call your father? The 'Darrow of Dallas'? He must have cast a long shadow. I bet that was a lot of pressure to live up to. Maybe that's why you cheated in law school?" Amir paused, apparently hoping I'd take the bait. I wasn't going to bite. "You were afraid of falling short, afraid you might disappoint him? Is that when everyone gave up on you? Is that why you got into intellectual property law? Make an easy buck, never try a case with true consequences, and hopefully avoid ever being compared to him?"

I didn't want him to know he was getting to me. But I had a feeling it was written all over my face.

"You might be the best patent lawyer in town, but that's a dubious honor, isn't it? It's like being the toughest guy in the smallest weight class. Don't you ever wonder if you could go toe-to-toe with the heavyweights? Could you do what he did? Argue a major case? Win a murder trial?"

I wanted to wrap my hands around his neck and squeeze until I was sure he'd never speak another word.

"Your flawless psychoanalysis aside, you're wrong about one very important thing," I said.

"What's that?"

"Not everyone gave up on me. There was one man who always believed in me, who always stood by me. Two nights ago, someone murdered that man."

"Having you stand beside me will make a powerful statement then. Your relationship to the victim, and your willingness to represent me, will have an impact on the jury," Amir said, confident in his strategic thinking.

I was not going to be used as a prop. And to be honest, I was more than a little insulted at the insinuation that my value was at all related to my personal friendship with Judge Gardner rather than my professional acumen in court. But perhaps that was the point of Amir's comment. He was trying to goad me.

"OK, Amir, I'll represent you," I paused for effect, "if you plead guilty."

He scoffed at the idea.

"We haven't seen what evidence the government has against you, but we do know that the district attorney plans to seek the death penalty. So this may be the only way for you to avoid execution."

"I won't take a deal. I don't see how the death penalty is any worse than life in prison."

"I can show you a recording of a lethal injection. It might change your mind."

I meant what I said. I also liked being the one to lay out his bleak options, making him imagine what it would be like to be strapped to a gurney and have poison pumped into his veins.

"I have come this far in life by trusting my instincts. If they charge me with this crime, I will not plead guilty. And I will not hire some out-of-town attorney. I don't want someone whose reputation as a top defense lawyer is already set in stone. I want someone who will feel like his entire life is on the line, right there with my own."

"Did you do it?" I asked. There was a two-ton elephant in the room, and I was tired of dancing around it. I'd made Abe and Layla uncomfortable, but I didn't care. Amir didn't offer an immediate response, so I pressed him. "Did you murder Judge Gardner?"

"I thought attorneys weren't supposed to ask clients if they're guilty," he replied.

"Well, as Layla just explained to you, I've never practiced criminal law, so I don't know what the hell I'm doing. But whatever you say right now is privileged, so it stays in this room. And I'm asking you, man-to-man, did you kill my friend?"

"No," he said flatly. "I did not."

It was weird the way he said it. I couldn't tell if he was lying, but it was clear that he wasn't overly concerned with whether or not I believed him. I found that disturbing.

"Will you take my case?" Amir asked.

"I'll have to think about it."

"You'll take it."

"You sure about that?"

"Yes, because sons never stop trying to please their fathers."

There was too much to consider, too many variables still unknown. This was a gut check moment. I envisioned myself taking the assignment, but I also thought about simply walking out the door. I tried to gauge my physical reaction to both options, but between the adrenaline, the exhaustion, the nicotine, and the hangover, I couldn't get a true read on myself. It was all instinct, save for one thought—I had a burning need to know if Amir was guilty. If I stood by and watched someone else handle his defense, I'd probably never know the full truth. Short of a confession, or new evidence implicating someone else, I'd always wonder if Amir had really killed Judge Gardner.

Then something else occurred to me. Any other lawyer would do their best to represent Amir, regardless of whether he had committed the crime. They would be ethically bound and subject to disciplinary action if they failed to do their job. But that didn't matter to me, not anymore. I was willing to risk it all, to forfeit my license to practice law itself, if it meant putting Gardner's killer behind bars—even if that killer turned out to be the man I was representing. If I confirmed Amir's guilt, I wouldn't hesitate to sacrifice myself in the name of justice for my friend. I would do what no other defense attorney would do; I would ensure that my client was convicted.

"You better hope I don't find out you're guilty," I warned.

PART II

CUI BONO

Who Benefits

· TEN ·

People divide the world into two parts. The line shifts depending on what the subject of division is, but the sides are always the same: Us and them. Old and young. Rich and poor. Powerful and weak. Red and blue. Black and white. Foreign and local. My objective in court was to draw the line in such a way that the jurors found themselves on the same side as my client. If I didn't like the way sides were being drawn, it was my job to adjust the line. Nearly every line can be redrawn. The only permanent demarcation is the line that separates the living from the dead.

Gerald Gardner was laid to rest in a simple plot at a cemetery on the northeast end of town. His headstone bore only his name and the years of his birth and death. It was clear from the short set of instructions found in his will that the judge wanted a modest funeral. That is what he received, with one notable exception: half of Marshall was in attendance, not to mention lawyers and colleagues from all over Texas and the country. Every intellectual property law firm sent at least one representative to pay their respects. If he had worried that his existence had been small, the mourners that filled the grassy hillside would prove otherwise. It was clear that Judge Gardner's impact on the world had been substantial.

I never removed my sunglasses, though I hadn't cried either. I'd always found my emotions took a respite when I was in public. I preferred it that way. As a procession of people tossed handfuls of dirt onto the coffin below, I made my getaway.

It had been six days since the judge had been murdered, four days since I'd agreed to represent the man suspected of killing him. Amir Zawar was arraigned twenty-four hours after I took the case. The DA officially charged him with first-degree murder, subject to the death penalty. Speaking on Amir's behalf, I entered the plea of not guilty. There seemed to be a growing consensus that my client was a fool for hiring me and that I was a traitor for representing him. I hadn't had a real opportunity to challenge either assertion yet, and with each passing day, I grew more concerned that at least one of them would prove to be correct.

I drove with the window down and a cigarette in my left hand. My phone buzzed and I used my right hand to remove it from my pocket. The truck stayed between the lines on its own. I didn't really care if it did or not.

The caller ID showed 269, and I realized that I hadn't added Layla to my contacts yet. She had flown back to New York with Honest Abe after the arraignment, but her return was imminent. Federal law requires that at least two attorneys be appointed to represent a client in a death penalty case. This case wasn't federal, nor was I a court-appointed lawyer, but the American Bar Association's guidelines were pretty much the same. A defendant who had been charged with a capital crime ought to have more than one lawyer, even if the lead counsel was the most seasoned criminal defense attorney in the country. In light of the fact that this was my first criminal trial ever, Amir couldn't argue with Honest Abe when he insisted that I not try this case alone. They agreed that, given her years of trial experience as a federal prosecutor and since they both trusted her, Layla would make an excellent addition to the team. The only person who didn't like that plan was Layla.

Layla had spent seven years as an assistant US attorney and seemed eager to put criminal law behind her. Unfortunately for her, she was the best possible lawyer for the job. She hadn't been at Gordon & Greene long enough to be a valuable member of a patent team, and she had more experience with murder cases than anyone at the firm. Amir had the potential to be a golden goose, so Abe intimated that Layla's path to partnership would be accelerated if she helped win their client's freedom. It was a good opportunity, albeit an undesirable one in her eyes, and she didn't really have a choice.

"What's new, Kalamazoo?"

"I'm at JFK. I'm boarding in a few minutes."

"You staying in Dallas tonight?"

"No, I'm getting the rental car and driving into Marshall late."

Tomorrow was Sunday, so she would have a day to get situated before we got to work.

"Did you see the email about the bench assignment?" Layla asked.

"No, I just left Gardner's funeral."

"Oh, right. I'm sorry."

"What'd the email say?"

"We've been assigned a trial judge."

"Who'd we get?"

"Judge Roy Whelan," she said, with the tone of someone who was hearing this name for the first time. "Is that good news or bad news?"

"Both."

Even though I was a couple minutes early, Layla was already waiting outside of the Fairfield Inn when I pulled up. She stood underneath the carport where guests unloaded their vehicles. I tried not to stare. It had only been a couple days since I'd seen her, and I had forgotten small details like her admirable posture and the way she always maintained eye contact.

"Hi," she said as she climbed into the truck.

"Welcome back."

I pointed to a pair of grande Starbucks cups between us. "The one on the right has cream, the one on the left is black. And there's sugar packets, real and artificial, in the glove box. Take whichever one you like." I was glad when she chose the one with cream. I preferred my coffee uncut. I drove the back way via Birmingham Road.

After his arraignment, Amir had been transferred to the Harrison County Jail on the east side of town. We'd made an unconvincing attempt to get him released on bail by highlighting that Amir had never been in trouble with the law, but D-Cal insisted that an outsider charged with murder, facing the death penalty, with ties to a foreign country and enough money to buy his own island, was the definition of a flight risk. So the county jail became Amir's new home.

The Harrison County Jail was a monstrous light brown building that gave off a repellent vibe. One look at it and you got the feeling that bad things happened inside but somehow the details never escaped those walls. Though not a prison, some of its guests have had extended stays there.

As Layla and I entered the secure facility, the first thing I noticed was the absence of sunlight. The white brick walls and mustard accents were brightly illuminated by lighting that belonged in a stadium. A sheriff's deputy escorted us into a short, dead-end hallway with four windowless doors on the right-hand side marked "Attorney 1A" through "Attorney 1D," the last of which had been reserved for us. We waited for Amir to enter through another door on the opposite side of the little room. His door had a small window, so I glanced through it. I hadn't spent much time around jails. I was struck by the emptiness of it all.

Another deputy led Amir inside but did not remove his wrist and ankle restraints before leaving. Amir wore an all-black outfit that looked like it was made from the material of a barber's cape. It was the official uniform of the county jail. It, like incarceration itself, was designed to strip a man of everything that made him who he was.

"How are you holding up?" Layla asked.

"I'll be fine."

"You look like you've lost weight," I noted. His sturdy frame had been slender, but he seemed skinny now.

"They've been serving me ham sandwiches most days. They don't get a lot of Muslims here," he said, resigned but frustrated.

"I'll talk to the guards on our way out," Layla offered.

"No. I think they're doing it to mess with me. You bringing it up with them will just make it worse," Amir replied. He was probably right. As long as he wasn't starving, it was better not to incur the wrath of the armed employees at the jail by having his lawyers tattle on them. I wasn't sure how tough Amir really was, but he seemed resilient, and I needed him to stay that way.

"We've got a potential problem, Amir," I said, turning to business. "Your case has been assigned to Judge Roy Whelan."

"You don't like him?" Amir surmised.

"Actually, I do. Every other judge in Harrison County comes by way of the DA's office. Whelan is the only one who was a defense attorney before putting on the robe."

"So he'll be sympathetic to our side?" Amir speculated.

"He'll be fair, which is about the best you can ask for."

"Then what's the problem?"

"I have history with his son."

I told Amir about my altercation with Samuel Earl Whelan earlier in the year. I explained that Sam was a mediocre patent attorney who gave us all a bad name and that I had embarrassed him on a number of occasions. I recounted the tale of him decking me in the middle of a trial after I called him a court jester. He was still up for review by the Texas State Bar's disciplinary committee and therein lay the potential conflict of interest for his father.

"So the judge hates you?" Amir concluded.

"Honestly, I hardly know the man. He's never been anything but pleasant to me even though I haven't hidden my contempt for his son."

"Why are you telling me all of this?"

"You have options, Amir." Layla jumped in, just like we'd rehearsed. It was better for her to lay out the choices so I couldn't be accused of trying to persuade Amir one way or the other. Plus, she had a calming effect on me and him. "Ordinarily, when a potential conflict of interest exists between the judge and a defense attorney, the defense can ask for the judge's recusal," she said.

"But we like this judge?" Amir had a brain for strategy. I'd give him that.

"We do believe he's better than the alternatives. So that potentially leaves you with a decision between the judge you want and the attorney you've selected."

"They can't make me fire my lawyer."

"No, they absolutely cannot. You have a right to be represented by the attorney of your choosing. But if you do insist on retaining James's services, you may risk a recusal by the judge."

"Even if we don't ask him to do that?" Amir was worried.

"That's correct. It is possible that he will simply recuse himself."

"And we can't do anything about that if it happens," I added.

"Or," Layla continued, "it is also possible that the DA will call for the judge's recusal."

"And that fucker probably will do that since we got a judge we like, right?" Amir concluded.

"That is a concern," Layla said. She and I allowed Amir to sit with his thoughts for a few moments, confident he understood the dilemma before him. This was one of the instances when all we could do was present the client with his options. He had to make the call.

"To hell with it. Let's roll the dice."

Judge Roy Whelan's office was in the old historic courthouse. His courtroom, however, was on the opposite side of the brick parking lot in the new Harrison County Courthouse, which hadn't really been new since the 1960s. The expansion had been necessary, but everyone from judges to the DA fought to keep their offices in the older building because it was more regal. So while the judge presided over a courtroom in the newer, uglier building, he kept his office across the street.

It was Monday morning, and all parties had agreed to a meeting in chambers so we could address the judge's potential conflict. Even if I'd known the judge better than I did, it would have been impossible to predict which way the meeting would go. We were prepared for a variety of outcomes.

Layla and I sat outside Whelan's office, watching his assistant transcribe a paper memo into a document on her computer. D. Calvin Lucas strode in at one minute to ten, able to perfectly time his arrival since his office was only seventy-five feet away from the judge's chambers.

"Hey, Euch. How you holding up?"

"So far, so good."

"It's a pleasure to see you again, Ms. Stills."

D-Cal was one of those rare former Texas high school football players who didn't pack on five pounds every year until middle age caught up to him. He was tall and still in great shape, his dark hair groomed with precision. His appearance was part of a larger package. When he spoke with women, he was a charming son of a bitch, or so he thought. Before D-Cal could sit, Whelan's assistant received a message on her computer.

"He'll see you now," she said.

Judge Roy Whelan was in his mid-sixties and conducted himself like a small-town judge who had no desire to inflate his own sense of importance. His demeanor was subdued, both inside and outside of the courtroom. He had a reputation for being fair, though not lenient. For the first half of his career, he'd been in private practice, representing clients in both civil and criminal court. When a vacancy opened up on the bench, he ran a campaign that focused on personal connections and relied largely on his genial reputation. He won convincingly and never looked back. Whelan and his late wife, Lenore, only had the one child. How two fundamentally bright and decent people spawned Samuel Earl, we'll never know.

The judge rose from his desk to greet us. He wore a light gray suit, and his robe hung on a coatrack in the back corner near shelves that held a collection of leather-bound books. As we found our seats, I took it upon myself to begin.

"I appreciate everyone making time to do this on such short notice. Judge Whelan, obviously, your son and I had a slight and unfortunate altercation a few months back. We have discussed the matter with our client, and none of us feels the event will in any way impede your ability to render impartial justice or preside over this case fairly."

In towns the size of Marshall, it's not uncommon for a judge to know one or both parties that come before the court. A passing relationship isn't enough to warrant a recusal. If it was, a small-town judge would find him- or herself stepping aside all the time. I felt I'd done a good job of commending Whelan for his ability to perform his duties with neutrality. But it could all be for naught if he'd already decided to hand Amir's case over to another judge.

"Thank you, Mr. Euchre. I am, of course, aware of the incident involving you and my son. My primary responsibility as a judge is to render impartial justice, as you say, and it is my hope that I am able to do so regardless of the unique circumstances surrounding any particular case. That being said, I'd like to give you, Mr. Lucas, an opportunity to be heard on this as well."

D-Cal couldn't have been thrilled when he learned that this case had been assigned to Judge Whelan, since there were other judges who'd been historically more biased toward the prosecution's side. But it wasn't a huge setback for him either. Not only was Whelan's reputation unimpeachable, but the potential conflict in question, if it were to have an impact on the judge, was sure to prejudice him against my side anyway, so D-Cal would be the beneficiary of any partiality. Additionally, while this promised to be the one and only case I'd ever argue before Judge Whelan, as the district attorney, D-Cal had trials in Whelan's court all the time. So D-Cal had to weigh his options carefully. If he did make a motion for recusal, he'd risk spoiling his relationship with the judge by questioning his ability to be impartial. Lastly, we were going to have a jury trial anyway, so while the judge could certainly make an impact, the verdict was ultimately going to be in the hands of twelve citizens of Marshall.

"The DA's office has complete confidence in His Honor's ability to preside over this case. I defer to the court's judgment." With that, D-Cal tacitly signed off on Judge Whelan.

I had come into this meeting hoping it would not result in a recusal. D-Cal's position made this all but guaranteed. Still, I thought it was the smart move on his part.

Judge Whelan stood up and moved toward the window. He put his hands in his pockets and jingled his keys, like old men do, while he weighed his options. "In light of the fact that neither side is calling for my recusal," he said, "and since it would seem we are all in agreement about how best to proceed, I find no reason to disqualify myself."

It was a substantial victory, but since it had come to us so easily, I immediately began to wonder if we had made a mistake. The facts didn't support my concern, but I worried anyway.

"Your Honor, since we are all here, I'd hoped to discuss two other matters." I figured I'd press my luck while everyone was in such an agreeable mood. "The defense is waiting on discovery from the district attorney."

D-Cal shifted in his seat. "Judge, we are still gathering evidence and compiling materials."

"We haven't seen so much as a police report, which has clearly been in the possession of the DA's office for over a week," I said.

"I'm not sure what Mr. Euchre is alleging, but my office has every intention of adhering to the proper rules of discovery."

"My client wants a speedy trial. We would like the earliest possible trial date, but that won't be achievable if we are subjected to delay tactics by the prosecution every step of the way."

"All right," Whelan interjected, not wanting the hostility level to rise more than it already had. "Mr. Lucas, please furnish the defense with everything you've got by the end of the week."

"Yes, Your Honor."

"What is the other matter, Mr. Euchre?" Judge Whelan asked.

"On the night of Judge Gardner's murder, our client was a guest in a residence owned by the law firm Gordon & Greene. It remains sealed off by the authorities, and we would like it back."

"A search is still underway for the murder weapon," responded D-Cal. "And since the accused spent most of the night on those premises, we believe there is a high probability the knife is hidden there."

Layla took her cue. "Not to jump too far ahead, Your Honor, but since the accused is innocent, no such weapon exists, at least not one that will be found on the property in question. Moreover, this house is used primarily as an office for the lawyers at my firm. We intend to use it as our base of operations in mounting a defense for Mr. Zawar, so we ask that it be unsealed as expeditiously as possible so we can get to work."

Judge Whelan looked to the DA. "Mr. Lucas, I trust you've already done an exhaustive search of the house?"

"We've searched it twice, but—"

"Search it a third time, and then unseal the property and return it to its owners."

"Yes, Your Honor."

We were three for three with our objectives for this meeting. For whatever reason though, I felt more dread as we left. I expected every case to have wins and losses along the way. I worried we were using up all of our wins too early.

ELEVEN

As Layla and I walked out of Judge Whelan's office, the DA jogged to catch up to us.

"Nice job in there, Euchre." There was no way this compliment was sincere. "Don't worry about the discovery. I have no interest in dragging this trial out."

"You're just naturally slow, D-Cal. I get it."

"I'm really going to enjoy this, Euch."

His confidence was intended to unnerve me. It was effective.

Layla and I exited the courthouse and looked out at the brick parking lot, still surrounded by a perimeter of yellow police tape. I doubted crime scenes in bigger cities would have remained locked down as long as this one had, but the authorities in Marshall weren't seasoned pros when it came to murder investigations. Still, I hoped they'd open it back up soon because it was a morbid reminder of Judge Gardner's death.

"Mr. Euchre."

At the base of the steps stood a young woman, maybe in her late twenties. She had cropped blond hair that was unevenly dyed blue at the tips. She was petite but carried herself like either she didn't know she was smaller than everyone else or she didn't care.

"Can I help you?" I asked.

"Have you hired an investigator yet?"

"I'm still reviewing applications."

"I'm Lisa Morgan," she said, almost as if that should mean something to me. It didn't, so I waited for more information. "I'm a licensed private investigator."

"You work here in Marshall?"

"I did my three years with an agency in El Paso. I recently moved back here to start my own company."

"What's your name?" I asked, knowing that she had just told me.

"Lisa Morgan," she said again.

I searched my memory for where I'd heard that name. "Lisa 'the Leg' Morgan?" I asked.

She smiled and made a kicking motion with her right leg.

The Leg had gone to Marshall High School more than a decade after I had, so I wasn't sure I'd ever spoken with her, but I definitely knew who she was. "Lisa," I said to Layla, "was the placekicker for the Mavericks a few years ago. You still hold the field goal record?"

"Sixty-one yards," she said proudly.

I looked at her left hand and saw the oversized Texas state championship ring on her finger. I was ashamed by how much envy filled my heart, especially at my age.

"I haven't heard your name in a long time," I said.

"I went to UTEP on a soccer scholarship. After I graduated, I got my PI license and worked out there for a while."

"You ever work a murder case?"

"Absolutely," she said, but she must have sensed my skepticism because she qualified her answer. "I observed several."

"Well, send over a résumé and I'll put you at the top of the pile."

She removed a résumé from a folder she held under her arm.

"How many candidates are you considering?" Her directness was a little jarring, but I recognized that it would probably prove to be an asset in her line of work.

"You are the first," I admitted.

"Hire me. You won't be disappointed."

"Do you think you can procure a police report?" I figured I'd test her resolve.

She reached right back into her folder, removed a file, and handed it to me. I looked at the first page. It was the arrest report for Amir Zawar.

"How'd you get this?"

"I'm good at my job."

I looked at Layla. She seemed equally impressed.

"Can I show you something else?" Lisa asked.

"Sure."

The Leg led the way like she was a general and we were her troops. Given her size, Napoleon came to mind. She approached the officer from the Marshall Police Department who had been tasked with guarding the crime scene.

"Back again?" he asked.

"I brought the boss this time," said the Leg as she held up the yellow tape the way a manager holds up the ropes of a boxing ring so their fighter can enter. Layla and I ducked under the tape and she followed.

"You've already inspected the crime scene?" I asked her.

"I told him I was your investigator. He let me right in. Cops like me."

The Leg led us to an area in the middle of the lot spotted with several evidence markers. "This is where the attack occurred," she began. "This big stain is the victim's blood. Notice there is one large pool and very little elsewhere, suggesting he was stabbed and bled out here."

I tried to remain as clinical as she was, but it was difficult. The bricks were darkened. Blood doesn't dry red, as it so often looks in the movies. It turns brown when oxygen hits it.

"Now look at this." The Leg called our attention to a line of evidence markers about sixty feet long. "Each of these has been placed next to a drop or drops of blood. You'll see that the drops tend to get smaller the farther away they are from the point of attack." We followed the trail. "What does this suggest to you?" she asked.

"The killer fled this way," I guessed.

"Right, and this is east. But your client was staying at a house on Franklin Street over there." She pointed southwest, almost the opposite direction.

"I'd expect him to run back home, to safety," I concluded.

"So would I," the Leg said. "But there's something else. Look at this."

She continued walking east, pointing out the drops of blood, most of which were accompanied by police evidence markers. We stopped at the last row of parking spots at the edge of the lot.

"There are five or six drops of blood here," she said as she knelt down.

My eyes then turned to three circles the size of softballs, one on top of the other, in the middle of the last parking spot. Maybe it was because the holiday season was upon us, but the figure they formed looked like a silhouette of Frosty the Snowman, minus the corncob pipe and silk hat.

"What are these?" I asked.

"Just oil stains. You can see the color is slightly different," Lisa said. "But focus on these little drops. Why, after the drops get farther and farther apart, presumably as the assailant fled, do they bunch up right here?"

"The killer stopped," Layla answered.

"That's what I think, too. But for what purpose?" asked the Leg.

"I don't know," I said.

"Neither do I," said the Leg, "but I have a guess. I think the killer attacked the victim back there, fled in a panic in this direction, and then stopped, got into his own car, and drove away."

I scanned the parking lot, trying to envision the scenario the Leg had just laid out.

"Is there any blood beyond this point?" I asked, thinking that even the slightest trace outside of the parking lot would shatter her theory.

"I couldn't find a single drop," she said.

"So the killer's car was parked right here the night of the murder," I said, allowing the information to settle.

"The night of the murder, also the night of the Christmas party," the Leg added.

"Can you get a list of everyone who was at the party that night?" I asked.

"Are you offering me the job?"

Since the Compound was still sealed, I'd decided to host our first official team meeting at my place that night. I chain-smoked two cigarettes and took a last-minute shower before Layla and Lisa arrived. I had to rush to get my clothes on when I heard a knock on my door.

"Right on time," I said as I welcomed them in from the cold December air. Lisa had picked Layla up at the Fairfield, so they arrived together.

"I don't know what kind of meeting you're running here, so I brought Red Bull and beer," the Leg said, as she headed straight for the living room and kitchen, which weren't separated by any kind of wall.

"Hi," I said to Layla.

"Jesus Christ, Euchre!" Lisa said from the other room.

The Leg had begun a self-guided tour. Layla and I joined her in the living room.

"Did this place come fully furnished?" she questioned.

"No?" I said, not understanding why she would ask that.

"It's pretty girly, don't you think?"

I hadn't looked at my habitat through anyone else's eyes in a long time. I had purchased the house, a three-bedroom on the outskirts of town, soon after my patent practice had taken off. I had to stretch my budget at the time, but I wanted a place I could grow into. It proved to be well within my price range as my career blossomed. I never did need all the space though.

"I was expecting matching leather couches and a TV the size of a horse." The Leg continued her critique, calling out items that supported her original hypothesis. "But you've got throw pillows that match accent pieces in every room. An antique apothecary table. Shelves lined with ornaments you probably never use. You have a painting of a bottle of perfume?"

"It's Parisian," I said defensively.

"Oh, it's *Parisian*," she said.

As the Leg moved to the fridge, I saw Layla looking around at my belongings as well. The Leg had made me feel embarrassed, but with Layla, I felt exposed.

"It just looks like it was done with a woman's touch. It's a compliment," Layla said.

We convened near the fridge where the Leg was putting drinks inside to keep them cold. "We doing caffeine or booze?"

"I've got a pizza on the way," I said.

"Booze it is." She removed three cans of beer from a twelve-pack.

"Natty Ice? Really?" I said.

"I'm a girl on a budget," the Leg replied.

"Spring for the Miller Lite next time. You can expense it."

We took our beers to the living room, where I found myself preoccupied with the excessive number of pillows on my sofa and chairs.

"I've reviewed the police report," I began. "Amir stepped outside to smoke some weed, locked himself out, and then broke a window in the rear of the house to get back in. This triggered a glass-break alarm inside the house that alerted Texas Warning and Alarm Systems, the security company that monitors the Compound. They called the police department, which dispatched a squad car. Two officers arrived on scene, found Amir inside the Compound, and, believing this to be a break-in, drew their weapons. They ordered him to the ground, handcuffed him, and called for backup. Three more squad cars arrived."

"Because it's Marshall and nothing exciting ever happens here," added the Leg.

"So while Jefferson and Ramirez, the original responding officers, continued to interrogate Amir about what he was doing on the premises, the second team went through the house looking for signs of burglary, while the third team broadened the search, presumably looking for an accomplice or Amir's car. What they discovered was the body of Judge Gardner in the parking lot, and thus a potential B&E turned into a homicide."

I took a sip of my Natty Ice and then placed it back on the mantel above the fireplace.

"They found his body at 3:00 a.m. As it turns out, I was the last person to see Judge Gardner alive. That was at 10:35 p.m., as he entered his courthouse. So that's our time-of-death range, but we should be able to narrow it down."

"I was hoping surveillance footage in the federal courthouse would allow us to pinpoint when the judge finally left his office for the night," said the Leg, "but, unfortunately, the cameras only cover the public entrance. Judge Gardner used his private one, so there's nothing of him coming or going."

"Maybe the guards saw something," I suggested.

"Nope. I spoke to both guards on duty that night. They said it was common for Gardner to work late. He'd come and go at all hours, but they didn't remember seeing him the night he was killed. I'll keep poking around though."

"All right," I said. "My guess is he was killed in the early hours of the morning, closer to three o'clock. The parking lot was packed that night because of the Christmas party. If the murder happened, say, before midnight, I'd expect someone from the party would have stumbled upon his body on the way to their car."

"I'll get that list of everyone who was at the party and start compiling a timeline of people's movements," the Leg said as she scratched some notes to herself on a pad that fit inside her palm.

"With Christmas being next week, people may start leaving town soon, so work as quickly as you can."

"What about the blood and DNA analysis?" Layla asked. Her prosecutorial background was sure to stress-test our case before it ever got to court.

"Still waiting on the results," I said. "Does it seem like it's taking an extraordinarily long time?"

"Not necessarily," Layla replied. "It's not an overnight process. Depending on how busy the FBI's lab is in Dallas, it could easily take weeks."

"All right, we'll set that aside for the moment. Hopefully the blood found on Amir won't be a match to Gardner's, and that will make it much easier to lay out our set of facts. The way I see it, we've got two strategies, and we may argue both of them simultaneously. The first is reasonable doubt. The prosecution's case is flimsy in a couple places, starting with motive."

"Amir's anger at Judge Gardner was on full display in open court only hours earlier," Layla replied, making the prosecution's counterargument.

"Every person on the wrong side of a judge's ruling has the same motive. It's there, but it's weak. Beyond that, there is no murder weapon. In fact, there is no physical evidence at all tying Amir to the crime."

"Yet," said the Leg.

"Right. So we'll push the reasonable doubt angle if it comes to that, but right now I want to focus our investigation on the second strategy: some other dude did it."

"Our client insists he's innocent, thus, if he is to be believed . . ." Layla's thought trailed off, so the Leg picked it up.

"We've got a murderer on the loose."

"Easy, Columbo. Let's take it one step at a time. Start with the people at the party. Conduct an interview with everyone who'll speak to you. I want to know who was there, when they departed, who spoke with Judge Gardner, and whose behavior was at all out of the ordinary."

"Abe would also like us to flag any mistakes the police may have made," Layla said.

"Does Abe think we need to be told to do that?" I asked, unsure of how Layla's boss had entered this conversation.

"It's safe to assume the police investigation was executed under the immediate presumption that Amir had to have been the culprit," said Layla. "Their approach was flawed from the start."

Any civil rights violations by the Marshall Police Department would ultimately leave it open to a police misconduct lawsuit. That litigation, however, would only be possible if Amir were acquitted in criminal court first. There was no question in my mind that Amir had already broached this topic with Abe and that Abe would acquiesce to his client's demand to seek retribution against the people who had arrested him. But with Layla's comment, I realized Amir was focused on the wrong battle at the moment.

"Tell Abe we'll keep him apprised of any issues we come across," I said.

"He also mentioned he's receiving a lot of interview requests from outlets all over the country," Layla added. "What would you like to do about those?"

"What do you think we should do?" I asked.

"Most defense lawyers crave publicity," she said.

"I'm a patent lawyer."

In Marshall, Texas, publicity usually meant prying questions from unwelcome strangers. All of us in the Eastern District had grown accustomed to the occasional out-of-town reporter coming to investigate the tiny town that hosted an inexplicably large number of patent infringement lawsuits. No one ever gave an interview.

"I could have Gordon & Greene handle all media," Layla suggested.

"That's fine by me," I said.

The Leg walked to the fridge and grabbed a beer for herself and one for me, which she tossed across the room.

"The police started with the assumption that Amir was guilty. The only way we're going to win is if we successfully point the finger at someone else," I said.

"Unless we avoid trial altogether," the Leg said as she opened her new beverage.

"And how do you plan to swing that?" I asked.

"By finding the real killer," she said with so much confidence I almost believed she would do it.

· TWELVE ·

After winning my last case, I hadn't expected to return my attention to patent law until late January. When Judge Gardner was killed, I'd put EDTX even further into the recesses of my mind. So I was surprised when Judge Knox, the magistrate judge who had served under Gardner for years, summoned me to his office in the basement of the federal courthouse before December had come to an end. I stared at Tammy Tex, Knox's assistant, as she went about her work. She wore a denim shirt that looked like a repurposed Texas flag. She avoided eye contact, and I assumed it was because there was no way to make small talk with the cloud of Gardner's death hanging so heavily in the building. It may have been the first time she hadn't been in a chipper mood in her whole life.

"Tammy, my investigator should be contacting you today regarding the invitation list to the Christmas party—"

"The little girl with blue hair? She stopped by earlier this morning and picked it up."

I nodded. The Leg didn't need to do that in person, but I suspected she made a habit of interacting with as many people as she could. She might need to return to sources for more information later, so it was good practice to foster those relationships.

Judge Knox didn't keep me waiting very long. He appeared in the doorway and invited me to join him in his office. I had seen him at the funeral, but we hadn't had the opportunity to speak. I was genuinely curious about the purpose of this meeting.

"Thank for you seeing me today, James."

"Of course, Your Honor."

"I've spent the past twenty-four hours making calls to firms across the country, and I wanted to meet with all the locals in person to discuss the court's calendar."

"I've talked with all the firms I'm currently working with," I said. "I told them I suspected we'd get a continuance on all cases in the Eastern District."

"As a matter of fact, I plan to adhere to the schedule Judge Gardner set. Patent trials will be held on their allotted dates."

It was common practice for Judge Knox to sit in for Judge Gardner from time to time. Gardner even lent his bench to Knox when he wasn't using it so that Knox wouldn't have to conduct all of his proceedings from his much smaller courtroom downstairs. But taking over the entire calendar seemed like an unnecessarily speedy solution to something that wasn't a pressing problem.

"What's the rush?" I asked.

"Part of Judge Gardner's legacy is the deftness with which he managed a large caseload. The burden falls on all of us now to live up to his standards."

"I appreciate that, but I just thought we would hit pause until his replacement had been appointed."

"It could be months before the president nominates someone. And who knows how long it might take the Senate to hold a hearing and confirm? If we put a halt to all of our cases, we'll be backlogged for years. And worse, parties will start finding other venues in which to file patent suits. The Eastern District may never recover."

What Knox said made a lot of sense. I didn't want to be argumentative, but this development complicated my life and threatened to eat into a big chunk of my expected earnings for the next year. My entire focus needed to be on Amir's criminal case.

"Judge, given that I'm involved in a murder trial, if I can get the parties in my patent cases to agree to postponements, would you be willing to push those trials until after my other work has concluded?"

"I'm afraid not, James. I sympathize with the situation you're in, but if I make an exception for you, every other lawyer before me is going to ask for leniency. If you can't perform your duties in these upcoming trials, I suggest you reach out to the respective law firms and let them know they need to secure new local representation."

I wanted to protest, but it wouldn't help. Judge Knox was intent on captaining this ship, and it was best that I not rock the boat.

"I understand, Your Honor."

There was a playful knock on my front door. I opened it, and the Leg continued to tap a melodic beat. "Hello," she said as she entered.

I saw Layla out by the car, on her phone. She spotted me in the doorway and motioned that she'd join us in a minute.

I closed the door and entered the main room. The Leg handed me a bottle of Miller Lite and cracked open one for herself as she plopped down on the couch.

"I went to see Judge Knox today," I said. "His assistant mentioned you stopped by."

"That woman is a trip," said the Leg. "Small-town Texas at its finest. Makes me miss living in a city."

"Yeah," I said. "Why'd you move back here anyway?" I asked with the bite that can only come from one Marshall resident to another.

"My life turned into a Marty Robbins song." The Leg lowered her voice and sang: *"Out in the West Texas town of El Paso, I fell in love with a Mexican girl.'"*

"Got your heart broken, huh?" I asked.

"Into a million pieces. I needed a change of scenery, somewhere I wouldn't think about her all the time."

"Did it help?"

"Not even a little," she said with a smile so big it had to be concealing a great deal of pain.

I lifted my bottle of beer toward hers. "To heartbreakers."

"God love 'em," she said.

Layla entered through the front door and then stopped, as if she was worried she should have knocked first.

"Come on in," I said.

"Sorry, that was an assistant in the DA's office."

"What'd they want?"

"I had requested a copy of the blood and DNA analysis. I spoke with a lab technician in Dallas this morning who said they completed their work two days ago. I think that's more than enough of a head start for the district attorney."

"We're going to have to anticipate that his office will be less than forthcoming whenever possible. What'd they say?" I asked.

"They claimed they only received the analysis today. They said they were reviewing it and preparing to forward it to us right when I called."

"That sounds like bullshit," I said. "Did you get it?"

"Should be emailed to us momentarily."

"What about our independent analysis?" I asked.

"I've already sent the materials to an expert here in Marshall," Layla said. "She should have something for us soon as well."

"Excellent. Now then," I said, unofficially calling the meeting to order, "I met with the magistrate judge today regarding some upcoming patent cases. Obviously, the lawsuit against Medallion, Amir's company, will be postponed. However, that is the only trial Judge Knox is willing to delay. He intends to keep Judge Gardner's docket intact. This means I will have to transfer all of my clients to other lawyers. But this brings me to another thought I had today about our case. Cui bono? Who benefits from Judge Gardner's death? What cases were coming down the pike in Gardner's courtroom that will now be held in Knox's? Let's take a look at the docket for any upcoming cases with parties who would have had a strong preference for Judge Knox over Judge Gardner. Maybe someone who has prevailed before the former and lost before the latter. Is there any party that would have reason to believe they would benefit from moving their case out of Judge Gardner's court?"

"You mean a party other than our client?" Layla said flatly. She was right. My theory did put Amir Zawar squarely under suspicion.

"Hold on a second," the Leg interjected. "You're talking about patent clients. That would mean someone coming from out of town to commit murder."

"Or hiring someone local to do it for them," I said.

The Leg sat forward. "I've already begun interviewing people who were at the Christmas party. Nearly every lawyer in town was there."

"Every lawyer in town knew where to find Judge Gardner, probably saw him leave the party, too," I said.

"Right. So forget clients who might have a preference for one judge over the other. What about lawyers? You must all have your favorite."

The Leg made a good point. It concerned me though because she was talking about my colleagues. I wasn't opposed to a fishing expedition, but this would piss off every lawyer in Marshall.

"Explore that line of thinking," I said to the Leg, "but be discreet."

"Damn it," Layla said as she read from her phone.

"What?" I asked with concern.

"The blood found on Amir matches Judge Gardner's."

· THIRTEEN ·

Layla and the Leg left my house early because we all had long days ahead. Even so, I stayed up well into the night, wondering if my client was guilty. As I smoked each cigarette down to the filter, I played the murder over and over in my head. With each beer I drank, my cognitive ability declined and, like water spiraling down a drain, my brain circled tighter and tighter around a single thought: Amir literally had the judge's blood on his hands.

I sat in my Dodge Ram, looking at the two coffee cups. They had become part of a familiar routine for me as I waited outside the Fairfield Inn. I'd been up early and had consumed more than enough caffeine, but I didn't want to show up empty-handed. I figured Layla may have expected a cup of Joe to be waiting for her. I could have just brought one but worried if I didn't get myself a cup as well it might seem odd. After about sixty seconds of fixating on my coffee order, I decided it was possible I was overthinking the situation entirely.

At the main entrance of the hotel, I saw a woman in dark jeans, a black blazer, jet-black hair, and black Wayfarer sunglasses stride toward a car. She looked like Tom Cruise in *Risky Business* except she was wearing pants. She carried a backpack over one shoulder like she was in college, though she was probably ten years removed from her undergraduate days. She saw me looking at her and shot me a grin. It was unnerving. Even though I wasn't sure if I'd ever seen her before, I got the sense she knew exactly who I was. I searched my memory, trying to place her. I came up empty as Layla opened the passenger-side door and climbed in.

"Do you know that woman in the sunglasses?" I asked. Layla looked in the direction I pointed, but the woman had already disappeared.

I took East End Boulevard for most of the eight-mile drive to the county jail. The farther away we got from the town square, the more run-down the houses looked as we sped by. The houses near the square weren't that nice to begin with.

We entered the facility, and I approached the sheriff's deputy who was manning the main desk. I gave him Amir's name. He picked up the phone and said, "We've got another one for Zawar."

"Someone else is visiting him today?" I asked. The deputy shot me a look that told me it wasn't his job to answer my questions.

After about five minutes, Layla and I were led to a private room, where we found the other visitor. He was stocky like a wrestler. His shirt and tie seemed uncomfortably tight around his muscular neck.

"Haq," Layla said, putting her hand out, "I didn't expect you until next week."

"I felt my presence was necessary," he replied as he shook her hand.

"This is James Euchre. He's lead counsel. James, Furqan Haq is the chief operating officer for Medallion."

We shook hands. I had read a little bit about Furqan Haq in *The New Yorker* piece on Amir. They grew up on the same block in Queens and had been best friends their entire lives. Like Amir's father, Haq's dad had immigrated from Pakistan and become a cabdriver, though he was still alive and enjoying a luxurious retirement thanks to his son's financial success. Haq had been working at a venture capital firm when Amir had the idea to create Medallion. Haq quit his job on the spot to team up with his old friend.

"Mr. Euchre, I'm concerned that Amir is still incarcerated."

"Unfortunately, he's not going anywhere until trial. There's nothing I can do."

"There's nothing anyone can do, or nothing *you* can do?" Haq shot back.

"He's been charged with first-degree murder," I replied, with an inflection meant to convey that Amir's current residence had nothing to do with any shortcomings in my legal abilities.

Haq nodded and I took that as a sign we could move on from the topic. "I want you to understand Amir can be impulsive," he commented, seemingly apropos of nothing.

"Are you saying he's guilty?" I asked.

"I'm saying he made a mistake hiring you."

"Uh-huh." I paused, trying to figure out how to handle my new friend. "Who the hell are you?"

"I'm the guy who looks out for Amir, especially when he's not looking out for himself."

Before I had a chance to react, a deputy brought Amir in and left him with the three of us.

"It's good to see you, Haq," Amir said.

"Amir, as I was just telling Mr. Euchre, we need to get you more impressive representation."

It was almost amusing how much he didn't care about what I thought of him or what he thought of me.

"You need a dream team," he added.

"No, Haq. Euchre's my guy."

"It's one thing to think outside the box; it's another to gamble with your life."

Amir shot his friend a look, and Haq stopped protesting. I wondered how much power he was used to wielding in his outside life.

"How long will you be in town?" Amir asked.

"As long as you need me," he replied.

"I appreciate that, but Medallion needs you more than I do right now."

Amir told Haq he wanted him back in California, and Haq reluctantly agreed to leave that night. Amir turned toward me and Layla. "So what are we talking about today?"

"Your case," I said. I then stared at Haq, intimating that it was time for him to vacate the room.

"Whatever you have to say to me, you can say it to him," Amir replied.

"Afraid not," I insisted.

"Haq is like a brother to me."

"I don't care if he's your identical twin. You and I don't enjoy attorney-client privilege with him in the room."

Haq was irritated, but I didn't care. He waited an extra beat. "I'll be back this afternoon." He knocked on the door, and a deputy let him out.

"So what's going on?" Amir asked.

"The blood and DNA analysis came back," Layla explained. "It was a match with the victim's."

"How is that possible?" Amir asked.

I paused, trying to assess the sincerity of Amir's question. It had rolled off his tongue so easily, and it absolutely would have been the first thing I'd expect an innocent man to ask. What I wondered, though, was whether or not Amir was capable of imitating an innocent man with that much accuracy if he was truly guilty.

"That's what we're trying to find out," I said. "You were never near the parking lot that night?"

"So you're back to accusing me?" he snapped.

"We are going to have to address how Gardner's blood got on your jacket. Either you went near the crime scene without realizing it or someone who was at the crime scene went near you."

"What do you remember about the officers who arrested you?" Layla asked.

"The two that first arrived, the pudgy one and the young one."

"Jefferson and Ramirez," she clarified.

"They were the only two I really spoke with."

"Did they stay with you in the Compound?" I asked.

"I'm pretty sure. I don't think they ever left me."

"And who transported you to the jail?" Layla asked.

"Those two, Jefferson and Ramirez. They put me in the cop car and drove me to the station."

"Did you interact with any other officers?" I needed something more than what he was giving me.

"I don't think so."

"Play it over in your mind," I advised. "If you remember anything else about that night, let us know."

I knocked on the door to tell the deputy we were ready to go, then I turned to Amir.

"Is Haq going to be a problem for me?"

"No."

It was odd, but I had become concerned I might get dropped from a case I hadn't wanted in the first place. I was all in now, and I needed to be sure the same was true for Amir. The deputy opened the door, and Layla and I walked out.

Layla and I left the jail and headed toward our next meeting. Dr. Marcia Jordan Cole was the director of the Lee P. Brown Criminal Justice Institute at Wiley College. She earned her bachelor's degree from Tulane University in cell and molecular biology, her master's in justice, law, and criminology at American University, and her PhD in sociology and criminology at Howard University. Layla had found Dr. Cole's name at the top of multiple lists of leaders in the field of DNA evidence. That she worked close by was an added bonus, especially if we ended up hiring her to testify as an expert witness. Layla had forwarded Dr. Cole all of the information we had on the blood tests and crime scene analysis. What we needed from Dr. Cole was a different narrative, supported by the evidence, that could exculpate rather than implicate our client.

Wiley College consisted of twenty-two buildings that sat on

seventy-seven acres of land within the town of Marshall. It was founded in 1873, but none of the original buildings were still standing due to a fire around the turn of the twentieth century. The school boasted a long tradition of courageous activism and was the alma mater of many notable figures, including civil rights leader James Farmer Jr. The school's 1935 debate team defeated the reigning champions at the University of Southern California, earning them the nickname the "Great Debaters."

The fall semester had finished, and there was almost no one on campus. Dr. Marcia Jordan Cole had an office in Thirkield Hall but asked to meet with us in a lab at the Baker Science Building. We found the door ajar. Inside the room, a sweet old lady was wrapping up an online lesson. She paused her instruction as we entered.

"Welcome. You must be Layla Stills." Dr. Cole greeted my colleague and then came to me. "And you are James Euchre, I presume?"

"Hello, Dr. Cole. Thank you for meeting with us."

She carried herself like an affable grandmother. I half expected her to offer us some fresh-baked cookies. She gave her student a final piece of advice. He was a man in his thirties. He wore an all-white jumpsuit. When he signed off, his video feed was replaced by a screen that read "Raymond Laborde Correctional Center."

"He's one of my Second Chance Pell Grant students," Dr. Cole said. She could see that this didn't mean much to me, so she elaborated. "The program was created to give incarcerated individuals student aid and access to education. Wiley College was one of three HBCUs to partake in the initial pilot program, and our students have been very successful. The government pays thirty-one thousand dollars annually to imprison a person. It costs two-thirds of that to educate one."

"Seems like an easy sales pitch," I said.

"You'd be surprised, Mr. Euchre."

We stood around a table in the back, on which Dr. Cole had laid out a presentation.

"Let's talk about blood," Dr. Cole began. "I've reviewed the police reports pertaining to Mr. Zawar's arrest, as well as the Federal Bureau of Investigation's laboratory analysis of the blood and DNA deposits found on your client's person. I saw no egregious errors in any of the work that was done, but if we take a step back, I believe what we'll see is that the authorities have a theory, and it controls the facts rather than the other way around."

"So you're skeptical, Dr. Cole?" I noted.

"I'm a scientist. It's my job to be skeptical. DNA evidence is more accurate than fingerprints and certainly more reliable than eyewitness testimony. The problem with DNA evidence, though, is that people, especially jurors, believe it is infallible."

"Is there a chance this analysis is wrong?" I asked.

"Not wrong, per se. Think of it like this: If you put a man on the witness stand, and he testifies to what he believes is true but, in reality, is factually incorrect, has he perjured himself?"

"No. Perjury requires the willful dissemination of information that is untrue. He'd have to know he was lying."

"Exactly. DNA evidence is never intentionally false. But the stories we extract from it aren't necessarily true."

"How do you mean?" I asked with sincere curiosity.

"If my thumbprint is found on a gun, then that print is demonstrable evidence that I must have touched that gun. The testimony the thumbprint is making is indisputable because a thumbprint doesn't show up in a place unless the thumb was there, too. Now, what if instead of a fingerprint, we find a single strand of my hair on that gun? The prosecutors or investigators may deduce that there is a good chance I was near that gun, but, in reality, the only thing it proves is the gun was in the same place as one of my hairs. Whether that hair was still attached to my scalp when it came into contact with the gun is an entirely different matter. It's possible that a strand of my hair could fly out of my car's windows, get carried by a gust of wind to a nearby home, get caught on someone else's sleeve, and then travel with that person until it falls to its final resting place on a park bench. If the gun in question were to pass by that park bench, it could pick up my hair, having never been within miles of me. And yet jurors implicitly trust DNA evidence so much that, if an officer of the law presents a theory, and the placement of DNA at a suspicious scene or on a suspicious object seems to support that theory, most jurors will make the mental leap themselves. That's the danger of DNA evidence."

She called our attention to a diagram she had sketched. I recognized it as a drawing, to scale, of the town center, with the three courthouses, the parking lot, and the Compound just off the square.

"This is your crime scene. Here is where the victim was discovered. The first question is: Can we conclude where his body was found is also where he was killed?" Dr. Cole smiled, seeing our rapt attention. "Yes," she said. "The fatal wound was a laceration of the carotid artery on the left side of the victim's neck. This caused severe bleeding immediately, as evidenced by the large pool of blood on the ground surrounding the victim's head and torso. There would have been no conceivable way to transport his body and bring the blood along for the ride.

"Now, here is the problem I have with the state's narrative of events," she continued, putting her reading glasses on as she turned to a police report. "The state's theory is that Mr. Zawar committed this murder, ran directly to this house two hundred and fifty yards away, broke in, and was apprehended within one hundred and eighty seconds. He didn't have time to change clothes or wash up. And, to that point, he was wearing the clothes he'd been wearing all day when the police arrived."

"So where is the flaw in their thinking?" Layla asked.

"If you were to stab a man in the carotid artery, resulting in enough blood loss to cause his death, I would expect to find either a great deal of the victim's blood on you or none at all." She paused but could see we needed more explanation. "Even with only minimal struggle, the proximity of the attacker to the victim in a stabbing case all but guarantees the transfer of blood and DNA. And not just traces but large, visible samples. Factor in the location of the particular wound; a lot of blood pumps through this area. That's why we can take our pulse by putting our fingers to our necks. Finally, puncturing an artery causes an expulsion of blood. Splatter would be certain. You put all of these ideas together and, well, it makes a mess. The attacker's clothes, hands, face, feet, everything would be tainted with the victim's DNA. There are only two reasons why this would not be the case. The first would be that the attacker was covered head to toe in some type of hazmat suit he carefully removed and discarded after the killing. This would require some planning to obtain the proper materials, which flies in the face of the state's theory that this was a crime of passion. The other reason would be that the attacker did an incredibly thorough job of cleaning up afterward. Your client didn't have that kind of time. And with what little time he did have, he didn't change clothes. In that case, I would expect to find visible samples of the victim's blood all over him."

"There was blood on his jacket and shirt cuffs," I said, worried I was poking a hole in Dr. Cole's theory.

"Look at the pictures of those spots of blood," she said, laying out the photographs. "If Mr. Zawar stabbed the victim in the neck, his arm, shoulder, and torso would have been hit with blood. There is only a very small amount near his hand, and it looks superficial. It didn't penetrate his jacket the way fresh blood would."

"How did the blood get onto our client?"

"I believe the most probable explanation is that it was transferred there."

"By an officer," Layla concluded.

"Precisely. If your client is innocent, then it's likely he was never in close proximity to the victim at all. Let's leave out the possibility that Mr. Zawar is being framed for this murder because, well, this isn't the movies. We need to reconstruct the narrative around the crime scene. Not just what happened, but *when* it happened. We have the victim in the parking lot and the accused in a house nearby. We have DNA linking them together. So if they never crossed paths, then someone who was in both locations picked up the victim's DNA and inadvertently brought it with him to your client."

"Like a gust of wind," I said.

"Correct, Mr. Euchre," said Dr. Cole. "And this would explain not only how it got there but also why the blood found on Mr. Zawar was a trace amount, and why the pattern was just a little streak on his left cuff."

"And is that actually what you believe happened, Doctor?" I asked.

"Yes, it is."

Relief washed over me.

"There is a problem, though," she continued. I braced myself. "According to the one police report I've reviewed, I don't see an explanation for how DNA got from the crime scene to your client. And you should anticipate the officers will dispute any suggestion that they did their jobs improperly. You'll need to find a way to prove someone became contaminated at the crime scene and then got close enough to your client to inadvertently transfer the blood onto him."

After another fifteen minutes of questions and answers, Layla and I were confident we had what we needed. Dr. Cole walked us out of the lab and down the hallway toward the main exit. I was thrilled not only because of the content of what we had just learned but also because of Dr. Cole's effortless ability to convey her knowledge to a layperson. She would play very well in front of a jury.

"You've testified as an expert witness before, Doc?" I asked.

"Several times," she replied.

"Well, obviously, you won't need travel expenses, but we will be more than happy to compensate you for your time," I said.

"My fee is reasonable, and I use the proceeds to supplement my students who need a little extra assistance."

"What made you want to work with felons?" I asked.

"I am one," she said with a smile.

· FOURTEEN ·

L ayla and I had a little time to kill before our meeting with the district attorney, so I gave her a tour of the town square. There were a few shops that got a lot of foot traffic, but mostly there were businesses related to patent law. Lots of locals had hung up shingles in one of the several buildings on the square. They liked having office space that was walking distance to the federal court. They also felt that it validated the work they were doing to have a physical place of business. I never saw the point in having any overhead.

As we strode the side streets of Marshall, I wondered when I'd be in patent court again. If Amir were to be acquitted, my hope was that Layla and I would team up for the lawsuit involving Medallion. I wanted her to see me in my element. This was not the most important motivation I had in proving Amir's innocence, but it was an added bonus to be sure. I also knew that Layla longed to move away from criminal law, though she hid any residual disappointment rather well.

We walked north for a few blocks and came upon the old Paramount Theatre. The marquee was intact, and it still bore the name "Paramount," though it hadn't screened a film since the 1970s. A true movie palace, the theater opened in 1930 and could hold 1,500 people. The proscenium surrounding the screen made the stage look like it was designed for live actors. Residents, including my grandparents, used to go there to see "the pictures." As I showed Layla the exterior of the building, we passed the side door, where Black moviegoers used to enter back in the day. The only seats available to them had been in the balcony. I didn't learn this until I was well into adulthood. These were the types of town secrets generations of white citizens had kept from their children.

As we passed a bank on our way back to the square, I looked in the window and saw a reflection of someone leaving the old Harrison County Courthouse. I glanced over my shoulder and spotted the same woman in Wayfarers I'd seen that morning at the Fairfield. Layla turned, but the woman's back was to us, and by the time she could get a good look, the woman had rounded the corner and disappeared.

"Keep an eye out for her," I said. "I think she's staying at your hotel."

We arrived at the DA's office with time to spare. Knowing D-Cal, I figured he would make us wait at least five minutes just to give us the impression he was busy and in control. True to form, he didn't emerge from his office until several minutes past the hour. He apologized for the delay though he didn't mean it. The entire meeting could have been conducted over the phone, but he'd been giving us the runaround, and I knew he'd have a harder time brushing us off in person.

His two assistant district attorneys joined us, as did Detective Elliot, who sat quietly off to the side, never one to call attention to himself.

"Where are we on discovery?" I got right to the one item on the agenda that mattered to me.

"Judge Whelan gave us 'til the end of the week. That's when you'll have everything. And I've already been in contact with your investigator. Awesome job hiring the Leg, Euch. Keeping it in the Maverick family. I love it." He looked at his ADAs. "She was the kicker on his high school's football team."

"Not my team, D-Cal. She's way younger."

"I know not *your* team, obviously. She has one of these." He held up his left hand to reveal his state championship ring. I assumed he wore it that day just for my benefit. He looked over at his audience. "I went to Longview. We played Marshall in '95. That was the first time me and Euchre went head-to-head."

It was hard to say what bothered me the most about D-Cal. It could have been his insistence on bringing up high school football every other time I saw him. Or that he did it just to piss me off. Either way, the only move I had was to pretend it didn't annoy me.

"Just like now, Euchre was playing defense and I was on the attack. We were down by four with a minute and a half to go. Sixty-five yards in five plays, capped off by a twenty-seven-yard bomb from yours truly right into the corner of the end zone. My third touchdown pass of the day."

"And not a single one thrown to my side of the field," I interjected, instantly regretting taking the bait. It made me look childish and petty in front of Layla.

"As riveting as high school athletics are," Layla started, "perhaps we save it for the reunion and focus on contemporary rivalries?"

I was embarrassed that Layla was forced to be the adult in the room.

"Beg your pardon, Ms. Stills," D-Cal said. "My team is wrapping up all the discovery for you as we speak. We'll put a nice little bow on it and make sure you have it tomorrow." D-Cal made it sound like he was doing us a favor rather than obeying a judge's order.

"And what about the Compound?" Layla asked.

"We'll complete our investigation of both the crime scene and the home by end of day," said Detective Elliot.

"You'll have it back tomorrow as well," added D-Cal.

"Great," I said. I stood up, ready to get the hell out of there.

"One more thing, Euchre."

"Yeah?"

"Should we at least talk about disposition?"

"Our client is innocent, so I doubt he'll be interested in a plea deal. But if you have an offer in mind, lay it down, and I'll see if he picks it up," I said.

"In the interest of saving the people time and money, I am prepared to offer LWOP in exchange for a guilty plea."

Life without parole was reserved for the worst offenders. Typically, it was the punishment given to a defendant who was found guilty of a murder that hadn't included special circumstances warranting the death penalty. It was hardly seen as a gesture of leniency since the convicted person was guaranteed to die in prison. I wasn't sure if D-Cal was just playing games or if he thought I was inexperienced enough in criminal law to consider this a real offer.

"As I said, our client is innocent, so the prospect of spending the rest of his life in a penitentiary will likely be unacceptable to him. I will, of course, relay the offer, but if he asks for my advice, I'll tell him to tell you to take your offer and shove it up your ass. That is unless you have a real proposition you'd like to make?"

"That's the best he's getting." D-Cal was so tickled to have a murder case that he would have done everything in his power to make sure it went to trial.

"Pleasure as always, D-Cal," I said as I headed for the door.

Layla exited the old courthouse first. I was two steps behind her, and by the time I made it through the doorway, I had a cigarette between my lips and my pink lighter in hand. I still considered myself a nonsmoker, but it was getting harder to make the case now that I was well beyond my single, celebratory, end-of-a-trial pack. Layla turned around, and I felt shame.

"It seems to me," she said, "that D. Calvin Lucas was a very impressive seventeen-year-old."

I laughed. I didn't know how I managed to get caught up in such stupid arguments and old feuds.

"Tonight's my last night at the Fairfield," Layla said. "I can't stand the thought of another dinner in that hotel room."

"Where would you like to go?" I asked.

"Take me to your favorite place."

I took Layla to a spot called Felix's, out on Karnack Highway. Back when I was a kid, it was a bar you didn't patronize unless you had a Harley-Davidson and you ran with your own crew. Somehow it had become the favorite watering hole for people who wanted to drink on the outskirts of town. In recent years, you were likely to see more pickups in the parking lot than motorcycles. You'd never see a rental car though. This place was for Marshall residents only.

We walked in and found a booth along the near wall by the window. I ordered Layla's whiskey and Coke directly from the bartender, a man we all called "Buck." He wore a bandanna on his head and ran his hand through his white goatee after he asked a customer for their order. I glanced at the beers on tap and selected a Bud Heavy just for the hell of it.

"What's good here?" Layla asked when I placed our drinks down.

"I'll let you in on a little secret: there is no good food in Marshall. The trick is to drink until you don't really taste it."

"Cheers," she said, clinking her glass to mine. "So this is your go-to spot?"

"My mom was a waitress here for a while. I used to come here after practice and do my homework in this booth."

"Did you always know you wanted to be an attorney?"

"It was the one thing I didn't want to be. Risk was too great that I'd turn into my father."

"You didn't dream of becoming a patent lawyer?"

"No one dreams of becoming a patent lawyer."

Our waitress came, and we each ordered a brisket sandwich with fries and another round. As the waitress left, I couldn't think of anything clever to say, so I took a big gulp of beer for inspiration.

"So did it work?" Layla asked.

"Did what work?"

"Your plan to not turn into your father."

I thought about it for a moment. "A little too well," I confessed.

She nodded, seeming to understand what I meant, or at least deciding not to pry.

"What about you, Kalamazoo? Your parents must be proud of their daughter."

"They are. My dad immigrated from Trinidad when he was a teenager. He became a history teacher at the same high school where my mom taught English. I think I became what they wanted to become."

"A lawyer?"

"Successful."

"You're an only child?" I asked.

"Is it obvious?"

"There's a loneliness to it," I said, speaking from experience.

"You think I'm lonely?" she asked.

I nodded.

"Well, I studied a lot in college. I basically lived at the library in law school. And I work seventy hours a week," she said. "What's your excuse?"

"People like me less the more they get to know me."

By the time our sandwiches came out, we were ready to order our third drink. The waitress set our dinners in front of us and then disappeared behind the bar. Maybe it was the beer buzz or maybe it was the company, but the brisket tasted better than usual. We both asked for more barbecue sauce when the waitress returned.

"What made you decide to leave criminal prosecution?" I asked between bites. I'd been wondering about it since we first met.

She covered her mouth because she hadn't finished chewing. "I just needed a change of scene."

"Oh, come on. I see you going toe-to-toe with D-Cal and the police, the US attorney, all of them. You're good at this. Something must have happened."

"I became disillusioned," she said with affect.

"Curse of the optimist," I replied.

"I'm a Black woman in America; I'm a realist when it comes to our system of justice. I also believe working to improve it is a worthwhile endeavor, and my best shot at making a difference was from the inside." I nodded, though I didn't totally buy it.

"Putting an innocent person in prison is the last thing I'd want to do," she said. "But there are fewer innocent people on trial than you might think."

Layla worked for a US attorney who, by all accounts, was an egomaniacal asshole. He liked putting bad guys in jail, and he measured his prosecutors by their conviction records. Layla's last case was prosecuting a low-level drug dealer who was believed to have had knowledge about a major distributor in Maryland and Virginia. The FBI had been working the case for nearly a year and was growing impatient. So agents broke down the dealer's door, cuffed him, searched the place, and found enough oxycodone and fentanyl to put him away for a decade.

"Problem was, they didn't have probable cause," Layla said. "They'd had their eyes on this guy for months, but he was smart, probably knew he was being surveilled, and he never slipped up. The feds were overzealous, or they just didn't give a shit, and one night they broke into his house. When I discovered this, I told the US attorney it had been a bad search and we ought to drop the case. He said it was a drug dealer's word against the FBI agents', so not to worry about it. I protested, but he ordered me to prosecute the guy to the fullest extent of the law."

"So you quit?" I asked.

"I put the FBI agent on the stand and set a trap. He testified that he'd spotted a pack of pills through the window, and this gave them probable cause to enter. But during my initial questioning, he'd described in great detail the burgers, wrappers, and empty beer bottles that got knocked off the kitchen table during the arrest. There'd been no mention of drugs. I then introduced photographs that clearly showed the only thing visible through the window, from the outside, was the kitchen table. The truth was, as the dealer had insisted all along, his drugs were hidden inside the box frame of his bed. The agent had never seen illegal narcotics prior to entering, and it was obvious he had perjured himself. The defense counsel made a motion to dismiss, and the defendant walked out that day a free man. The FBI agent was suspended, and my boss gave me an hour to draft a letter of resignation and pack up my things. I left quietly and decided I was done trying to fight the good fight."

"No interest in switching sides, becoming a high-priced criminal defense attorney?" I asked.

"An unintended by-product of criminal prosecution is when the rare innocent person goes to prison. Getting a guilty client exonerated and set free isn't an unintended by-product of criminal defense; it's the objective. No way was I going into that line of work."

"Yet here you are, representing a man accused of murder."

We hadn't discussed our personal opinions about our client. Perhaps we knew the only way for us to do our jobs was to ignore, at all costs, the massive blind spot regarding Amir's guilt or innocence.

"You think he did it?" I asked.

"I hope not."

We finished our meals and decided not to order another drink. We were going to pass a couple of bars on our way back into town, and I figured I might suggest one of them as we drove by. We stepped outside and the cool night air gave me a jolt. I mindlessly reached for my Marlboros.

"Can I get one of those?" she asked.

"I thought you didn't smoke," I said.

"I thought you didn't either."

"Objection! Argumentative."

"You going to give me one or not?"

I shook one out of the pack and handed it to her. Then I struck the pink lighter and lifted it toward her face, protecting it from the wind with my other hand. Her eyes held mine for an extra beat as she inhaled. The end of her cigarette glowed bright orange. She kept the first breath in and then slowly let the smoke escape.

As I lit my own cigarette, a car peeled into the parking lot with the reckless abandon of a teenager or a drunk driver. The tires screeched as it stopped at the fence and backed into the last spot so the car was facing forward, as if on display. Everything about it, from its design to its custom matte black paint job, resembled the Batmobile. For some inexplicable reason, it had a yellow racing stripe down the center of it. I recognized the Mercedes-AMG GT because there was only one of them in Marshall. There was only one asshole in town who would drive a car like that.

When Samuel Earl Whelan's short body stepped out of his Mercedes, I felt the joy of the entire evening spill out onto the ground.

"Fuck, Euchre, you just can't stay out of my way." He approached us with extra strut in his step. "Who's this?"

"Layla Stills," she said with some force.

"She's with Gordon & Greene," I added.

"Good for her," Sam said.

"Remember how you were talking about unintended consequences?" I asked Layla. "Well, Sam is the walking embodiment of unintended consequences. He's Judge Whelan's son."

"Euchre, if you want me to make that pretty little face of yours look bad, just say the word."

My right hand was down at my side, holding my cigarette. I let the Marlboro fall and must have instinctively clenched my hand into a fist because the next thing I felt was Layla's fingers curl around my wrist.

"James."

I didn't budge. She moved in front of me and looked me dead in the eye.

"You do this, and it'll screw up our case." She was right. The fact that we'd had a previous run-in months earlier was one thing, but if I got into a brawl with the judge's son in the lead-up to our trial, either

Amir would get assigned a new judge or he'd need a new attorney. Neither of these was likely to benefit our client.

"James," she said again.

"Yep. Let's go," I agreed.

She released my wrist, and we headed toward my truck.

"It's good to see you listening to a woman," Sam called out after us. "Too bad you couldn't have done that for your wife."

I was instantly torn in two. Half of me wanted to explain to Layla what he meant. The other half wanted to tackle Sam and swap punches until one of us was unconscious or dead. But Layla was right; that would have ended badly for me either way. So I climbed into the truck and shut the door.

A feeling of awkwardness hung in the air, and Layla and I both sensed it. The truth was, we hardly knew each other. Sam's comment had pierced a hole through the fragile casing of our relationship, instantly deflating whatever had existed only moments before. The fact I had been married wasn't exactly something I was obligated to mention. But even if the omission wasn't a sin, it had implications. We drove back to the Fairfield in total silence.

· FIFTEEN ·

I woke up to incessant banging on my door. It was unclear whether the person knocking was intentionally keeping a beat to the throbbing in my head or if it was mere coincidence. Either way, as I stumbled through my house, trying to throw a shirt on while lacking the dexterity to button it, I took note of the incriminating evidence around my living room: the beer bottles, the whiskey tumblers, the ashtrays. It would be obvious to anyone that I'd ended my night on a low note.

The knocking finally stopped when I opened the door. I squinted at the midmorning sun and could barely make out the Leg and Layla behind her.

"Jesus Christ. How's the other guy look?" The Leg patted me on the arm, a congratulations for still being alive. They both entered the house, Layla's eyes scanning the room. Twelve hours earlier, things had been so different. I wondered if she was shocked at how rapidly I could descend into the darkness, or perhaps she wasn't surprised at all.

"Maybe you should whip up a Bloody Mary. Little hair of the dog, Euch?" The Leg grinned at me, still finding all of this amusing.

"Coffee," I managed to say. While a pot brewed, I took a quick shower. After five minutes under the steam, I felt marginally improved. I chugged cold water directly from the sink faucet and took three aspirin. I made a feeble attempt to dry off before putting on pants and a collared shirt, rolling my sleeves up as I emerged from the bedroom to join Layla and the Leg.

"I've got good news, bad news, and annoying news," my investigator offered. "Pick your poison."

"Let's start with the good news followed by the bad. Maybe by the time we get to the annoying news, it'll have sorted itself out," I said.

"Doubtful," replied the Leg.

Layla received a text message and stepped out of the room for a moment while Lisa began her report.

"I may have a lead," the Leg said.

"What is it?" I asked.

"I've been digging into the lawyers at the party. Multiple witnesses told me that when Judge Gardner announced he wasn't retiring, the magistrate judge became visibly angry."

"Judge Knox? Come on," I said incredulously.

"I thought it was far-fetched, too, but there may be something to it. I haven't been able to pinpoint exactly when Knox left the party, but it was as things started winding down. He got into his car, which was parked in the same parking lot where Gardner was killed—"

"Where in the parking lot?" I asked.

"I don't know yet. But after he leaves the party, his whereabouts are up for grabs because he's unmarried and lives alone. He's got no alibi."

I couldn't tell if the Leg was weaving an impossible story or if my hungover brain was incapable of absorbing it, but something didn't fit for me. Knox had clerked for Judge Gardner the first year Gardner was on the bench. Then he'd practiced patent law for ten years before becoming the magistrate judge under Gardner. He worked for him, he learned from him, he respected him.

Layla returned, with a steaming cup of coffee she held with both hands. Realizing it was for me, I stood up to take it from her. "You didn't have to do that," I said sheepishly.

"You look like you need it." Her comment, like my coffee, wasn't cut with any unnecessary saccharin.

I sat back down and returned to the Leg. "So what's your theory? The magistrate judge kills his boss because he wants his job?"

The Leg shrugged. "It's motive."

"There's at least a dozen viable candidates for that job," I said, "and it's anybody's guess who'll get the nomination. To kill a man on the off chance that you're going to be his replacement . . . I don't know. It feels weak to me." I lifted the mug toward my mouth. "And was that the good news?"

"You know what aichmomania is?" the Leg asked.

I shook my head no, gulping the coffee.

"It's an obsession with knives," she said. "Judge Knox owns hundreds of them. He buys them from all over the world, orders them online mostly. They're on display in his house. He's got every type and size you can imagine. He calls himself a collector. I'd call him a fanatic."

This was good news, potentially. It didn't make him a murderer, but jurors love an unsolved mystery. They like to put some of the pieces together themselves. We weren't in some-other-dude-did-it territory yet, but we were working on it.

"All right, it's thin, so keep at it," I said, trying not to sound too optimistic. "Now hit me with the bad news."

The Leg looked to Layla, signaling that it was her turn.

"The district attorney emailed the rest of the police reports," Layla began. "According to the officers, no one touched our client or went within arm's reach after they were near the victim."

"Assuming those reports are accurate, there was no opportunity for one of them to transfer blood from the crime scene onto Amir?" I asked.

"Assuming they're accurate."

"Well, then let's assume they're inaccurate. How would we prove that?" I asked with some irritation.

"Unfortunately, these reports are the best indication of what transpired because the notes within were made contemporaneously.

We would need testimony from one of these officers contradicting what's in these reports, and even then we'd be relying on faulty memories that would be months old by the time we got to trial."

I exhaled a frustrated breath. My head was still pounding. I thought about a cigarette, but it would only make the pain worse.

"All right, now do your best to annoy me," I said to Lisa.

The Leg reached into her pocket and pulled out her phone. She flipped through the apps while she spoke.

"Amir gave an interview," she said while pulling something up on her screen.

"When?" I asked with dread in my voice.

"Yesterday."

She placed her phone in front of me. It was open to an article with the headline "Rideshare Prince Shares All: Murder in a Small Town." I looked at the byline. The journalist's name was Charlotte Mayhew, and there was a photo next to her name. Even in her headshot she wore Wayfarer sunglasses.

"Let's go talk to our client."

The three of us agreed to meet at the county jail. Layla told the Leg she'd catch a ride with me. To be honest, I'd hoped to drive alone so I wouldn't have to use what little brain power I had for small talk or, worse, real conversation.

Layla climbed into the passenger seat of my Dodge, and we followed the Leg's car away from my house. I lowered my window and found my Marlboros. "You want one?" I asked.

"No, thank you."

The response felt cold, though I had no idea if it really was.

The first inhalation made me dizzy. I figured I'd stabilize by the time I was halfway through the cigarette though. I just needed silence.

"So last night . . ." Layla let her words hang and then dissolve, like a phrase written by a plane in the sky.

"I'm sorry about how it ended," I said. "Sam and I go way back. But I shouldn't have let him get to me."

I expected her to respond immediately, but she didn't. She seemed to be thinking about what I said and how it impacted what she had intended to say.

"We don't know each other very well," she started. "We're all entitled to our secrets." With one simple statement she managed to forgive me my trespasses, while also constructing a wall between us. I didn't know how I could change the situation or if I even wanted to. All I knew was that I felt entirely alone again.

The Leg was already at the entrance to the county jail when Layla and I arrived. We signed in and were taken to Attorney 1A, the closest of the four rooms where lawyers and their clients meet. When the deputy left, I told Layla and the Leg not to mention Judge Knox. I wanted to be the one to present Amir with that theory. I wanted to see how eagerly he would accept an alternative. An innocent man is skeptical. A guilty man will jump at the opportunity to blame anyone other than himself since he knows all substitutes are equally flawed.

While we waited for Amir, the three of us traded notes on Charlotte Mayhew. Originally a software engineer, Mayhew had worked for several tech companies, bouncing around Silicon Valley for years. Finally, she grew tired of trying to gain admittance into the brotherhood of assholes and decided she'd start a blog offering an insider's perspective into the tech world. She was known for being a blunt interviewer and a dogged reporter.

"She's cute, too," said the Leg.

"That's helpful, thanks," I replied.

After a few more minutes, Amir entered. He noticed the Leg and seemed to be sizing her up, even before the deputy had exited the room.

"Who's this?" Amir asked.

"This is Lisa Morgan. She's our investigator."

"Do she and I enjoy attorney-client privilege?"

"Her work product related to the case is protected, as is this discussion we're about to have because it pertains to our trial strategy," I said with annoyance in my voice. He had asked a perfectly reasonable question, but I wasn't in the mood to deal with Amir's attitude. He sensed the condemnation in my tone.

"I want to protect myself. Certainly you can understand that."

"I'd be more sympathetic to your concern for privacy if you weren't giving interviews to journalists from inside your jail cell," I said. I was frustrated, so I stood up and moved around.

Lawyers likely fell over themselves vying for Amir's business, but this wasn't corporate law, and I wasn't looking to rack up billable hours. I was going to run this case as I saw fit, or I was going to remove myself from the situation entirely.

"Where I get confused, Amir, is how you go from promising to keep your mouth shut to volunteering your entire version of events to a member of the press."

"First of all, my *version of events* is the truth. And second, my reputation is also on the line. It's called the court of public opinion."

"If you die by lethal injection with your reputation intact, you gonna consider that a victory?" I asked. "You have no idea the impact this could have on a potential juror."

"A lot of townsfolk 'round these parts read Silicon Valley blogs?" Amir asked sarcastically.

"No, but reporters from *The New York Times* and *The Washington Post* do. And if they find out you're giving interviews, there will be a whole lot of people down here, and this thing will turn into a spectacle. But none of that is as damaging as your quotes in that piece."

"I spoke the truth."

"You called the Marshall Police Department 'a racist descendant of the Ku Klux Klan.'"

"I know what this town used to be and I know what it still is. You see anyone else here who looks like me?"

"We fight this case in court, not in the media," I insisted.

"Are you going to attack the police for racial bias?"

"You weren't profiled because of your appearance, Amir. It's not like they got a call that a murder had occurred, and then spotted you and thought, 'Hey, he looks like a criminal. Let's arrest him!'"

"You think it's that simple?" Amir asked.

"They responded to an alarm for a break-in. They went to the house where the alarm went off. They didn't know who they were going to find inside."

"But once they saw me, they stopped looking for anybody else."

"And I'll make that argument, but I'm not making it the way you want me to. Any juror who believes there's racial bias in policing is going to see it without me pointing it out. There will be others on that jury, though, people who have family members in law enforcement. You want to guess how big the Blue Lives Matter movement is in East Texas? We aren't going to convince twelve citizens of this town to acquit you by arguing that you're the victim of racist cops."

Amir looked to Layla. "What do you think?" he asked her.

"When I was a prosecutor," she said, "I always knew I was winning a case when the defense attorney argued racial bias."

"But do you think this is about race?" he asked.

"Any time a person of color is on trial in America, it's always about race," Layla said.

I returned to my seat and looked at my client. "I want you to understand, we will be looking for prospective jurors who are open-minded and want to hear your side of the story, but if any of them read what you had to say in the press, they will get kicked from the jury."

"All right," he said.

"No more interviews?"

"OK."

"Good," I said, thinking we were done arguing.

"But what are you doing to publicly promote the fact that I didn't do what I've been accused of?"

"We are following up on leads and exploring every possibility," I said. "The best thing I can do is find an alternative theory that proves, in a court of law, you didn't commit this crime."

"That shouldn't be an impossible task for you since I didn't do it."

"You do have a motive, Amir." I felt he needed some reminding.

"Because I didn't like being sued for patent infringement in Judge Gardner's court? I would imagine that is true of any CEO whose company has faced a lawsuit in Marshall, Texas. So if that's the list of suspects, let's get Tim Cook down here and see where he was on the night of the murder."

"Tim Cook didn't stand up in court and threaten to kill the judge," I said too loudly.

"I didn't threaten to kill him."

"You shouted, 'I'll fucking kill you.'"

"I was shouting at the bailiff who was trying to break my arm!" Amir raised his decibel level to match mine.

"That wasn't entirely clear, nor is it how the prosecution will tell the story, so maybe you will finally learn you're better off when you keep your fucking mouth shut!"

I stood up. Amir could push my buttons about as well as anyone I'd ever met.

"To your point," I said, lowering my voice and trying to bring some calmness to the conversation, "we are running the names of every person who was party to a lawsuit in the past year, as well as all of those on the upcoming docket, to see if anyone may have had anything to gain from Judge Gardner's death. However, there is one other angle we're currently exploring." I paused, having cast my line like a fly fisherman, letting it float over his head for a moment.

"What is it?" Amir asked.

"There's a man by the name of Jay Knox. Maybe you've heard of him."

Amir shook his head. "No."

"He's the magistrate judge for the Eastern District. He served under Judge Gardner for the last ten years. Eyewitnesses say that Judge Knox appeared agitated on the night of the murder when Gardner declared he had no intention of retiring. This announcement came as a surprise to many, including, presumably, Judge Knox. We're just starting to scratch the surface on this theory, but I wanted to keep you in the loop." I had dangled the hypothesis above my prey and then teased it back, waiting to see if he'd take the bait.

He looked at Layla and then at Lisa before landing back on me.

"I don't buy it," Amir said.

I glanced at Layla.

"Judge Gardner was a thousand years old," Amir continued. "He would have died soon anyway."

"He had a lot of good years left," I said defensively.

"Whatever. You're telling me this guy, Knox, he served under him for a decade and then all of a sudden becomes so impatient with the old man that he offs his boss?"

Amir's skepticism had two consequences. The first was, it renewed my faith in him that he might be innocent. The second was, it made me question the plausibility of Knox myself. But all we needed was a clear alternative theory, a red herring that could buy us reasonable doubt.

"There is one other item we need to discuss with you," Layla said, sensing that I was done. "We would like to ask for a delay, and I'm confident it'll be granted."

"A delay for what?"

"For your trial. We could probably be in court in under a hundred days, but since we are still running an investigation, an investigation we hope will bring to light the actual culprit, I see no harm in biding our time. A delay of at least eight months would be well within reason."

"Every day I spend in here is a day my company falls further behind," Amir said. "Every day I'm here is another day I have to hold on tighter to everything I've built. It is imperative to the survival of my business that I get out of this jail and out of this town as soon as possible. No delay."

Layla looked at me. We both knew it wasn't worth the fight. Win or lose, this trial was going to begin on time.

SIXTEEN

As we exited the jail, I noticed a spotless black town car parked near the entrance. The hired driver sat motionless behind the wheel. A rear door was open, and I could see the passenger working on his laptop inside. When Furqan Haq saw me approaching, he closed his computer and stepped out of the vehicle.

"Good morning, Mr. Euchre."

"I thought you were leaving town," I said.

"Some things came up. I'm on my way to the airport after I see him."

"What's your agenda?"

"Protecting my friend."

"Then we're on the same team," I said.

Haq let out a little laugh laced with disbelief. "Amir is a once-in-a-generation mind," he said. "He could be the next Steve Jobs."

"And you're Wozniak?"

"I'm the guy who would have ripped out my own pancreas and given it to Jobs so he'd still be alive today. Amir's parents are gone. I am his only family. And with the money and the success, I've seen a thousand people like you try to use him to advance their own careers with no regard for what matters to him. You aren't looking out for Amir."

"You mean I'm not looking out for Medallion."

"They're the same thing."

"No, they're not," I said. "And the fact that your primary concern is for your company rather than your *family* is more than a little troubling. But you're right, I don't give a damn about Medallion or the money you stand to lose."

"This has never been about money. Medallion is more than a company; it's a new way of organizing the world. I don't expect someone like you to see the big picture."

"Enlighten me."

"Amir is an existential threat."

"To who?"

"To anyone who benefits from the world as it is and fears the world as it could be. We can shatter millennia of power dynamics in which the rich subjugate the masses."

"With a single rideshare app," I replied.

"Medallion is an idea, and if we can prove that it's achievable, then we will transform the economy so that individuals are no longer controlled by the people who pay them. That's disruption of the highest order. When that is your mission, you make powerful enemies."

"You think this is a conspiracy?" I asked.

"I don't think someone set him up if that's what you mean, but throughout history, revolutionaries have been taken out by the powers that be, one way or another. If it's not outright assassination, sooner or later an opportunity presents itself for the system to destroy what threatens it. For us, it started with city commissions voting to ban our operations. Next, it was patent infringement lawsuits intended to shut down Medallion for good. Then, one night, a backwoods police force and a racist justice system stepped up and volunteered to carry out Amir's execution. It wasn't a plan, per se, but it was a happy accident. It was a perfect opportunity to eliminate a radical idea. I say Amir and Medallion are the same thing because that's how the world views them."

"That's a fascinating story," I said. "Maybe you understand the world better than I do. But I know Marshall, Texas. And a jury here won't give a damn about your revolution. They care that one of their own was killed. That's where I come in. You are making my job more difficult and that could cost Amir his life."

"I would never put him in harm's way," Haq said.

"Really," I said, "then tell me this—who facilitated his interview with Charlotte Mayhew?"

His expression was all the confirmation I needed.

I tailed the Leg's car back toward town. We turned onto East Houston Street, and as we approached the main square, we could see that a crowd had gathered outside the federal courthouse. I looked to Layla, who seemed as curious as I was about the commotion. There were hundreds of people, dozens of reporters near the steps, and three news vans. I parked next to the Leg.

"What the hell's going on?" I said as I climbed out of the truck.

"Is that for us?" the Leg asked.

We headed straight for the crowd, not sure what we'd find. A podium had been placed at the top of the steps leading to the federal courthouse. An old man in a blue suit with a gold pin on his lapel exited the courthouse and flashed a politician's smile as he walked to the microphones. "Good morning, folks. It is always good to be in Marshall, Texas."

"Senator Brookberry," I said to the Leg. She nodded. Brookberry had been elected to the United States Senate in 1980 and had been a fixture in Texas politics my entire life. A few weeks earlier, he had told the press this would be his final term. He would not seek reelection. There was only one reason the senior senator from our state would be standing in front of cameras at the federal courthouse for the Eastern District of Texas.

"I am very pleased to announce I have spoken with the president of the United States of America. I have given him my official recommendation that Judge Jay Knox be nominated to serve as the next federal judge in East Texas. The president has accepted my recommendation and will be sending Judge Knox's name to the US Senate for confirmation early in the new year."

I hadn't realized Knox was standing behind the senator until his name was said aloud. Knox was obviously on the short list, but I was surprised he was being nominated, and with such speed. As the senator put his arm around the magistrate judge, I homed in on Knox's face. I couldn't help but think that he didn't look surprised at all. Maybe he wasn't. Maybe everything was going exactly according to his plan.

As I watched Jay Knox humbly prepare for his moment, I felt my body fill with rage. Guilty or not, Judge Knox was unequivocally the biggest beneficiary of Judge Gardner's death. Our alternative theory of the murder now had an indisputable motive.

"What was that you said, Euchre?" The Leg leaned in close to me. "Cui bono?" Her words struck like lightning. "I'd say that's a pretty big fuckin' bono."

PART III

IN CURIA

In Court

My original plan to drink and smoke my way through the remainder of December no longer seemed practical given that I was charged with defending a man accused of murder, a man I no longer believed was guilty. But it didn't seem fair to me that I should have to completely abandon my holiday plans either. So I made myself a deal. I would devote twelve hours every day to Amir's case, and then the other twelve hours were all mine. There was one looming activity that needed my attention.

My three-bedroom house looked the same way it had when my wife had been there. It seemed pointless for me to redecorate, to replace furniture and other things simply because they might remind me of her. The house had been ours. So unless I wanted to sell it and move someplace new, there was no escaping my memories of Amy. There was one room that needed to be dealt with, though, one room I'd been avoiding for a very long time.

The three-car garage was detached from the house, and there was a studio above it. I never went in there. That was her place. That was where she painted, where she read, where she went to shut out the world. But after four years, it was time to clean it out. I'd resolved to tackle this project by the end of the year, and with only a few days left in December, the time had come.

I carried my second beer of the evening into the studio. It smelled of dust and old paint. I couldn't remember the last time I'd set foot in there. I'd never cleaned it. It was exactly how Amy had left it. The walls were lined with canvases, some painted and some bare, resting on the floor. Three easels stood in the center, two were unused and one was a work in progress. I used to tell her that her abstract art frustrated me. I was always trying to unscramble the mess and extract the true meaning, to decipher the message. She told me that wasn't the point. Now, surrounded by the bursts and swirls of color was as close as I'd ever come to her again. I found the paintings haunting, though I had no idea if that was the intention of the dark waves of various hues collapsing into one another. I couldn't crack the code. Her art, much like Amy, remained an enigma.

I gathered a bucket and cleaning supplies from the kitchen, and I grabbed a bottle of Jack. I drank and worked for a long time, until every inch of the studio had been tended to. I couldn't throw out any of her paintings. I carried them down to the garage and covered them with a tarp in the corner. It took me all night.

As I stood in the doorway, I turned back to the room I had just scrubbed bare. I felt no better, and possibly worse, than I had several hours earlier. I had removed all evidence of Amy from the room.

I turned off the single dull light and locked the door.

The only person I saw on Christmas was Amir Zawar. I visited the county jail to deliver some books he'd requested. We attempted to make small talk. As lonely as I'm sure he was, my company didn't seem to help at all. It was awkward and I left quickly.

I kept in regular contact with Layla and the Leg. The district attorney's office had sent over more discovery than we were prepared for. D. Calvin Lucas flooded our little operation with as much material as he could. The Compound was unsealed. We would use it as our base of operations when Layla returned. The DA's office had seized so many items from the house that the evidence list was twenty-five pages long. That was nothing compared to the witness list, which included half the town of Marshall. Every person who had been near that federal court or at the party was on the list. There was no way the district attorney planned to introduce most of this in trial, but he knew if he listed everything and everyone, we'd have a hard time figuring out what he did intend to use. He also knew we would waste a lot of time looking into things that would prove useless.

Meanwhile, the Leg was burrowing deeper and deeper into the rabbit hole that was Judge Jay Knox. We were still hoping to uncover the figurative smoking gun, but the circumstantial evidence was piling up. We believed we would have a very compelling narrative for the jury when the time came for us to present our defense.

Layla had gone from New York to Kalamazoo to spend the holiday with her folks. If I was working twelve-hour days, I had a feeling she was working sixteen. We'd communicate throughout the mornings and afternoons, checking in on each other's progress, cross-referencing one another's work. Usually, we'd hop on the phone in the evening, just before quitting time and brief each other on our developments. A couple of nights we did this via video because we had some visuals to share. More than once, our conversation transitioned seamlessly away from the case. We didn't talk about anything of particular importance. The important thing, I guess, was that we were talking.

"What did Santa bring you this year?" I asked when she called me on Christmas night.

"Oh, this was a very exciting Christmas in the Stills house," she said. "I got a new charger for my laptop and headphones."

"Beats coal, I guess."

"I left my charger in New York and had planned to buy a new one when I got back to Texas, but Apple doesn't have a store in your lovely little town."

"And it never will," I said. "Apple has no stores anywhere in the Eastern District."

"You're kidding me," she said. "In the hopes that, if they didn't do any business there, no one would be able sue them for patent infringement in EDTX?"

"Yep."

"Did it work?"

"Nope. And if they'd asked me, I'd have told them to go the Samsung route instead." That company had given out scholarships to Marshall High graduates and, some winters, put up the Samsung Ice Skating Rink, right across the street from the courthouse, for all the jurors to see.

"Is there an ounce of shame to any of this?" Layla asked.

"Sure doesn't seem like it," I said. "But this is the life you've chosen. Welcome to patent law in East Texas."

Aside from my client, I was discovering that the most frustrating aspect of criminal defense was the power imbalance between the individual accused and the omnipotent state leveling the charge. The district attorney and I were on opposing sides, so I was, for the most part, willing to accept his lack of assistance. But the police are, theoretically, neutral. In practice, nothing could be further from the truth. These two entities make up that historical coupling of law and order, and neither one gives a damn about the presumption of innocence.

D-Cal was making it all but impossible for me to interview the officers who were dispatched the night of Judge Gardner's murder. I had pored over every word in their police reports, but I wanted to hear their stories from their own mouths. I wanted to watch them search their memories for what really happened. I also needed to know if any of them were open to the idea that they'd apprehended the wrong man.

I pulled off of Victory Drive and into the Pine Hill trailer park. Detective Elliot had moved into a single-wide mobile home after his second divorce. He had openly boasted that he wanted his third wife, should he ever get one, to have nothing to take from him when she left. My suspicion was he wanted his domicile to match his life, simple and small.

When Detective Elliot opened the door to his trailer and found me on the other side, he rolled his eyes. "This must be my lucky day," he said as he motioned for me to enter. He was frying eggs and a piece of ham in the same pan on the stove. He asked if I wanted some, but I passed. We stood while he cooked.

"I have some questions about the Gardner investigation, but no one will talk to me," I said.

"Ask your questions."

I had to proceed delicately. Cops didn't take kindly to performance reviews from defense lawyers.

"Is the Marshall PD, or anyone else for that matter, looking into other suspects?"

"We have our suspect."

"My concern is that the investigation zeroed in on my client too quickly and may have overlooked some things."

"Believe it or not, I want the man who killed Judge Gardner to be caught and punished. Justice is the only thing that matters to me. I've reviewed the evidence, and every piece points to your client." He spoke with a reassuring tone, though it didn't change how I felt.

"If I had another theory, would you look into it?"

A bit of grease jumped out of the pan and onto his undershirt. He either didn't notice or didn't care.

"I'm not asking you to go in guns blazing and arrest somebody else; I'm wondering if you'd be willing to do the slightest bit of investigating if I pointed you in the right direction," I said.

He flipped his eggs and they crackled. They were already too browned for my taste.

"It's been my experience that defense theories tend to be straw-grasping fantasies with no real merit whatsoever. Now, if you want to share your theory, and if I find it unusually compelling, perhaps I'll be motivated to investigate. But if it's nothing more than a lawyer's desperate attempt to save his client from conviction, then you're wasting both our time."

I had a tough decision to make. My goal wasn't to catch the real killer. That's not what my client needed, nor was it what the Texas Disciplinary Rules of Professional Conduct demanded. Judge Knox was my best hope at winning Amir's freedom. He was our one chance to point the finger at someone else. He was my ace in the hole. If I gave him to Detective Elliot at that moment, I'd be showing my hand early in the game. I'd also risk Elliot relaying our strategy to D-Cal, who would then be able to prepare accordingly. I decided, given Elliot's aversion to helping me, it wasn't a risk worth taking.

"I do hope the Marshall Police Department will review its investigation and revisit it with an open mind," I said.

"I appreciate the unsolicited advice, Jimmy." He turned the burner off and grabbed a plate. "I liked you better when you were a patent lawyer."

"So did I," I said. "So did I."

· EIGHTEEN ·

January and February flew by. Amir had agreed to pay me the same fee I normally took for a patent case, but the workload was significantly greater. So was the pressure. I didn't take a day off in nine weeks. Layla and I prepped exhaustively, and she gave me a crash course in criminal procedure. The only saving grace was that this was D-Cal's first murder trial as well, though he had the Marshall Police Department and the FBI in his corner.

Finally, it was the night before the trial was set to begin. I'd spent two weeks weaning myself off liquor, and by that I mean I was down to my trial limit of three drinks per night. That particular evening though, I hadn't had a sip yet, and my sobriety, combined with my anxiety about being in court the next day, was really starting to show. As the Leg watched me and Layla rehearse some moves, it was clear my performance was getting worse.

"We should call it a night," Layla said, gracefully throwing in the towel for me. "You're ready. At this point, we're over-preparing."

"Right," I said, not buying it.

I stood up, glad to be done. We had turned the Compound into the headquarters for the Amir Zawar defense. The dining room table was covered with books and legal documents that left a trail into the living room. There was evidence of our hard work everywhere. I hoped it was going to pay off.

I followed the Leg out the front door, then stopped and turned to face Layla. I wanted to thank her for staying on the case. Instead, she spoke.

"Try to get some sleep."

She had cursed me. I didn't sleep a wink.

We convened in front of the new Harrison County Courthouse, an ugly, tan, rectangular eyesore that, cruelly, was forced to stand across the brick parking lot from its much more attractive predecessor. The interior was lined with cold hallways and uniform doors that led to offices of low-level bureaucrats who rubber-stamped business licenses and admonished people for using the wrong forms. There was nothing majestic about it at all.

We took the elevator up to the criminal courts and stepped off to discover a packed hall. We expected a few curious onlookers but nothing like what we found.

"The jury pool?" Layla asked me.

I shrugged. We were beginning jury selection that morning, so it was possible the potential jurors had congregated in the hallways while they waited to be called. In the federal court, they would have had their own room. As we pushed our way into the courtroom itself, we found that it, too, was crowded. The faces all blended together, though I did spot a woman in Wayfarer sunglasses. Charlotte Mayhew was not the only member of the press in attendance. I glared at her and she smiled back.

Layla and I moved to our table on the left side of the court. D-Cal and his two assistant DAs were already at their table on the right. He grinned and gave me a salute. I looked around to see how many people's eyes were on me and then discreetly used my briefcase to shield my hand from everyone except D-Cal while I flipped him the bird.

When Judge Whelan entered the courtroom, he seemed taken aback by the size of the crowd as well. "Those of you who were called here for jury duty need to see the clerk at the end of the hall," he announced.

We all waited for a mass exodus of confused jurors, but there wasn't one. Everyone in there was a spectator. In patent litigation, I'd grown accustomed to my cases being of almost no importance to the outside world. However, a murder trial, especially in Marshall, Texas, was an event worth watching live.

Judge Whelan asked the guard to bring in the defendant. Amir took his seat at the end of the defense table, next to Layla. His Honor ran through a few procedural items and then reminded everyone in the audience to remain quiet as the first batch of prospective jurors came in.

Layla and I had agreed to tag team jury selection. It was not uncommon to have local counsel handle voir dire in patent trials. We had a better feel for our fellow townspeople than the big city lawyers. It was also the jurors' first introduction to the legal team, so locals helped ingratiate them to their respective sides.

"You want me to start?" Layla asked. I assumed she offered because she thought I looked nervous.

"No, I've got it."

As I rose to my feet, I started with the same opening line I always used. "Go Mavericks," I said as I approached the jury box. It was a reference to our high school mascot, though it doubled as the name of Dallas's NBA team for anyone who hadn't gone to Marshall High. Ordinarily, I'd get at least half a dozen "Go Mavericks" in response. Sometimes I'd even draw out an "Amen." These jurors gave me nothing, and their silence told me everything. There's a whimsical side to trial law, and it served me well in EDTX. But in criminal court, where one man's life had been taken and another's was on the line, my attempt at levity had missed its mark. These potential jurors took this matter very seriously, and my cavalier opening had done nothing except make me look like a fool. If I'd had my way, we would have kicked that entire panel of jurors and started fresh with a new twelve.

The defense and prosecution went back and forth all morning. There were thirty peremptory challenges between us. D-Cal and I could each dismiss fifteen jurors without giving a reason. Challenges for cause were unlimited. If we wanted to kick a juror, we would try to get them dismissed for cause to preserve our peremptory challenges. The reasons for a cause challenge are laid out explicitly in Texas statute and largely fall under three categories: 1. A juror is physically or mentally unable to perform their duties; 2. A juror has some affiliation with the case and/or has their own issues with the law, like a felony conviction, thereby rendering them unable to serve on a jury; or 3. A juror is biased. Most arguments between the defense and the state revolve around this third justification.

The term "voir dire" is often misattributed to Latin when it is, in fact, derived from Old French. It means "to speak the truth." Its purpose is supposed to be to ask potential jurors to speak truthfully so the court ends up with twelve unbiased triers of fact. In reality, we are all biased. Therefore, each side is doing everything in its power to make sure that as many of those dozen jurors as possible are biased in their favor.

Layla and I had a list of questions meant to guide us toward jurors we believed would be sympathetic to a client who was decidedly an outsider. We were looking for people who understood what it meant to be falsely accused, suspected of something they didn't do because of how they looked or who they were. We were looking for people who questioned authority and didn't jump to conclusions just because someone had been arrested and charged with a crime. Short of that, I was looking for rule breakers.

D-Cal sought people who walked the line. He wanted individuals who didn't prize their individuality. He needed jurors who obeyed the laws of the state and felt that those who did not should be punished accordingly.

Of course, as anyone who's been on a first date can tell you, it's impossible to ascertain who a person is with just a few questions and answers. So while this should have been an intricate and delicate process, one brazen pattern emerged rather quickly.

"Your Honor, may we approach?" Layla called for a sidebar. I followed her to the bench. D-Cal and his two lackeys joined us.

"Ms. Stills?"

"Your Honor, the district attorney has challenged the first three jurors of color."

"I can use my peremptory challenges for any reason at all."

"No, you can use them for *almost any reason,* or you can use them for no reason," Layla said. "But the one reason you can't use them is to compose an all-white jury."

Judge Whelan needed to take control before things got out of hand. "Mr. Lucas, do you wish to use one of your challenges on Juror Seventeen?"

"Yes, Your Honor."

"Very well." The judge looked over to the witness stand. "Juror Seventeen, you are dismissed. Thank you for your service." He returned his attention to the lawyers at his bench. "Ms. Stills, your objection is noted for the record. Mr. Lucas, I trust that your challenges will be more varied, and believe me, this will be a jury that represents our entire community, be that in age, gender, and, yes, race. Let's not have this conversation again. Return to your places."

He had issued the warning we wanted, and that was the best we could hope for. Our second problem had no solution. D-Cal was allowed to ask every prospective juror what his or her feelings were on the death penalty. If they were morally opposed to it, or simply had any "conscientious scruples" about execution, then the state could challenge them for cause. It wouldn't even cost D-Cal any of his fifteen peremptory challenges to weed out every single person who opposed capital punishment. This inevitably made the jury more likely to render a guilty verdict. People who believe in harsher punishments also tend to believe that if you're on trial, you must deserve to be there. On this front, there was nothing we could do but watch as one juror after another was excused for saying such radical things as "I believe only God should be allowed to take a life."

In the end, jury selection took two days. We ended up with six white people, four Black, and two Hispanic. There were seven men and five women, the reverse of how I would have preferred it, but I could live with what we got. As Judge Whelan prepared to adjourn court for the day, D-Cal rose to his feet.

"Your Honor, we have an unusual request."

"Go ahead, Mr. Lucas."

"In light of the attention this case appears to be receiving, I suggest the old courthouse might be a more appropriate venue for our trial."

The old Harrison County Courthouse hadn't been home to an actual trial in half a century. The courtroom inside was much larger than Judge Whelan's court though. Its historic ambience made it the perfect setting for the biggest trial in Marshall's history. Though unexpected, the proposition was sort of like pointing out that the marquee tennis match at Wimbledon ought to be played on Centre Court; it just made sense.

"Would you like to be heard on this, Mr. Euchre?" Judge Whelan asked as he turned to our table.

I envisioned this new venue, and it made me nervous. I had spent my career between the modest federal courtroom and its even more humble magistrate companion in the basement at the Eastern District. I never needed a big stage. I was comfortable in Judge Whelan's understated courtroom. However, I didn't want to show any sign of hesitation. I had a hunch the train had already left the station. Besides, what better place for me to argue my only murder case than the grandest courtroom in Marshall?

I stood up and buttoned my jacket. "Your Honor, I second the DA's request."

· NINETEEN ·

Judge Whelan scheduled the trial to begin every day at 9:00 a.m. on the dot. Layla and I convened at the Compound at seven o'clock to prepare for opening arguments. I'd adhered to my three-drink rule the night before and felt sharper than I had since December. I'd completely given up on being a nonsmoker though, so the morning combination of fresh nicotine and coffee was fueling my every move.

One of the benefits of using the Compound as our office was that we could walk to court. As we made the short trip, I couldn't shake the thought that this was the same path the prosecution would claim Amir had taken on his way to killing Judge Gardner. I avoided looking in the direction of the crime scene as we passed it. I knew the bricks were still stained with blood.

The old Harrison County Courthouse was half office building, half museum. The first time I stood inside it was on an elementary school field trip, learning about this history of our town. There were exhibits of famous Marshall residents, including heavyweight champion George Foreman, renowned journalist and presidential adviser Bill Moyers, and Mrs. Lady Bird Johnson, whose inaugural gown was on display next to a suit worn by her husband, Lyndon.

The courtroom itself was a lawyer's dream, like stepping onto the set of *To Kill a Mockingbird.* The main floor was made of stained mahogany that matched the several rows of seats fanning out to either side like pews in a church. The tables for attorneys faced each other on opposite ends. Between them stood an elevated bench for the judge. Two-story windows rose behind his chair. The side walls were curved, as was the balcony that overlooked the main floor. The courtroom had been renovated with central air-conditioning but seemed like it should be sweltering and filled with townsfolk fanning themselves with rolled-up newspapers while William Jennings Bryan and Clarence Darrow argued about the existence of God.

We took our seats at the table on the left. The maximum occupancy was 150 people, but I doubted the fire chief was going to enforce it. Nearly every local patent attorney had come to watch the first day's proceedings.

There were reporters from every major paper in Texas and a few from out of state. They sat together in a couple rows that had been reserved for the press. There was one reporter who sat elsewhere. Charlotte Mayhew had found a seat in the middle part of the middle row. She didn't blend in. Perhaps she wasn't welcome around the rest of her colleagues, or maybe she felt there was information to be gleaned by sitting among the people. Either way, her presence in the courtroom annoyed me.

Furqan Haq sat toward the back. He was in regular contact with Amir, but he had decided he didn't want to interact with me at all. That was fine by me.

I spotted the Leg in the second row. She still had investigatory work to do, but I wanted her in court on the first day. It was important that she hear D-Cal's opening statement, as it might alter the direction of her sleuthing. But now I had a second task for her.

I waved her over to the rail and got in close so no one could hear us. "That tech reporter is here," I said.

"I saw."

"Keep an eye on her, would you?"

"You got it," she said.

I nodded, and the Leg headed back to her seat just as Judge Whelan entered the courtroom.

"Ladies and gentlemen of the jury, my name is D. Calvin Lucas and I am the district attorney here in Harrison County. I appreciate each and every one of you for answering your civic call to duty and lending the judicial system your time and attention. The circumstances that bring us here today are as unfortunate as they are unpleasant. I apologize in advance for the graphic nature of what we'll be discussing over the next several days. You will find it disturbing. Indeed, I am disturbed by it every minute of my day."

D-Cal was laying it on a bit thick, but his tone had a ring of authority to it that would go over well with the jury. I scanned their faces, looking for any crack, any skepticism, but I didn't see any yet.

"The defendant, Mr. A-mir Za-war," he said, intentionally making the Pakistani name sound difficult to pronounce, "had been a guest in our town for one day. In that one day, he had a hearing in the federal courthouse right next door. Mr. Zawar and his attorneys stood before Judge Gerald Gardner, the victim in this case. Judge Gardner issued a ruling that did not go Mr. Zawar's way. That ruling threatened to destroy Mr. Zawar's business. And he didn't like that. How do we know? Because Mr. Zawar's immediate reaction to Judge Gardner's decision was so vicious that it landed him in jail. Mr. Zawar lost his temper, and in front of a courtroom full of people, he looked the judge dead in the eye and declared, 'I will f-in' kill you . . . I will f-in' kill you.' Later on that same day, in the dead of night, in the parking lot right outside, someone killed Judge Gerald Gardner."

The prosecution's opening hit all the notes that we expected, from Amir's outburst in patent court, to his contempt for Judge Gardner, to his proximity to the scene of the crime, and finally, to his arrest. Still, D-Cal played the notes with a level of skill that suggested we had better not underestimate him. He knew how to tell a story, how to connect, and he was compelling. There was only one element in his statement that caught us off guard.

"Mr. Zawar had the perfect vantage point to stalk his victim. He watched Gerald Gardner enter his courthouse after the judge left the party and then patiently bided his time, waiting for his moment to strike. When the judge reappeared, Mr. Zawar took the knife he'd been holding in his hand, crept down Franklin Street to the parking lot outside of this very building, snuck up behind Judge Gardner, and stabbed him, stunning his victim. Mr. Zawar raised the knife one last time and pierced the judge's neck, fatally wounding the man he had sworn to kill just hours before. As the judge's body fell to the ground and blood spilled out onto the bricks beneath him, Mr. Zawar disposed of the murder weapon and absconded into the darkness."

Layla quietly scribbled a note on a yellow legal pad and then twisted it counterclockwise so I could read what she'd written. "Knife?" I shrugged ever so slightly. The prosecution had not offered a weapon during the pretrial phase. It would be a violation of the rules of discovery if D-Cal had found it and failed to turn it over to the defense. But there was something about the way he kept referring to this knife, this murder weapon, that suggested to all of us that he intended to reveal it in due course.

All in all, D-Cal had successfully laid out the prosecution's case and laid blame in the bloody hands of our client.

As the lawyer for the defense, I had the option to deliver my opening statement before the state began calling witnesses, or I could wait until the state's case was completed. Part of me wanted to delay and let the prosecution present its entire case so my opening could attack it all, piece by piece. But the other part of me felt that I couldn't let the moment pass. D-Cal's opening had lasted just over ninety minutes. He'd teed up his case nicely, and I worried that if the jury didn't get a response from me now, it'd be nothing but fairways and greens for D-Cal. So when Judge Whelan asked if I wanted to make my

opening statement, I said yes and walked toward the jury box, hoping to blow the prosecution off course.

"You know what the difference is between a good conspiracy
theorist and an insane man?" I asked as I got closer to my audience.
"The insane man tells you what he believes and demands you believe
it as well. The conspiracy theorist simply invites you into the conversation. Let me illustrate. Imagine you and I are walking down the
street and a man approaches us and says, 'I know who killed JFK!'
Would we want to stop and have a chat with him? Hell, no. We'd
cross the street and avoid eye contact, am I right? That man's crazy."
I got a few smiles and nods from the jurors, and it felt promising.

"Now, imagine we're sitting at a bar and the man next to us says,
'If Lee Harvey Oswald truly acted alone, why did Jack Ruby, a night-
club owner and known associate of the criminal underworld, murder Mr. Oswald two days later, preventing us from ever knowing the
whole truth?' It's intriguing. It gives you just enough to make your
brain start filling in the missing pieces. You'll see that the state's case
against my client is riddled with holes. What Mr. Lucas is going to do
at each and every turn is ask you to bridge the gaps for him. But with
each new gap, I want you to ask yourselves, 'What's missing here?'
Because those holes are where reasonable doubt lives. Those absent
pieces are where the truth lives. Mr. Lucas cannot bridge those gaps
because those gaps are where my client's innocence lives."

I scanned my jury, making sure that I was connecting with every
member before I continued. "Gerald Gardner was a federal judge and
an important fixture of our community. When he was killed, every
member of the Marshall Police Department worked this case. Agents
from the Federal Bureau of Investigation were brought in. The US
Marshals Service offered to help. Hell, the Texas Rangers were on the
job for a beat. And, of course, we had the district attorney's office. All
of these institutions were devoted to a single mission: proving that
Mr. Amir Zawar had committed this crime. As we proceed, I want
you to ask yourselves, with all those agencies and all those resources,
how is it that Mr. Lucas is still coming up short? It's not for lack of

manpower. And it's not for lack of effort. Every agency in Texas lent a hand and every inch of our town has been investigated, so why won't the district attorney be able to prove what he has come here to prove? Why can't they solve this case? I want you to think about that as they construct their theory, missing piece by missing piece. I promise you they are going to ask you to bridge those gaps for them."

I felt unsure of my opening. On the one hand, I was revealing to the jury how D-Cal intended to pull off his magic trick. On the other, our defense strategy was designed to do the exact same thing. We intended to redirect suspicion toward Judge Knox, but the Leg was still searching for the smoking gun. Without it, all we had was an incomplete theory with gaps that needed filling. I worried I couldn't undercut the prosecution's strategy without damaging my own. The burden of proof was on the state though, so, technically speaking, if neither side proved its theory, the defendant should go free. But anything can happen in a jury room.

D-Cal called his first witness, Sergeant Jefferson, to the stand. I remembered my brief interaction with the curt officer outside of the police station on the night of the murder. In the three months since I'd seen him, it looked like he'd aged another five years and put on a few more pounds. His lumbering walk to the witness stand made me doubt his ability to chase a suspect down on foot. I wondered if he'd ever had the speed to catch one.

Jefferson set the scene for the jury. He and his partner, Sergeant Ramirez, were out on patrol when they got a call from dispatch informing them that an alarm had been tripped and the private security company had called for police assistance.

The Leg had looked into this several weeks ago. Because the law firm owned the Compound, and it was often vacant, the home insurance company insisted that a security system be installed. Honest Abe had taken care of that the previous year. When Amir broke the window, he triggered an alarm.

Jefferson and Ramirez arrived at the Compound in under five minutes after receiving the call, at about 2:35 a.m. The security company had informed them the breach was in the rear of the house, so they moved there first. They found the broken window and a light on inside. When they saw a figure move, they opened the unlocked door and entered, guns drawn.

"We encountered the suspect in the main hallway on the primary floor." Jefferson was one of those cops who, when testifying, thought bigger words would make him sound smarter. "I issued an oral command for the suspect to get on the ground. He complied, at which point myself and Sergeant Ramirez apprehended Mr. Zawar. Sergeant Ramirez continued to search the premises while I attempted to conduct an interrogation."

"What do you mean you attempted?" D-Cal asked.

"The suspect was highly agitated and uncooperative."

"How so?"

"From the moment I handcuffed him, he kept shouting that he hadn't done anything wrong. Of course, I'm looking at a broken window and a man who entered a house he doesn't own. So already I know he's being untruthful. I tell him he's only making matters worse by lying to an officer of the law, but he continues to verbally assault us, calling us names I'd rather not repeat in a court of law."

D-Cal did a good job of eliciting testimony about Amir's state of mind. Jefferson painted a picture of an unhinged man, panicked and irrational, resistant to authority.

"Who arrived next?" prompted D-Cal.

"Officer Meacham and Officer Fairchild. I instructed them to assist Sergeant Ramirez with his search of the house. Officers Chapiteau and Hodges showed up in a second car and conducted a search of the perimeter for potential accomplices."

"What made you believe there might be accomplices?"

"The suspect's behavior was suspicious. He grew more impatient rather than subdued. He demanded that we call his lawyer, who could straighten everything out. He made it clear he wanted us gone, and quick." Jefferson testified that several more minutes passed with Amir becoming more and more enraged. "Then Officer Chapiteau radioed dispatch for assistance and a 10-79."

"What's a 10-79, Sergeant?" D-Cal asked.

"It's the code for a coroner."

D-Cal led Jefferson through Amir's arrest, placing him in the squad car and driving him to the police station. D-Cal would have to call one of the other officers to the stand to describe the crime scene because Sergeant Jefferson didn't leave the Compound until he drove Amir to jail. He had never gone to the parking lot or seen Gardner's body.

Finally, it was our turn to cross Jefferson. We'd decided the best division of labor was for me to take anything that related to our theory that someone else, namely Judge Knox, was the true killer. Layla would handle the arrest, the DNA evidence, and the more technical aspects. I also wanted to watch a damn fine attorney cross-examine a local police officer and make him look like Barney Fife.

Layla walked to the podium with confidence and placed her notes in front of her, though she'd rarely refer to them.

"Sergeant Jefferson, you testified that your instincts told you Mr. Zawar was lying, is that correct?"

"His demeanor suggested he was being untruthful."

Layla furnished Jefferson with a copy of his report from the night of the murder, and she kept a copy for herself.

"During your impromptu interrogation, did you ask Mr. Zawar what he was doing at the house?"

"Yes, he said he was a guest—"

"And did that turn out to be untruthful?"

"He said he was unsure who owned the house—"

"Sergeant, please answer the question I asked. Was Mr. Zawar telling the truth when he told you he was a guest in the house?" Layla repeated herself, keeping her tone steady.

"That turned out to be accurate, yes," Jefferson said.

"And did Mr. Zawar tell you why he had broken the window?"

"He claimed he had locked himself out."

"And did that statement turn out to be accurate?"

"According to him."

"During this attempted interrogation, as you call it, did Mr. Zawar say anything that turned out to be untrue?"

"Once my backup arrived—"

"Sergeant, I'm asking about these first few minutes, while your partner was searching the house and while you were conducting an interrogation of my client. Did Mr. Zawar provide any answers to you that were false?"

"No."

"So your instincts failed you?"

"I wouldn't say that. He turned out to be hiding something much bigger," Jefferson asserted.

Layla had done a good job of landing some early jabs. Jefferson was on his heels. What Jefferson tried to pass off as reliable police intuition was textbook racial bias. Still, Layla had to make that clear without coming right out and asking because the witness would never admit it. We also had to be careful about playing into D-Cal's narrative of Amir as an outsider.

Layla moved on, turning to the moments after Gardner's body had been discovered. She asked Judge Whelan if she could approach the witness, and he allowed it. She called Jefferson's attention to a key moment in his report and asked him to read it aloud.

"'Officer Chapiteau's search of the surrounding area resulted in the discovery of a dead body in the parking lot of the town square. Victim appeared to have been stabbed.'" Jefferson finished reading his own statement.

"How was this information relayed to you, Sergeant?"

"By Officer Chapiteau."

"To be clear: Officer Chapiteau discovers the body and then returns to the house to tell you what he found?"

Jefferson must have sensed that Layla was laying the groundwork for how Gardner's blood made its way from the crime scene to our client in the Compound. The sergeant paused and thought for a long beat about his answer.

"He radioed the information back to me, as I recall."

"He radioed? You're certain he didn't tell you this face-to-face?" Layla's incredulity was evident.

"Officer Chapiteau used the radio because he never left the crime scene," Jefferson assured her.

"In your report, it doesn't specify how he relayed this information to you. Is that unusual?"

"Not particularly."

"Do you see the eight lines in your report that are highlighted in blue?"

"Yes."

"Can you read those for the court?"

"'I radioed to dispatch that we had a suspect in custody.'" He moved to the next highlighted line. "'Officers Meacham and Fairchild radioed their position and ETA.'" He read the next six highlighted lines, each time with mounting frustration at the realization that he used the word "radioed" in his report over and over.

"Your report is very detailed about the means of communication with your colleagues. You even specify your communications with dispatch are over the radio when that is surely implicit. So why doesn't your report make it clear that Officer Chapiteau radioed his findings back to you at the house?" Jefferson didn't offer an immediate response, so Layla plowed ahead. "Isn't it possible Officer Chapiteau walked from the crime scene to the house and told you what he'd discovered?"

"That's not how I remember it." Jefferson's confidence was shaken. Layla was never going to get an arrogant cop to admit wrongdoing, but she had exposed the discrepancies in his own notes, and we hoped the jury believed he was hiding something.

My truck and the Leg's car were at the Compound, so we walked back with Layla.

"You want me in court again tomorrow, boss?" the Leg asked.

"No. If you've got things to follow up on, I'd rather have you doing that."

Judge Knox's nomination to replace Judge Gardner complicated her investigation. A federal judgeship isn't like a seat on the Supreme Court, which is to say the vetting process isn't nearly as exhaustive. It is a lifetime appointment, though, and the United States Senate attempts to do its due diligence. In a way, this was helpful because there were several people, from the government to the media, digging into Knox. However, it also meant Knox was on guard. He didn't know my team was looking into him, but he knew he was being vetted by other groups, and his defenses were up.

"That works for me," the Leg said. "I've got to speak with someone at Homeland Security tomorrow."

"Homeland Security?" My interest was piqued.

"Let me get into it before I tell you more."

I agreed to wait for her report. She got in her car and drove away.

"How did we do today?" I asked Layla as we arrived at my truck.

"The DA is doing a solid job of laying out the details, but we're exposing the right cracks."

"Yeah. Day one really took it out of me," I confessed.

"Get some rest tonight. We're ready for tomorrow." Layla's confidence made me feel better as I watched her walk up the steps to the Compound.

On my drive home, I enjoyed my first smoke since that morning. I was thinking about the next day in court, but I realized a big part of my motivation was to impress Layla. It wasn't the first time my thoughts had wandered in her direction. I vowed to put her out of my mind for the night. I was successful until I tried to get some sleep. With nothing else to distract me, I couldn't stop thinking about her.

TWENTY

Day two of the state's case picked up where day one left off. D-Cal called other members of the Marshall PD who had responded that night. Officer Meacham had searched the Compound, and Officer Hodges had helped secure the crime scene. They colored in the picture of a brutal murder and a volatile Amir Zawar, whose presence in our town was suspicious and, without saying as much, unwelcome. For our part, we countered the same way we had with Sergeant Jefferson. We pointed out inconsistencies in their versions but still needed to make the case for the transfer of DNA from one of the cops to our client. Unfortunately for us, the officers knew what we wanted. They had each been adamant that no one who was near Gardner's dead body had ever gone anywhere close to the Compound.

Officer Chapiteau was the last one to take the stand. He was in his late forties, at the point when age starts to catch up with most men. But Chapiteau kept himself physically fit. In fact, he looked like the poster child for law enforcement. He was sturdy and confident without the air of dickishness that can so easily accompany a badge. D-Cal walked him through his initial call from dispatch to assist Jefferson and Ramirez. When Chapiteau and Hodges arrived at the Compound, they were told to fan out. It was Chapiteau who first walked toward the parking lot.

"I was on the far side of the town square, opposite the building we are currently in," Chapiteau testified. "I was looking past the parking lot, and that's when I noticed a dark shape on the ground. At first, I thought it was a coat that maybe someone had dropped. But as I approached it, I realized it was, in fact, a person."

D-Cal took Chapiteau through every move he made after discovering Judge Gardner's body. The officer sent a request, using his radio, for a coroner. He notified the other officers that he had discovered a dead person. "How did you inform your colleagues about this?" D-Cal asked.

"Over the radio."

"Did you at any point walk back to the house?"

"No, I remained with the body until the scene was secured. Then I went back to the station."

D-Cal turned the witness over to me. There were gaps in Chapiteau's testimony that we were going to fill, he and I. I didn't know what we'd use for mortar though.

"Officer Chapiteau, you said you approached the figure in the parking lot and discovered the body. Was he already dead?" I wasn't going to waste time with him, the fourth cop to testify in two days.

"Yes."

"How did you know?"

"He was unresponsive."

"So you attempted to get him to respond?" He paused, so I decided to keep pressing. "Did you try to talk to him?"

"I called out 'sir' repeatedly," Chapiteau said.

"Did you check his vitals?"

"Didn't need to."

"Did you touch him at all?"

"I kept my hands off of him."

"Did you nudge him with your boot?"

"No."

"How'd you know he wasn't just passed out?" I asked with skepticism.

"He didn't look drunk; he looked dead."

"You hung back and relied on your ability to assess his state visually?"

"Pretty much."

"You made no contact with him whatsoever?"

"I may have poked at him with my nightstick," he admitted. That was all I needed for step one of two. Potentially, there was now DNA on Chapiteau.

"Do you recognize that man sitting at the table next to my colleague, Ms. Stills?" I asked the officer, pointing at Amir.

"Yes, I do."

"Is this the first time you've seen him?"

"No."

"Did you see him at the house where he was arrested?"

"I was never at that house. I believe the first time I saw him was at the police station that night."

"Sergeant Jefferson testified that Mr. Zawar was a . . ."—I looked down at my notes for the quote—"'noncompliant arrestee.' Do you know what he meant by that?"

"From what I heard, he was argumentative with the arresting officers and resisted being transported to the jail."

"Your Honor," D-Cal said as he stood up, "I ask that the last answer be stricken from the record as speculation since Officer Chapiteau was not with the prisoner during transport."

I couldn't have asked for a better objection. Without knowing it, D-Cal had played right into my hands.

"Your Honor, Officer Chapiteau's testimony regarding the transportation of my client is not speculation because he was there." I turned to the witness and asked, "Isn't that right, Officer?"

Chapiteau had clearly hoped to avoid talking about this, but Judge Whelan wanted an answer.

"I did assist in getting the prisoner from the squad car into the jail, yes."

"Why was that necessary?" I asked.

"The prisoner was not cooperative, and we had to restrain his arms and his legs just to get him out of the vehicle. Sergeants Jefferson and Ramirez asked for help to ensure the safety of themselves as well as their prisoner."

"You must have gotten pretty close to Mr. Zawar?" I asked.

"I got into the back seat with him and had to forcibly remove him."

"Did you still have your nightstick on your hip?"

I've always loved the moment when I can see that a witness wants to lie but realizes on the spot that he won't get away with it.

"Yes, I did."

The state's final witness for the day was the Dallas County medical examiner. Dr. Jesse Fillmore was a jolly scientist who seemed to enjoy talking about his work with anyone who would listen. Despite being D-Cal's witness, he seemingly had no agenda other than to relay his scientific findings to the court. He was clearly smart and also skilled at talking about complicated subjects in a way that laypeople could comprehend. He had a habit of summing up his technical thoughts with everyday language. He was a good witness and a nice break from all the police officers.

Dr. Fillmore's autopsy report placed the time of Judge Gardner's death between 11:45 p.m. and 2:30 a.m. This was roughly the window we had been working with all along. His body had been discovered around 2:55 a.m., and the parking lot didn't empty out until a little before midnight, meaning if Gardner had been killed earlier than that, there would have been a high probability someone would have discovered his body on the way to their car. But by midnight, the only cars left in the lot likely remained there until the next morning. They probably belonged to people who'd enjoyed the party and opted not to drive drunk.

Dr. Fillmore came to court with blown-up drawings of the outline of a body and two *x*'s showing where Gardner had been stabbed. "This first wound was to the left side of the victim's chest, about four centimeters below the clavicle, or the collarbone," he told the jury.

"What makes you say it was the first wound?" D-Cal asked.

"The ectodermal tissue, the skin above the pectoral region, was pierced but not the muscle. The penetration was not severe, and the resulting hemorrhaging was minimal. It suggests that this wound stunned the victim, but it certainly did not cause his death."

"And tell us about the other wound," D-Cal said.

"The weapon entered the left side of the victim's neck with considerable force, penetrating three to four inches deep with a half-inch heel to the blade. Then, while inside the neck, the object was pulled, doing significant damage to the carotid artery as well as the larynx. There were major arterial and venous injuries due not only to the depth of the wound but also to the subsequent movement of the blade from the side to the anterior, down toward the thyroid. The victim lost a great deal of blood rapidly, but even if he'd received immediate medical attention, morbidity was almost a certainty. You stab someone in this part of the neck, you're likely going to kill him."

It was a gruesome description of how Judge Gardner had died, and what was perhaps even more helpful to D-Cal was that it didn't seem like the medical examiner was intentionally trying to disturb people. He was just telling it like it was. It was a combination of vivid descriptions and uncensored language that left everyone with a visceral reaction. When D-Cal turned the witness over to me, I rose to my feet and felt a little lightheaded. I had skipped lunch, not having much of an appetite after the morning's testimony.

"Dr. Fillmore, let's back up for a moment. How did the Dallas County medical examiner become involved in a murder case that occurred in Harrison County?" I asked with as much fake curiosity as I could muster.

"There are no full-time medical examiners in this part of the state."

"Why is that?"

"There aren't many people who live here, so you don't have that many deaths."

"And even fewer murders?" I asked.

"Precisely. In fact, a lot of the coroners in these parts are either physician assistants or even funeral directors. Their experience is largely with natural deaths and automobile accidents."

I doubted that anyone saw my reaction to these last words, but the mention of a car crash brought on fleeting visions of roadside wreckage, ambulance lights, and emergency responders. I looked down at my notes that I'd left on the podium and took a moment to reorient myself. I had completely lost my bearings. I glanced back at our table, as if something there would jog my memory. All I could see was Layla and a slightly concerned look on her face. I focused on my notes and then closed my eyes, blocking out everything except my conversation with the medical examiner.

"Doctor," I said, returning to the world of the living, "is it fair to say that here in Marshall, Texas, we just simply aren't equipped to handle a crime like murder?" I could feel D-Cal wanting to object. This was, of course, a shot at the police and the district attorney. Without besmirching my hometown, I was trying to paint a picture of a provincial murder and a bunch of rural authorities who were in over their heads.

"This is certainly out of the ordinary in a small town."

"Let's turn to the victim's body. Was there any indication of a struggle?"

"Very minimal, if at all. There were some marks on the victim's palms, but those could have easily come from his fall to the ground. For the most part, there were no signs of a fight."

"No skin under the victim's fingernails?"

"No."

"No foreign blood or DNA on his person?"

"None."

"Knuckles weren't injured? No scratching, bruising, anything like that?"

"None whatsoever."

"And the fatal wound, am I correct in assuming the attacker made one motion, inserted the blade into the victim, sliced toward the front of the neck, and that was the end of it?"

"It was one point of contact. The blade moved and then was removed."

"Would you say it was done with skill?" I asked.

"Objection, Your Honor. Calls for speculation." D-Cal's tone intimated that he expected Judge Whelan to agree with him.

"He's a medical examiner, and his opinion is that of an expert," I responded.

"I'm going to sustain the objection, Mr. Euchre."

I'd find a way to make my point whether D-Cal liked it or not. Still, he had messed up my flow, and that pissed me off.

"Doctor, how many autopsies have you conducted involving victims who were stabbed?"

"Over the years, I'd put it in the hundreds."

"Is it typical to see one wound do this much damage all on its own, or are fatal stabbings more often the result of several puncture points?" I asked.

"It is more common to see multiple entry wounds."

"So whoever did this knew how to use a knife?"

"Objection!"

I didn't even care that this one was sustained. I'd made my point. The jury was picturing a killer who knew his way around a blade. Amir Zawar was not that person. I would reveal someone who was in due time.

After D-Cal handled a brief redirect of the medical examiner, Judge Whelan excused the witness, and we adjourned for the day. As Layla and I carried our evidence boxes out of the courthouse, the Leg spotted us from across the parking lot and sprinted our way.

"Jesus, Lisa, what was your forty-yard-dash time?" I asked.

"Better than yours," she said.

"What's so urgent?" Layla asked.

"I think I know who the prosecution is going to put on the stand tomorrow."

Every night we had to prepare cross-examinations for all the witnesses we thought D-Cal might call the following day. I'd told the Leg to keep her ear to the ground for any potential trial strategy from the other side, as it might spare us from any unnecessary preparation.

"Who is it?" I asked.

"Judge Jay Knox."

· TWENTY-ONE ·

At the Compound, I hunkered down with Layla and the Leg for a long night of strategizing. Our plan had been to get through the government's case and most of our defense before calling Judge Knox to the stand. He was supposed to be one of our last witnesses, so his testimony, and our theory about him being the murderer, would be fresh in the jurors' minds as they deliberated. More importantly, it would buy extra time for the Leg to find anything we could use against him. We had not planned for the prosecution to call Knox. Casting suspicion on the future federal judge was a risky ploy. Making the move too early could be catastrophic.

"How sure are you they're going to put him on the stand tomorrow?" I asked the Leg.

"I've been tracking his movements pretty closely. Tammy Tex is way too forthcoming with his travel schedule."

Knox had been flying back and forth from Texas to DC to meet with senators before his confirmation hearing. He was still presiding over the Eastern District, so he would fly home to work for a few days here and there and then head back to Washington. The Leg had learned Knox was landing at Dallas/Fort Worth that night even though he had nothing on the docket at EDTX that week.

"Did you not prepare at all for this?" the Leg asked.

"There was no reason to think D-Cal would use Knox," I said defensively.

"He was on the witness list," she said.

"Everyone at the party that night was on the witness list," I said.

"He was also in court," Layla declared, having apparently stumbled upon a realization as she thumbed through a file in her lap.

"What?" I asked, bracing for the worst.

"Forget about the Christmas party. Judge Knox was in Gardner's courtroom when Amir was held in contempt. The prosecution needs a witness to testify about Amir's outburst, his temper, his statements allegedly threatening Gardner."

"Who better than the next federal judge?" I asked rhetorically.

The testimony Judge Knox could give regarding Amir's behavior in court that day wasn't our biggest concern. Someone was going to provide that testimony, but I had assumed it would be Gardner's court clerk or the bailiff since both were on the witness list. The real dilemma was whether to seize the moment and present our bombshell theory tomorrow, or risk waiting to call Knox back to the stand during the defense phase of the trial.

"First question, are we ready for him now?" I asked, looking at the Leg.

"Give me an hour to compile what I have on him, but yeah, I can give you everything I've got," she said.

"But you're still hoping to get more?" I asked.

"I'd love to find a murder weapon or, short of that, at least go through and test his entire collection of knives for Gardner's DNA. But sadly, I don't have subpoena power."

"We're not going to get the police to investigate Knox, at least not until we draw suspicion his way in court," I said, remembering Detective Elliot's lack of interest in helping when I spoke to him in his trailer.

"OK." The Leg stood up and threw her backpack over her shoulder. "Let me go put together a presentation." She headed to a small room in the rear of the house that she'd commandeered weeks earlier for her office. The door closed, and I looked to Layla, who had stood up and was staring at the unlit fireplace. I could tell something was bothering her. I walked over to where I could see her face.

"You disagree?" I asked Layla. She remained silent, so I pled my case. "There are good reasons for us to launch a surprise attack tomorrow. It'll catch them off guard, it'll play better for us with Knox as one of D-Cal's witnesses, and it may even cause the police to get off their hands and do some real detective work. Maybe they find something, and we get the charges on Amir dropped without ever getting to our defense or a verdict."

"It's too risky," she said.

"I don't like how it looks if we watch this pitch pass us by," I said. "If we have to call Knox back to the stand a second time, the jury will wonder why we hesitated."

"If you take this shot and miss—"

"Judge Whelan will almost certainly afford us more leeway with Knox as a witness for the prosecution."

"Leeway to ask questions whose answers we don't yet know," Layla replied. "You could lose this case tomorrow, James."

I usually welcomed skepticism, but Layla had shattered my confidence.

"You're probably right," I said. "But let's prep for both strategies. You work on a cross that responds to Amir's outburst in court. And if we see the opportunity to hit him with everything we've got, I'll be ready. Otherwise, we stick to the plan and bring Knox back during the defense and take our shot then."

Layla's eyes danced from one side of my face to the other. She had my attention. "If you accuse Jay Knox of murder, you will have made a lifelong enemy of the next federal judge of the Eastern District of Texas."

"Layla—"

"You'll never practice patent law in Marshall again."

"Are you worried about me?" I asked.

"I want to make sure you understand the consequences."

"I'll be careful," I said.

Judge Jay Leonard Knox stood next to the witness stand the following day. As he put his left hand on the Bible and raised his right hand toward God, I imagined him taking other oaths. I pictured him standing before the Senate Judiciary Committee, cameras flashing, swearing to tell the truth. Then I envisioned him on the steps of the federal courthouse, pledging to fulfill his duties as the new federal judge of the Eastern District. He looked the part of a Texas judge. He had an aura of a 1950s father dressed in his Sunday best, ready to drive the family to church in a station wagon. He projected a sturdy image. But I knew he could be rattled.

Judge Knox took his seat on the witness stand and the district attorney asked him to introduce himself to the court. "My name is Jay Knox. I am currently the magistrate judge for the federal court of the Eastern District of Texas, right across the street from here."

"As the magistrate judge, you worked with the victim in this case?" D-Cal asked.

"I worked *for* him, I would say. That was Judge Gardner's court. As the magistrate judge, my duties were to oversee any hearings or cases that Judge Gardner didn't have the time on his calendar to handle. He referred to the magistrate judge as an understudy. He told me on my first day, 'You have to know the lead part just as well as the star of the show and be ready to step in at a moment's notice.'"

"It sounds like the two of you were friends?"

"Dear friends. He taught me a lot. He was, quite simply, one of the finest men I've ever met."

I could see D-Cal was going to milk Judge Knox's testimony for every drop. And Knox, for his part, came with the goods.

"Judge Knox, do you recognize the defendant, Mr. Zawar?"

"I do."

"Are you familiar with his company, Medallion?"

"I am."

"The afternoon of December tenth, what would tragically become the last day Judge Gardner was seen alive, Medallion had a hearing in the Eastern District. Were you aware of that?"

"I was. There was an eligibility hearing, a hearing to determine if a lawsuit has enough merit to warrant going to trial. It was originally going to be in my courtroom because Judge Gardner was presiding over a patent trial that week. However, the trial ended several hours earlier than expected, and since the lawsuit involving Medallion would ultimately end up in Judge Gardner's court anyway, he opted to oversee the eligibility hearing that day as well."

"And you were relieved of your duties, shall we say?" D-Cal asked.

"I was."

"Did you clock out early?"

Judge Knox smiled. His charm was working on the jury.

"No, I stayed at the courthouse to catch up on work. I had prepared for the eligibility hearing, so I decided I'd sit in on Gardner's court and watch how it unfolded."

"Can you tell us what happened at that hearing?"

"In the simplest terms, the lawyers representing Medallion were asking Judge Gardner to dismiss the lawsuit against Mr. Zawar's company. Judge Gardner rejected that motion, and the case was set to go to trial. As Judge Gardner issued the ruling that the motion to dismiss had been rejected, Mr. Zawar had an outburst."

"What did he say?"

Knox turned for a moment to Judge Whelan. "I ask the court to excuse my language. I want to be as accurate as possible."

No one would have given a shit if he cursed without first getting approval, but Knox was being overtly deferential to Judge Whelan, and I'm sure that played well with the jury.

"He said, 'This is fucking bullshit.' Judge Gardner heard that comment and asked Mr. Zawar to stand up if he wished to address the court. Mr. Zawar asserted his statement."

"Did this surprise you?"

"The Eastern District was Judge Gardner's kingdom, and he deserved respect. To see a guest in his courtroom show such contempt was shocking."

"Did Judge Gardner lay down the law at that point?"

"As a matter of fact, no, he did not. He gave the defendant every opportunity, but Mr. Zawar wouldn't help himself."

D-Cal had Judge Knox read the court transcript from the eligibility hearing, giving the jury the word-for-word replay of what Amir had said. Judge Knox recounted how I had stood and attempted to get Amir to take a seat, only to be pushed to the ground by my client. Knox painted the picture of a violent and unhinged Amir resisting any attempt at being subdued.

"Ultimately, the bailiff and the defendant's own lawyer wrestled him to the ground. He had to be physically restrained," Knox said.

"And was Mr. Zawar silent at that point?" D-Cal asked.

"No. He said one more thing."

"What was that one thing?"

Judge Knox addressed the jurors directly.

"Again, I apologize for the vulgarity. Mr. Zawar looked Judge Gardner dead in the eye and shouted, 'I'll fucking kill you.'"

The district attorney let this hang for a long beat.

"Did you see Judge Gardner after that?" he asked Knox.

"Yes. We both attended the annual Christmas party for the legal community that night. I didn't get much of a chance to speak with him, though we wished each other season's greetings and said we looked forward to seeing one another in the new year. That was the last time I saw him."

D-Cal had done his best work of the trial with Judge Knox on the stand, though I didn't want to give my opponent too much credit. The witness was exceptional in his own right and very comfortable in court. In the span of less than two hours, Judge Knox had ingratiated himself to the jury and described the victim in a way that made his death seem all the more tragic. He presented Amir not only as someone who had threatened to commit murder but as the type of volatile person who was more than capable of carrying out such a threat. It was the perfect testimony, especially if the witness had an ulterior motive.

As D-Cal returned to his seat, Layla scribbled a note on her legal pad. She turned it so I could read what she'd written: "Don't do it. You'll get your chance later."

"Your witness, Mr. Euchre."

Typically, I liked to walk around while I questioned witnesses, but with this one, I buttoned my jacket and went directly to the podium, where I planned to remain for the duration of my examination. I wanted it to look like a showdown. Judge Knox was literally and figuratively on a pedestal, and I was going to knock him off.

"Judge Knox, you described my client as being highly agitated in patent court. Do you happen to know how much his company was being sued for?" I asked.

"Not off the top of my head."

"Would it surprise you to hear that the number is north of a hundred million dollars?"

"No, that doesn't surprise me."

"With a hundred million dollars on the line and potentially the future of his company at stake, were you really surprised that Mr. Zawar's emotions were running a bit high that day?"

"I was surprised at his inability to contain them," Judge Knox responded.

"You've never seen a client lose their cool?"

"Not in Judge Gardner's court. People know better."

"Have you ever seen Judge Gardner get under anybody else's skin?" I asked.

"Judges make tough rulings, and people aren't always happy with the outcomes."

"Did Judge Gardner ever get under your skin?"

I'd caught him off guard, but he was smart enough to recognize a trap.

"Not in that way, no."

I glanced in Layla's direction. She subtly yet clearly shook her head back and forth, but it was like telling a drunk not to imbibe after he'd already broken the seal. I looked back at my witness.

"Do you recall the case of *Jansen versus Westward Aviation?*" I asked.

Knox gave me a look that said "How dare you?"

"Yes, I remember that case."

"Was it in your court?"

"It was a patent suit that was ultimately tried in Judge Gardner's courtroom."

"But . . ." I said in a tone that suggested to everyone there was more to the story. Knox was like a dog, refusing to go on a walk. He wanted me to expend energy pulling on the leash. I wasn't going to play his game.

"But there was a Markman, a pretrial hearing, in the magistrate court first."

"Did this hearing have any consequence in the actual trial?"

"I assume you would like to discuss a certain point in that trial when my ruling from the Markman hearing became an issue." Knox was letting me know he wasn't afraid of me. "Judge Gardner halted the proceeding to review my ruling, and having found it substandard, he summoned me into his courtroom to explain my decision."

"How did that make you feel?" I asked like I had no idea.

This moment was legendary in EDTX. Judge Gardner was not known for micromanagement, but Knox's faulty and confusing ruling in the Markman hearing had caused a problem for Gardner's own trial. The old man decided to haul Knox's ass into court and deal with the issue once and for all. The lawyers who were present that day dined out on the story for months.

"It was a good learning experience for me. I was a green judge, and

I had made an error. Judge Gardner brought it to my attention, and it never happened again."

"How did you feel at the time, as you stood before a courtroom filled with attorneys, while your boss reprimanded you for your mistakes?"

"It was unpleasant."

"Were you embarrassed?"

"It was a humiliating experience, Mr. Euchre."

"Did it make you angry?"

"I don't recall."

"Did you raise your voice?"

"I got defensive, and I said, perhaps louder than I should have, that he was making a mistake airing his grievances in public. But I took my admonishments, and when I left the courtroom, I cooled off."

"Isn't it possible that my client did the same thing? That, like you, he had a heated exchange with Judge Gardner in court and then cooled off?"

"Objection, Your Honor. Calls for speculation." D-Cal was happy for an opportunity to break this up. I'd made my point, or so he thought.

"You've been nominated to be the next federal judge of the Eastern District?" I asked.

"I have."

"Congratulations. How did that come about?"

"It's an Article III judgeship, meaning it's by presidential appointment, subject to confirmation by the United States Senate."

"So the president chose you? How did he reach that decision?"

"You'd have to ask him, Mr. Euchre."

"Does he solicit recommendations when appointing a new judge?"

"It's common practice for one or both of the senators from the state in which a judge is being appointed to suggest potential nominees."

"And in your case that was Senator Brookberry?"

"That's correct."

"Did you know Senator Brookberry intended to recommend you?"

"He called me the day before and told me he'd be submitting my name to the White House."

"What I mean is, did you know well in advance that, should a judgeship become available, Senator Brookberry had plans to put your name forward?"

"I was as surprised as anyone."

"Surprised? Had you never heard speculation that Judge Gardner might retire and you might be named his successor?"

"There are a lot of rumors in a courthouse. I work with facts."

"Here's a fact: Senator Brookberry came to Marshall this past November, and the two of you went hunting together. Correct?"

"I had seen him a few months earlier in Washington, and he mentioned that he'd like to catch himself a white-tailed deer. I told him I'd be happy to host if he ever wanted to go out to Caddo Lake and bag one."

"How long were you out there?"

"Seven or eight hours."

"Did the senator tell you that he was contemplating retiring?"

"He mentioned he was missing Texas and might want to spend more time here."

"Did you talk about your future, about possible jobs you might be interested in?"

"We talked about deer, Mr. Euchre."

"OK." I pretended to give up on this, hoping to lull him into a false sense of security. "Judge Knox, I know you were in Washington yesterday and that you flew back specifically to be with us today. You've been flying back and forth a lot?"

"I have. It's a lot of work to confirm a federal judge. A lot of people to meet."

184 · JOEY HARTSTONE

"Have you been flying commercial?"

"Objection, Your Honor, what's the scope here?" D-Cal wanted to protect his prized witness.

"I'll get there quickly, Judge," I promised.

"Very quickly," Whelan insisted.

I turned back to Knox.

"No, I've been flying private," he said.

"Is there a reason for that?"

"Given the circumstances, and how frequently I'm traveling, it's more convenient."

"Is that the only reason you're not flying on commercial flights?" I asked.

He adjusted in his seat, letting me know that I was, again, inconveniencing him with my questions. "As a matter of fact, there is a minor issue that's being remedied as we speak, but a couple months ago I was placed on the No Fly List."

"By the Department of Homeland Security?" I said, trying to make it sound as serious as possible.

"Yes."

"Why was that?"

He paused for a moment, as if waiting for Judge Whelan to intervene. There was no lifeline offered.

"Six months ago, I was flying to Florida. I'd forgotten to remove some items from my carry-on bag. They were discovered by airport security."

"What kind of items?"

"Knives."

"Like kitchen knives?"

"Hunting knives, Mr. Euchre."

"How many?"

"Eight or nine."

"That's a lot of knives."

"I'm a collector."

"A collector who owns hundreds of knives? Thousands?"

"Somewhere in that range."

"Do you have any with blades that are four to six inches?"

"Certainly."

"Do you know the term 'aichmomania'?"

"It means an obsession with knives."

"Are you an aichmomaniac?"

"Objection, Your Honor! Is Mr. Euchre serious with this line of questioning?" I thought it possible D-Cal's astounded tone was sincere.

Judge Whelan used two fingers to wave me and D-Cal over for a sidebar.

"Mr. Euchre, you've wandered far off the beaten path."

"This is the state's witness, Your Honor. I'd like some latitude here."

"I'm going to sustain Mr. Lucas's objection and ask that you either get to your point or end your cross-examination. Understand?"

"Yes, Your Honor."

"The objection is sustained," Whelan declared for the court.

I returned to the podium. I didn't have much time left.

"Let's go back to the Christmas party. You said you didn't have a chance to speak with Judge Gardner?"

"Only in passing to wish him Merry Christmas."

"Do you remember anything else about Judge Gardner that night?"

"Of course. My assistant, Tammy, gave a toast in his honor, and then Judge Gardner said a few words."

"What did he say in his speech?"

"He said he had enjoyed his tenure as judge in the Eastern District for the past twenty years and that he hoped he could serve twenty more."

"That must have been disappointing to hear," I suggested.

"To the contrary, I, like you and everyone in our community, would have been happy to see Judge Gardner never leave the Eastern District."

"But you wanted his job."

"I don't know that I'd given it much thought at that point."

"OK, let me put it another way. There was wide speculation that Judge Gardner was going to retire. Your hunting buddy, Senator Brookberry, has the power to recommend to the president who Gardner's replacement will be, but he had just announced his own retirement. So his recommendation to the president was good only if a vacancy occurred before his term expired. You're next in line, but the clock is ticking. Then Judge Gardner declares he has no intention of stepping down, that he wants to stay on for another twenty years. You weren't the least bit disappointed?"

"No, I was not."

"If witnesses who were at the party that night testify that you looked visibly unhappy to hear the news Gardner wasn't retiring, would they be lying?"

D-Cal jumped in. "Objection, Your Honor. This line of questioning is beyond the scope, calls for speculation, and counsel is now badgering the witness."

I couldn't pause. I couldn't wait for the ruling. I had Knox in the crosshairs.

"In front of your colleagues, your professional community, Judge Gardner dashed your hopes of getting his job. Everyone knew you were in line for his seat. You weren't embarrassed?" I demanded.

"Your Honor!" D-Cal protested.

"You weren't humiliated?" I continued.

"Mr. Euchre!" Judge Whelan interjected.

"You weren't angrier at Judge Gardner than you'd ever been in your entire life!" I shouted.

Judge Whelan banged his gavel, and the trial came to a halt. "I want to see counsel in my chambers. Right now."

Whelan dismissed the jury, and everyone else stood up. I spotted Detective Elliot in the back of the courtroom, next to the door. I grabbed my briefcase and headed his way. As I approached, he stared ahead blankly.

"You gonna look into it now?" I asked.

"No, Jimmy, I'm not," he said.

I scoffed in disbelief and then shoved the door open on my way out.

TWENTY-TWO

A benefit to having the trial in the old Harrison County Courthouse was that Judge Whelan's office was in the building, so we didn't have far to walk. Layla and I followed D-Cal and his two assistant prosecutors, staying several steps behind them.

"So?" I asked. "That went better than I expected."

She shrugged. "We're not done yet."

Judge Whelan had already removed his robe by the time we entered his office. Everyone, including the judge, remained standing. We knew better than to speak. The sound of Whelan's keys jingling inside his pocket broke the momentary silence.

"Mr. Euchre, is it the defense's intention to present an alternative theory about who committed this murder, or is it simply your strategy to cast wild aspersions in as many directions as possible to muddy the state's case?"

I hesitated. That was apparently the wrong move because Judge Whelan got louder.

"Please tell me you can at least definitively say it's one or the other. Because wandering down the middle of the highway on this one is a very dangerous place to be," he continued.

"Your Honor, in light of the circumstantial nature of the state's case against our client, I believe it's well within our right to mount a

defense that implicates a different suspect who had the same opportunity, better means, and a stronger motive to kill Judge Gardner."

"Mr. Euchre, I am putting an end to your examination of this witness. If, and I underscore *if*, you choose to mount a defense based on
accusing someone else of this crime, then you will first present this
court with some evidence that substantiates your theory."

"That's a problem, Your Honor. The murder investigation has
been myopic from the start, and we can't broaden its scope because
the police don't work for us," I responded.

"Mr. Euchre, welcome to criminal law."

I could feel D-Cal's glee as he watched this unfold.

"Tomorrow, Mr. Lucas, I will give you the opportunity to redirect the witness if you want it?"

"Absolutely, Your Honor."

"You're giving the prosecution another crack at him, but you're
cutting me off?" I demanded.

"You wove a hell of a mess today. I will allow the DA to rehabili-
tate his own witness. If you want another shot at Judge Knox, you are
free to call him back to the stand during the defense. However," the
judge continued, "let me say that on a personal note, I can't think of
anything more harmful to a patent attorney's career than to accuse
the next federal judge of the Eastern District of Texas of murdering
his predecessor."

Judge Whelan adjourned court early, but Amir's ride back to the
county jail wasn't until the end of the day. We decided to spend a
little time with our client, who was across the street at the new courthouse because it had a secure holding cell. As we crossed the parking
lot, I commended the Leg for her investigation, which had yielded
information about Judge Knox's knife collection as well as his inclu-
sion on the No Fly List. There was still more work to be done, but it
was a solid start. Since Knox would be on the witness stand again the

following morning, he would stay in Marshall overnight. I asked the Leg to keep an eye on him.

She broke off from us and went back to the Compound to get her car. Layla and I continued to the new courthouse. As we rode the elevator, I could feel my leg bouncing, my foot nervously moving up and down. I was still amped up from Knox's testimony. When the elevator reached our floor, the doors opened, and Charlotte Mayhew was standing in the hallway, waiting to go down. Her Wayfarer sunglasses were in her left hand, her notepad in her right.

"Hello," the journalist said. Her demeanor bugged me.

"You are not to speak with our client," I said, as I stepped off the elevator and she stepped on.

"Oops."

She pressed the button. I put my hand in the elevator to prevent it from closing.

"Do I need to explain this to you?" I asked.

"Are you offering to give me an interview?"

"Amir is on trial for his life. I know you don't give a shit about that, but talking to you could interfere with his defense."

"If a journalist can ruin this trial for you, you ought to be much more worried about the state of your case," Mayhew replied. She smiled at me as I let the elevator doors close.

The guard took us into the holding room, where we found Amir pacing back and forth. He lit up when we entered.

"Holy shit, Euchre, that was an incredible cross!"

I motioned for him to sit down. "We had a good day, but we're going to need a few more like it."

"I really didn't believe Knox had anything to do with this until you backed him into that corner," Amir said with excitement. "That asshole may have done it!"

I set my briefcase down and rested my hands on my hips.

"I said no more interviews until after the trial."

"Mayhew asked, but I told her no," Amir replied.

"I'm trying to save your life here."

"And you're doing a bang-up job. You just accused a federal judicial nominee of murder!"

I couldn't let Amir's elation distract us from the job at hand. Layla explained to him how we expected the rest of the state's case to unfold. D-Cal would do a redirect in the morning with Judge Knox, but if we needed another round with him, we would have to call him during the defense phase. As they talked, I saw something in Amir's demeanor that I had only seen one other time. He exhibited the same enthusiasm as he had in the restaurant when he talked about creating his company. I saw the same expression he had worn when he spoke about his father and the business he was building to honor him. I saw hope.

Layla and I got a bite to eat and returned to the Compound. I was finally coming down from the rush of adrenaline, and she seemed drained as well.

"Got anything to drink around here?" I asked.

"Twelve presumably delicious bottles of wine in the kitchen that can't be opened," she said.

"Did Honest Abe tell you they're off-limits?"

"No. The DA confiscated the corkscrew."

Lucas had included everything with a sharp point on his list of potential evidence. By now he'd certainly tested all of them for Gardner's DNA and come up dry. He could have returned them, but he was just being a dick.

"It's a tragedy," she lamented.

"Let me see what we can do." I walked to the kitchen and returned with a bottle of pinot noir and two glasses. I sat down next to her on the couch.

"Looks good," she said. "Now let's see you get it opened."

I used my house key to cut the foil sleeve off the top. Then I grabbed my pink lighter. I sparked a flame and held it to the neck of the wine, just below the cork, and I slowly rotated the bottle.

192 · JOEY HARTSTONE

"I like my wine medium-rare," she said.

"When you're a teenager in Marshall, you do a lot of drinking in the woods. Bottle openers and corkscrews can be hard to come by."

"That's why, in Kalamazoo, we drink our wine out of boxes."

I continued to spin the bottle slowly.

The cork started to eke its way upward and finally shot out as if from a bottle of champagne. The loud pop made Layla laugh. I filled the glasses with two healthy pours. She pulled her feet onto the couch and snuggled up to her glass of wine, putting her nose to it. I just dove in and took a gulp.

"Do you think Judge Knox could have done it?" I asked.

"It's plausible," she said. "We'll see what the jurors think."

"Assuming this will be my only murder trial, I'd really like to win it and retire undefeated," I said.

"I know you didn't dream of becoming a patent lawyer. Was the original plan to go into criminal law?" Layla asked me.

"Not sure I had a plan, though criminal law wasn't it."

"I read about your father." I wondered what she had discovered, and what conclusions she might have drawn. "The best trial lawyer in all of Texas."

"I don't know," I replied. "Texas is a big place."

"I imagine the prospect of being measured against him was daunting."

"It wasn't that," I said. "I didn't want to be like him."

"You failed," she said. "You are a very good trial lawyer."

I felt a rush. I wasn't sure if it was the fear that she was breaking me down or just seeing right through me. Without thinking, I let my hand fall to my leg, and then, with the back of my fingers, I gently found her foot, which had wandered close to my knee. I paused before glancing up, knowing that the look on her face would either tell me I had made a huge error in judgment or, perhaps more frightening still, that I hadn't.

Her eyes locked onto mine. I froze, waiting for a sign in either direction, but her face was impossible to read. Then she reached over and set her glass of wine on the coffee table and returned to the same position she had just been in. I set my glass down, and as I did, she leaned back, waiting for me. I moved toward her, though we were still inches apart. There was nothing else I wanted in that moment except her. As we kissed, the wine tasted even sweeter on her lips.

It was only by a small miracle that we managed to hear the beeping from the keypad on the front door as the code was entered and the lock opened.

"What in the holy fuck is going on down here!" Honest Abe made his presence known in classic Rabinowitz fashion. We could hear his footsteps followed by the sound of his suitcase being rolled behind him on the hardwood floor. By the time he'd made his way down the hall and into the living room, Layla and I had straightened up and separated like a couple of teenagers who'd nearly been caught in the act. Abe looked at the two of us for a short beat.

"Who wants to explain this catastro-fuck to me?"

I stood up, but before I could speak, he continued.

"Who the hell are you to accuse Judge Knox of murder?"

I was overcome with relief that Abe had not witnessed me and Layla on the couch, but I had to shift gears immediately because relief was not the expression he wanted to see on my face.

"I didn't accuse him outright," I said.

"I think your point was crystal clear!" Abe screamed at me.

"It's a theory we've been exploring," I said, defending myself.

"You don't call an audible halfway through a witness's testimony."

"I had to go with my instincts."

"Your instincts have royally fucked us, Jimmy!" Abe's face was turning red, and I wondered if I'd recognize the warning signs of a heart attack if they presented themselves.

"How did you get here so quickly?" I asked, probably focusing on the wrong thing at that moment.

"When I heard my legal team was in court accusing Jay Knox of murder, I figured it was an appropriate use of the company jet to fly directly to Marshall since, you know, we are patent lawyers, and

Knox is about to become the most important patent judge in the whole fucking country."

"I have to represent my client," I insisted. "For what it's worth, Layla thought it was a bad idea."

"That's because she's smarter than you. It's quite possible you ended your career today."

"That was a risk I was willing to take."

"It's also possible you just destroyed Gordon & Greene's ability to represent clients in the Eastern District, and that is a risk you're not authorized to take!"

He stopped screaming and exhaled a deep breath.

"Knox is going back on the stand for redirect tomorrow?" Abe asked.

"Yeah."

"Good. You're going to keep your goddamn mouth shut and pray that I can mend our relationship with His Honor."

"Knox might be guilty," I said.

Abe ran his hands through his hair as if he were trying to force the frustration out of his head. We were going to spend the rest of the night, he said, figuring out how to fix the mess I had created. Then he disappeared upstairs. Layla began cleaning up the wineglasses. Gone was all evidence of what we'd been doing minutes before.

· TWENTY-THREE ·

Layla texted early the next morning to suggest we meet at the courthouse rather than the Compound. I was happy to delay seeing Honest Abe anyway. I found the Leg waiting for me in the parking lot, nursing a coffee. She had on the same clothes she'd worn the day before.

"Long night?" I asked.

"I staked out Knox's home until the sun came up."

"Please tell me you got something."

"Like what?" she asked. "Were you hoping you scared him so much he took the murder weapon he'd been hiding and threw it into a dumpster, where I was able to retrieve it?" I don't know why I always seemed to bring out the sarcastic side in people, but it was undeniably one of my gifts.

"That would be nice, yeah," I said.

"Sorry, Euch. The judge drove straight home from court and stayed there all night. The district attorney did stop by for about an hour and a half."

I told the Leg she ought to go home and get some sleep, but she wanted to see how the rest of Knox's testimony unfolded.

When we walked into the courtroom, the first thing I noticed was that the number of reporters had nearly doubled. From the looks of it, there were TV and print journalists, and nearly all of the new additions were from New York and DC. Apparently, word had gotten out that the president's nominee for the federal bench had implicitly been accused of murdering his predecessor. There was a chance this might cause a delay in Knox's confirmation process or put an end to it entirely.

Layla was standing near our table. She saw me but turned her attention toward Abe, who was talking with the bailiff. By the time I'd made my way over, the bailiff was carrying a fourth chair to our table.

"What's this for?" I asked.

"As long as Knox is on the stand, you and I are going to be whispering distance from one another," he said.

"Welcome to the team," I said, not hiding my dissatisfaction.

Abe took the seat between Layla's and Amir's chairs. When our client arrived, Abe chatted him up like they were old friends. I couldn't tell if Amir had any sense that Abe's purpose here was more to look out for his firm's interests than his client's.

I spotted Furqan Haq in the back of the crowded courtroom. He had been in and out most days, still running Medallion in Amir's absence, but evidently the promise of Knox's testimony was too enticing to keep the COO away. Haq saw me looking at him, though neither one of us so much as nodded at the other.

Judge Whelan took his seat and brought the jury in. He reminded Knox that he was still under oath as Knox made his way to the witness stand. Then D-Cal was given the floor.

"Judge Knox, on behalf of the entire community, I'd like to thank you for taking yet another day out of your busy schedule to be with us."

"No problem," said Knox.

"I'd also like to apologize for what transpired yesterday and for defense counsel's attempt to smear the name of a highly regarded judge."

"Your Honor, I object," I said, rising to my feet. "As much as I know we'd all love to listen to the prosecutor's own personal narrative of events, I'd prefer to wait until his closing argument to hear them." I could feel Abe looking at me. My objection was valid, but he wasn't happy with my tone.

"Let's get to the questions, Mr. Lucas," said Judge Whelan.

"Mr. Euchre's theory, laid bare yesterday, was that you, Judge Knox, may have had something to do with the murder for which Amir Zawar has been charged. Is there any truth to that theory?" D-Cal asked.

"No, there certainly is not," replied Knox.

"We've established that you own knives. It's also been pointed out that you inadvertently wound up on the No Fly List. Did Senator Brookberry know about either of these things when he recommended you to the president?"

"Yes, he saw my knives when we went hunting together. And I mentioned to him my little misfortune with the TSA and Homeland Security."

"And did the president of the United States know about these things when he nominated you to the federal bench?"

"I disclosed all of this to the White House so as to avoid any surprises," Knox said confidently.

"Then what we have here is a desperate defense theory, constructed like a house of cards, built solely on the foundation of motive. That motive being that you, Judge Knox, were so covetous of Judge Gardner's job that you would end his life. And the defense's theory, as I understand it, hinges on one moment at the Christmas party when Judge Gardner announced his intention to remain in his post for another twenty years. This public announcement prompted you to hunt down your colleague, a dear friend and mentor, and murder him in cold blood so that you could take his seat on the bench."

"Objection, Your Honor." Abe wanted me to be silent, but I couldn't take it anymore. "Can counsel either ask a question or excuse this witness?"

Judge Whelan seemed willing to let D-Cal go on until I protested, but since I had formally objected, he had to rule accordingly. "Mr. Lucas, the objection is sustained. Please get to your questions."

"Yes, Your Honor." He paused, as if trying to piece his thoughts together until inspiration struck. "Judge Knox, you testified yesterday that the last time you saw Judge Gardner was at the Christmas party on the night of his murder?"

"That's correct."

"And that's the last time you spoke to him?"

"Yes, it is."

"Is that the last time you interacted with him in any way?"

"No."

I glanced over my shoulder at the Leg. She gave me a slight shrug as if to suggest she had no idea to what Knox was referring.

"What was your final interaction with Judge Gardner?" D-Cal asked the question like he was a magician, demanding everyone's attention as he prepared to complete his trick.

"After Judge Gardner left the party, he sent me a private email, which I received and responded to immediately on my phone, while I was still at the party," answered Knox.

D-Cal walked back to his table, where one of his assistant DAs handed him a thin stack of papers, separated into three identical packets. D-Cal presented one to the court clerk as official evidence, one to Judge Knox so he could refer to it during his testimony, and then he walked the third one over to me and delivered it with a wink. I tried to skip ahead, but D-Cal was leading Knox directly to the point anyway.

"Judge Knox, can you read for us the message you received from Judge Gardner?"

Knox noted the time and date as 11:08 p.m. on the night of the party, and then he read from the email. "'Dear Jay, I want to apologize for my remarks this evening. I can imagine you felt blindsided. The truth is, I fear that my existence is completely wrapped up in this court and that, should I step aside, I will, in essence, cease to exist. But I've been reminded that life doesn't have to be quite so small.'"

Hearing the words of Judge Gardner, words that referred to his last conversation with me, was difficult. He had tried to give me direction that night, about moving on with my own life, but now it seemed maybe he had taken some advice from me instead.

Knox continued reading, "'Early in the New Year, I will announce my retirement. You have served me loyally and patiently as magistrate judge, and it is my sincere hope that you will be named my successor. You have certainly earned it. I have no doubt you would make a fine federal judge. Let's reconnect in January and discuss this transition of power and how best to proceed. Sincerely, Gerald Gardner.'"

There it was, from beyond the grave, an email that destroyed my theory. Judge Knox didn't need to kill Judge Gardner because Knox already knew what no one else did: Gardner was going to retire.

"And just to be clear," D-Cal began, "you not only received this email prior to Judge Gardner's murder, but you read it as well?"

"I read it and responded while still at the Christmas party. I thanked him for his kind words and said I looked forward to seeing him in the New Year."

"Thank you, Judge Knox. No further questions." D-Cal looked in my direction as he returned to his seat.

"Mr. Euchre?" Judge Whelan called out.

My brain raced for a strategy, anything I could do to undercut what had just happened. But then I glanced at Abe, and he slowly but firmly shook his head left to right. His eyes conveyed a clear message: "Don't even fucking think about it."

"I have no questions, Your Honor," I said from my seat.

Judge Knox was excused from the witness stand.

Judge Whelan granted a short recess after Knox's testimony was complete. I walked over to Amir because I could see his spirits were fading fast.

"He didn't kill the judge," Amir said flatly.

"We got his love of knives out there; we got his means and his ability. True, his motive is no longer viable, but I'll keep Lisa on it, and if there's more to it, she'll find it." I wasn't going to lie, but I also didn't want my client visibly dejected in view of the jury or the press. "Remember, all we need is reasonable doubt. We don't have to prove our theory to win."

"It'd help if we believed our theory, though." Amir was right. "That was our big play, and not only did it fail; it backfired."

"It wasn't ideal," I conceded.

"What's the plan now?"

There was nothing I could say that would give him hope, nothing truthful at least.

"Yeah, that's what I thought."

In the hallway that led to a portico, Layla and Abe had found a quiet spot. I joined them for the postmortem on Knox's testimony. It was shitty news, no two ways about it. But Abe had bigger concerns. He needed a few minutes with Knox before he headed back to DC.

"What are you going to say to him?" I asked.

"I'll say 'I'm sorry' in as many ways as I can think of. I'm going to throw you under the bus obviously and then drive it over you as many times as I can. The partners at Gordon & Greene will need to write a formal letter in support of His Honor's nomination to the federal bench. God help you if I end up having to testify before the United States Senate to explain what the fuck happened here this week."

I couldn't say that I was sad to learn Abe wouldn't be joining us back in court.

When Judge Whelan returned, D-Cal called Sergeant Ramirez to the stand. Ramirez was Jefferson's young partner, and predictably, he didn't provide anything new. It was uneventful testimony, though it was probably wise for D-Cal to reset the case he'd already laid out and try to erase Judge Knox from everyone's mind. The DA walked the witness through the call for the break-in, the initial encounter with Amir, the subsequent search of the surrounding area, and the eventual arrest and transportation back to the police station. It took a couple of hours, but the point was made: Amir was still the obvious suspect.

Layla handled the cross.

"Officer Ramirez, when you got the call for the break-in, did you do anything before heading to the house?" she asked.

"No, ma'am."

"You didn't stop to get a coffee or use the restroom?"

"The call was for a potential crime in progress, so we responded immediately."

"The medical examiner lists the time of death as somewhere between 11:45 and 2:30, based on tests he administered nearly a day later. Did you see the dead body?"

"No. I stayed in the house."

"The prosecution's theory is that my client happened upon Judge Gardner in the parking lot, killed him, and then ran back to the house where he was a guest, broke a window, and you arrived almost immediately to arrest him. Does it strike you as odd that my client wasn't covered in blood?" Layla asked with a great deal of curiosity in her voice.

"There was blood on his person, ma'am."

"How much blood?"

"It was visible."

"If it was visible, why didn't you see it?"

Sergeant Ramirez gave a confused look, prompting Layla to retrieve a copy of his police report and walk it over to the officer.

"Is this the report you made following the arrest of Mr. Zawar?"

"It is."

"Show me where you describe finding blood on my client."

"I don't think it's written in there."

"Sergeant, if you found blood on a murder suspect, isn't that something you would include in your report?"

"There are photos that show blood on him."

"Where?"

202 · JOEY HARTSTONE

"On his sleeve."

"Where were the photos taken?" Layla asked, clarifying her original question.

"At the police station."

"There are no photos at the house, no photos during the arrest, in which my client is shown with blood on him?"

"No."

"There's no mention of blood on him, in your arrest report or any other report, until after he arrived at the police station?"

"I'm not sure."

"Maybe that's because the blood wasn't on him until after he arrived at the police station."

"Objection, Your Honor. Is the witness here to testify, or is counsel just going to do it herself?"

Judge Whelan nodded in agreement with D-Cal. "Sustained."

"Let's look at the timeline," Layla said, undeterred. "When the other officers discovered the victim's body in the parking lot, when was it presumed that the crime might have occurred?"

"Generally sometime that night. I mean, how long can a dead body remain in a public square without being discovered?" Ramirez asked.

"But did it look like it had just happened or like the body had been there for a few hours?" Layla pressed.

"Objection, witness already testified he never saw the body," D-Cal reminded the judge. "Calls for speculation."

"Sustained."

Layla had to find another way to get to her point.

"Did anyone administer CPR to the victim?" she asked.

"No."

"When the call went out, did it say someone was severely injured or that someone was dead?"

"I believe it was a call for a dead body."

"So your theory was that Mr. Zawar killed the victim and then sprinted back toward the house to hide. He broke a window, the alarm went off, and you arrived within minutes. Then how do you explain that when Judge Gardner was discovered in the parking lot, there was no attempt to save him? There was no attempt to revive him. Doesn't that suggest to you that the responders believed he'd been dead for quite some time?"

"All I know is it was the middle of the night and the only two human beings we found were your client, breaking into a house, and a dead body a few hundred feet away."

There weren't big points to be won on this cross, but Layla had done a good job underscoring that none of these young officers had ever handled a murder investigation and that their theory of events had holes.

As we exited the court, Abe called Layla's cell phone and asked that we meet him at his plane. While I drove us the 4.6 miles east to the Harrison County Airport, I called the Leg to see if she had any intel on the remaining witnesses for the district attorney. She said she'd pressed her sources but hadn't yet been able to get anything out of them. I was tired and drained from the whole Knox fiasco and was thrilled to stop worrying about the case for the night.

"Do you think it's possible Amir was never going to get a fair trial?" I asked Layla.

"You're not going to like my answer," she replied. "No. I don't think Amir was going to be treated fairly. But I also think he's guilty."

She was right—I didn't like her answer one bit.

We pulled up to the small parking lot at the local airport. It was a public facility used almost entirely for corporate jets and private lessons. I had done a few hours of flight training there a couple years earlier in a Cessna 182 but never saw it through to completion. I loved flying but realized I didn't have anywhere to go.

Layla and I found Abe out on the tarmac by the Citation CJ4 owned by Gordon & Greene. The two pilots were doing their final walk-around inspection as we arrived.

"How'd it go with Judge Knox?" Layla asked.

"He agreed to speak with me, which was charitable. I apologized for what transpired in court, gave Euchre up for sacrifice, and offered to do whatever I could to make things right." Knox had shaken Abe's hand and left it at that. "Assuming he gets confirmed, we'll find out during our first few cases whether or not he holds a grudge," Abe said with dread in his voice.

I couldn't predict one way or the other how Knox would treat the lawyers from Abe's firm, but I was pretty sure he would not be quick to forget about me personally. That problem would have to wait until after Amir's trial though.

"I've got to get back to New York. But I want updates at the end of every day. I want to hear about any trial strategy that might impact our work *before* that strategy is implemented. No more audibles. Is that understood?" Abe said with authority.

"I got it," I answered, though that was all I could say. This was the second time he'd issued this admonition.

"And you," Abe said, turning to Layla, "you're blowing a golden opportunity to impress the partners at the firm."

With that, he climbed into the jet, and Layla and I watched as it taxied into position at the end of runway 33 and then raced forward, reaching just over a hundred knots before lifting off into the air.

On the drive back to the Compound, Layla and I were quiet. I was craving a Marlboro, but I found myself even more fixated on something else.

"How did Abe know I'd called an audible with Knox?" I asked, staring straight ahead.

"You told him you were following your instincts," she replied. "That's what you said to him last night."

"I said that in response to him berating me for changing our original strategy and not waiting to attack Knox during the defense phase." Layla didn't look at me. "How did Abe know what our original strategy was in the first place?" She remained quiet, so I continued. "You told him?"

"James—"

"Did you call him yesterday and tell him he'd better get down here?"

"He came because he was worried about the firm's relationship with Judge Knox."

"He got here so quickly. You called him, right?"

"Yes, I called him."

I pulled up to the Compound and kept the truck in drive.

"See you in court," I said.

Layla climbed out, and I drove away.

· TWENTY-FOUR ·

I arose with the sun the next morning, deciding that sheer will-power was all I needed to overcome my hangover. After a quick shower and shave, I put on one of my nicer suits, slicked my hair back, and headed out. I wasn't necessarily looking for trouble, but I sure was hoping trouble would find me.

The morning cigarette hit the spot just as "Tougher Than the Rest" came on the radio. It wasn't my favorite Chris LeDoux song, but it was perfect for my drive in. It was my sincere hope that some-one would make the mistake of trying to fuck with me that day.

I marched into the courtroom, and the Leg chased me down at the rail.

"What's up?" I asked.

"The next witness is the guy from TWAS," she said. "Sorry, I just got it this morning."

I arrived at the table where Layla was sitting with Amir. As I unpacked my notes, Layla stood.

"You didn't give me a chance to explain last night," she said.

"No explanation necessary. I'm here to work."

Before she could respond, Judge Whelan entered. The jury was brought in, and D-Cal called Jeremy Crawford to the stand. Craw-ford was a twenty-nine-year-old employee of Texas Warning and Alarm Systems, the home security company that Abe had hired to install the alarm in the Compound. We'd reviewed the alarm system but had honestly written off this witness as one of the many fillers on the district attorney's list whom he had no intention of calling. Since we were wrong about that, I was slightly unsettled thinking about what else we may have been wrong about with the security system.

"Mr. Crawford, what is your job title and description?" D-Cal began.

"I am an alarm dispatcher. I monitor our systems remotely, am the first to see when an alarm gets tripped, and I field calls to and from the customers, as a sort of counterpart to the emergency police dispatcher."

Crawford was the kind of guy who didn't have the fortitude to enlist in the military or join the police force but still fancied himself some sort of officer of the law. He tried to sound like a cop when he answered D-Cal's questions.

"Were you working the night of December tenth and into the early morning of December eleventh?"

"Affirmative."

"What occurred, on your end, involving the house on South Franklin Street where the defendant was staying?"

"At zero two thirty, a glass-break alarm was triggered."

"And what is a glass-break alarm?"

"It's not always possible to secure every pathway into a house. Sometimes residents don't want an individual sensor placed on every single window, so instead we have an alarm that detects the sound of glass breaking. When it gets tripped, we know that a window has been breached."

"OK, so a window is broken, and then what happened?"

"I confirmed on my monitor the address of the house and that the alarm was still activated. Then the next thing that happened was the sensor on the rear door to the property was disengaged."

"What do you do at that point?"

"Given the alarm and the sequence of those two events, it fits the model for a common break-in. A window is broken, and the burglar reaches his hand through and unlocks the door. I tried the phone number listed on the account, just in case the alarm went off acciden- tally. But there was no answer, which usually there would be if the owner of the house was home while the alarm was blaring. So I called 911 to let the police know I had a possible break-in and they should deploy officers immediately."

I got the sense this guy was thrilled to be a part of a murder trial and was probably bragging to friends that he was the key witness.

"Are there any cameras on the property in question?" asked D-Cal.

"Negative. No cameras inside or around the perimeter."

"What about motion sensors?"

"No. The only sensors on this property are on the doors."

"In other words, you can't tell if someone is inside or outside of the house, but you can tell when a door is opened and closed?"

"Correct."

"Prior to 2:30 a.m., was there any other activity?"

"Yes. At 19:57 on December tenth, the front door was opened."

"That's 7:57 p.m.?" D-Cal didn't need this wannabe cop confusing the jurors.

"Yes, 7:57."

This aligned with the statement Amir had given to the police that night. Abe and Layla brought Amir to the house at about eight o'clock.

"And after that?"

"The front door was opened again thirty-nine minutes later." This, too, matched Amir's statement. That was when Abe and Layla departed for the hotel, leaving Amir alone for the night.

"Between 8:36 p.m. and 2:30 a.m. were any doors ever opened?"

"Yes. The front door was opened and closed three times. The first time was at 10:33 p.m. The door opened and closed. Then, six min- utes later, the front door was opened and closed again, suggesting someone had stepped outside for a quick smoke or something."

I leapt out of my chair. "Your Honor, while I'm sure the court appreciates the insight of a man who serves our community as an alarm dispatcher, I'm going to have to object to blatant speculation on his part about what was occurring inside or outside of this house given the only information he had was that a door was opened and closed." It was a wordy objection, but since D-Cal had clearly coached his witness to provide a narrative he couldn't possibly have borne witness to, I thought I'd take the liberty to make my entire point to the jury as well as to the judge.

"The objection is sustained." Judge Whelan looked at the witness. "Please keep your testimony confined to information and facts rather than speculation and assumptions."

"Yes, Your Honor."

I glanced at D-Cal as I returned to my seat. I didn't know what he had planned, but he was out of his mind if he thought I was going to let this pimple-faced security guard pull that kind of bullshit.

"You said that the front door opened twice, first at 10:33 and then again at 10:39, six minutes apart. And there was a third door opened?"

"Yes."

"When was that?"

"The front door opened again at 11:24 p.m. and closed one minute later."

"And after that?"

"Nothing until the glass-break at 2:30 a.m."

"So it's reasonable to say the defendant left the house at 11:24 and didn't return until over three hours later?"

"Objection, Your Honor. Calls for speculation." I let my indignation show.

My objection was sustained, but it didn't matter. The facts were coming out either way. Amir had opened the door to the house at 10:33, perfect timing to have seen me and Judge Gardner walking through the parking lot. He could have easily witnessed Gardner entering the federal courthouse, where we now knew he was writing an email to Judge Knox. Amir could have gone back inside and devised a plan. Perhaps he grabbed a weapon. Then he exited the

Compound one final time, lying in wait for Gardner to walk back to his car.

In trial the day before, Layla and I had laid the groundwork to expose what we thought was a hole in the prosecution's case. We assumed D-Cal's theory was that, at around 2:30 a.m., Amir ran out of the Compound, stabbed Judge Gardner, and then ran back to the house. This left questions about why there wasn't more blood on Amir and why the detectives hadn't found a murder weapon. But this new theory, a theory supported by the sensors on the door, was that Amir would have had time to watch Gardner's movements from the house, wait for him to reemerge from the federal courthouse, murder him in the parking lot, and then spend nearly three hours going God knows where to clean himself up and hide the evidence.

We had made a huge mistake. Since the house alarm had never been armed, and because Amir had told us he never left the property, we'd failed to confirm that with the records from the sensors on the doors. Even more egregious, we had trusted our client.

It was my turn to cross-examine the witness. The problem was, aside from his attempts to speculate, this witness was testifying to unimpeachable facts. Still, I had to take a shot.

"Mr. Crawford, what percentage of alarms that go off turn out to be false or accidental triggers by the owners of the homes?"

"A decent amount."

"Ballpark it for me."

"I don't have those numbers off the top of my head."

"How many alarms go off on a typical night of work for you?"

"Anywhere from a couple to ten or more."

"On most nights, isn't it true that all of those alarms are false or accidental?"

More than anything, this kid didn't want to admit that his job was basically to call the owners of these properties and help them turn off the alarm systems they had inadvertently triggered themselves.

"Yes, I suppose that's accurate," he admitted.

"In the course of your work at TWAS, how many times have you participated in a criminal investigation?"

"It happens more than you'd think."

"How many times when it's not just you cooperating with an insurance company and a claim of stolen property?" I asked.

"It's rare," he admitted.

"Rare like this is the first time?"

"Perhaps."

"I'll take that as a yes."

I couldn't really do much to challenge his testimony, so I figured the next best thing was to make him look like he didn't belong there. I spent another twenty minutes asking about false alarms and how a glass-break can be triggered by other loud noises. None of my questions applied to the case at hand, but they were intended to muddy the waters and make this witness's testimony forgettable in the minds of the jurors. Ultimately, though, the problem remained. We had three hours in Amir's night that were now unaccounted for.

With no recess after Crawford stepped down, D-Cal called Detective Elliot to the stand. My stomach turned. I had a hunch that D-Cal had been saving the lead investigator for something special. The detective made his way to the witness box with a slight limp that was befitting of an old gumshoe. The bum leg slowed him down a little, a quality that probably lent itself to a methodical investigative style. He swore to tell the whole truth and then sat down.

Detective Elliot had been a cop in Marshall for my entire life. He was one of the only detectives in town who'd ever worked a murder case. He was well known and well liked. His demeanor on the stand was plain and unpretentious. He gave the impression that his pride wasn't on the line and that his only agenda was to answer questions honestly. He was, in short, the perfect witness for the prosecution.

"Detective Elliot, I want to turn to your investigation of the home on South Franklin Street where the accused was staying. Did you search that property?"

"Searched it three times."

"When were those searches conducted?" D-Cal asked.

"The first was done on the morning of December eleventh, a couple hours after the arrest of Mr. Zawar."

"What were you searching for?"

"Any clues or information that could either connect him to the murder of Judge Gardner or exclude him as a suspect in the investigation."

"What did you find in that first search?"

"Nothing."

"Nothing that confirmed his guilt or his innocence?"

"Nothing to persuade me in either direction."

"Then you conducted a second search?"

"Two days later. We brought in a full forensics team from Dallas, and we expanded our efforts to include hair fibers, fingerprints, basically anything that might have DNA, visible or microscopic."

"What did you find?"

"Again, nothing of consequence. We found several fingerprints, but they all matched lawyers from the firm that owns the house and Mr. Zawar, who was a guest there."

"All right, let's turn to the third search. When was that conducted?" I could feel D-Cal building to something big. The fact that I had no idea what it could be was terrifying.

"The final one was done nine days after the night of the murder."

"Can you walk us through that search, Detective?"

"We had spent the previous week broadening our scope to the outside of the house, surrounding properties, and an expanded perimeter that included the parking lot, the town square, and beyond."

"What were you looking for?"

"A murder weapon."

I glanced at Layla, and she looked as concerned as I was.

"Your Honor, may we approach?" D-Cal was taking us into potentially dangerous territory, and I wanted the judge to weigh in before irreversible damage was done. Judge Whelan waved us toward him.

"What is it, Mr. Euchre?" he asked.

"I'd like to know where Mr. Lucas is going with this line of questioning," I said.

"Keep watching, Euchre," D-Cal said.

"Your Honor, the district attorney has flooded my team with discovery, most of which covers phenomenally unimportant documents and items that he'll never introduce in this trial. But nowhere among all the potential evidence in his discovery is there mention of a murder weapon. He has teased this idea from the very beginning, and if he intends to present a weapon now, without first disclosing it to the defense, I will move for an immediate mistrial."

Judge Whelan shifted his glance from me to D-Cal. "Mr. Lucas, can I trust that you've adhered to the rules of discovery?"

"Judge, we have no murder weapon to produce. And Euchre has seen all of the evidence we've got." There was something about the arrogant way D-Cal delivered this information. It was so carefully worded, like he was trying to thread a needle.

"All right," said Whelan, "let's continue."

As we turned and moved away from the bench, D-Cal walked close enough behind me to whisper without anyone else hearing what he had to say.

"You're going to love this next part, Euchre."

I returned to my seat, filled with dread.

"Detective Elliot, I believe you were searching for a murder weapon? Did you find one?"

"No, I'm afraid not. After an exhaustive search and our third sweep of the house, we had no murder weapon."

"Did you find any knives or blades in the South Franklin house?"

"Certainly. It's a house, so it had knives, scissors, and sharp objects, primarily in the kitchen."

"Did you suspect any of these were the murder weapon?"

"There was nothing to indicate one had been used in that manner.

No blood or hair could be seen with the naked eye, but we bagged and sealed every knife and instrument and sent them to the FBI lab in Dallas for testing."

"How long did that testing take?"

"Several weeks to go through everything."

"What were the results?"

"One by one, every item came back clean. No DNA from the victim. No DNA from the defendant."

"In total, how many items were tested?"

"We tested thirty-one items."

"How many knives?"

"Twenty-one. Eight dinner knives that were part of a forty-piece silverware set that also included sixteen spoons and sixteen forks, which we didn't test. And then there was a stainless steel knife set, the kind that often comes with a wooden storage block. That set had thirteen knives of various sizes and one pair of scissors. We tested the entire fourteen-piece set."

"And all came back clean?"

"That's correct."

"It was a dead end?" D-Cal said.

"I thought so. But there was one more item we found during our third search that needed to be tested. A knife magnet strip was attached to the wall next to the stove."

"Why did you test that?"

"All of the knives in the set were fastened to the magnetic strip, so we thought it was possible DNA from a knife could have been transferred to it."

"And what did the lab discover?"

"No DNA anywhere on the magnetic strip."

"So you struck out?"

"Not exactly. As I read the report on the magnetic strip, something else occurred to me. When you have a knife block, you have a specific place for each of the knives. There are usually six or eight steak knives at the base and then an assortment of larger knives and the scissors above them. But, as I mentioned, this set didn't have a knife block. If it did, I would have seen right away that this wasn't a fourteen-piece set. This set is sold with fifteen pieces. One knife was missing."

I resisted the urge to look at Amir because I knew if a juror caught me, it would appear that even his own attorney thought he was guilty. I would have paid any amount of money, though, to see the expression on his face.

"Did you figure out which piece was missing, Detective?" D-Cal continued.

"I found the same knife set online and matched the original fifteen pieces to the fourteen we had in our possession. The missing piece is called a slicing knife."

Right on cue, D-Cal carried an exact replica of the knife in question past the jury box and toward the witness stand.

"Is this the make and model of the missing knife, Detective?"

"It is a match," Elliot replied.

Layla rose to her feet. "Your Honor, we object to this so-called evidence being introduced without any discovery offered to the defense." She had probably expected me to make that argument, but legal tactics were the furthest thing from my mind in that moment. I was stunned by the revelation itself.

"Your Honor," D-Cal said, "how can the state be expected to turn over evidence that doesn't exist? The whole point is that the knife is missing."

Judge Whelan thought for a moment. "The objection is overruled."

"Your Honor—" Layla said.

"Your objection is noted, Ms. Stills. Have a seat."

With that, Layla returned to her chair. D-Cal moved on. He received permission to hand a copy of Judge Gardner's autopsy report to the witness.

"Detective, did the medical examiner conclude anything about the weapon used to kill Gerald Gardner?"

"Yes. He concluded that the two stab wounds were made with a sharp object, at least four inches long and half an inch from top to bottom."

While still holding the knife in his hand, D-Cal asked his final question. "What are the specifications of the missing knife, the exact replica of which we have right here?"

"It has a four-inch handle with a six-inch blade, approximately half an inch high at its heel."

I stared at the table and felt the air move as D-Cal walked by me on his way to his seat. When Judge Whelan asked if I had any questions, I couldn't bring myself to speak. I was thinking about Amir and what I would say to him, or do to him, the next time he and I were alone. After an extended moment of silence, Layla rose and requested a recess. It took every ounce of my strength not to leap across the table, grab Amir by the throat, and beat him to a bloody pulp for killing my friend.

PART IV

RES IPSA LOQUITUR

The Thing Speaks for Itself

· TWENTY-FIVE ·

Res ipsa loquitur is a legal doctrine in tort law. It permits a court to infer that an injury was caused by negligence—not because someone proves the negligence occurred but rather because the nature of the injury itself could not have happened absent negligence in the first place. It's not a phrase often uttered in criminal cases, but I was struck with how pertinent it was to Amir's set of circumstances. There was no discovery of a murder weapon to suggest that Amir had killed Judge Gardner, but the absence of the weapon was itself incriminating. The textual translation for the Latin term is "the thing speaks for itself." At that moment, the missing knife was doing all the talking.

I followed Layla down a hallway in the new courthouse toward a sheriff's deputy, who had been tasked with transporting Amir to and from the county jail. The deputy opened the door he'd been guarding and we entered the holding room. I stayed up against the wall, as if the extra few feet between me and my client would protect me from my impulses. Layla sat down, joining Amir at the little table.

I thought back to the night of the murder and the first time I'd shared a room like that with Amir. Back then, he had looked small and scared. I had been convinced, without any evidence, that he had killed Judge Gardner. The difference now was that I had evidence.

I also felt the rage of having been tricked into believing in his innocence in the first place.

"I never touched that knife," Amir said quietly. He looked at our
faces and he must have seen defeat, if not skepticism. "I don't even
think I was ever in the kitchen."

I looked to Layla to gauge her reaction. She looked at the ground,
but her face didn't reveal anything.

"I didn't do it!" Amir protested, his voice growing louder and
more desperate.

"We will continue to make that case," Layla offered. "Today was
a setback, but we are going to make it very difficult for the jury to
convict you on evidence that doesn't exist."

"That's it?"

"We'll be back in court in twenty minutes. Let's get through the
rest of this day." Layla was calm, though not reassuring. "Then we'll
take the three-day weekend to rethink our defense strategy."

"You don't believe me," Amir said.

Layla didn't immediately respond, so I stepped in.

"Where were you, Amir?" I asked.

He stared at me, reading my face. He realized he had lost me as a
believer. I had no intention of hiding that from him. I'd started the
day hoping for trouble, for a fight. I didn't expect it would be with my
client, but at least I had somewhere to focus my rage.

"Where'd you go for those three hours?" I said, clarifying my
question.

"I went for a walk."

"That's a long walk," I said through gritted teeth.

"I had just spent half the day in a federal detention facility, and I
needed some fresh air."

"Then why'd you lie? Why'd you say you only stepped outside for
a few minutes to smoke?"

"I knew it would look suspicious if I admitted to being out of the
house for several hours right around the time the judge was murdered."

"The problem with that answer, Amir, is you told this lie right

away, supposedly before you even knew Gardner had been killed."
I paused briefly to see if he'd compound one lie with another, but
he didn't. "The officers placed you in handcuffs, believing you had
broken into the house. You told them you had stepped outside for
five minutes. It wasn't until the third set of officers arrived later that
anyone bothered to search the area. And it was several more minutes
before the dead body was discovered. In your statement, you claimed
that the first you'd learned of a killing was when you arrived at the
police station. Yet you told a lie fifty minutes earlier because you
were afraid your true whereabouts would make you look like a suspect for a murder you say you didn't yet know had occurred."

He stared at the floor for a long time, trying to unravel the mess he
had so masterfully woven. "You need to put me on the stand," he said.

"I can't put you on the stand, Amir."

"Why not?" His anger started to shine through.

"Two reasons. The first is that it's unethical for a lawyer to put a
client on the stand and elicit testimony the lawyer knows to be false.
Since everything that comes out of your mouth is a lie, I can't expect
you to tell the truth in the witness box. And second, it's an absolutely
idiotic strategy. After you're convicted but before you're executed,
you are going to hire another team of lawyers, and those lawyers
are going to appeal your conviction on the grounds of any and every
claim they can concoct. I will not let them add ineffective assistance
of counsel to that list, which they most certainly would claim if I put
you on the stand because only a lawyer who is a total fucking moron
would let you testify."

"Don't I have a say in the matter?" he asked.

"Actually, you do. Because I don't have to be your lawyer anymore."

"James," Layla said.

"I told you the day after you were arrested that you wouldn't want
me representing you if you were guilty. You should have listened to
me, Amir." I stood up and moved for the door.

"You know what I think?" Amir asked.

"I truly couldn't care less."

"You're scared. You finally have a case that matters, and you're terrified you're going to lose. So, true to form, you'd rather just quit."

"The jury is going to convict you. They believe you did it. And the reason I know that is because I believe you did it. I'm getting you a new lawyer."

"I don't want a new lawyer."

"I don't give a shit."

I opened the door and walked out.

I marched underneath the rotunda and toward D-Cal, who was speaking with his two assistant DAs. They stopped talking as I approached.

"Come with me for a minute," I said.

"I'm not really in the wheeling and dealing mood, Euchre."

"It's not about that."

He walked with me as I jogged up the stairs toward Judge Whelan's chambers. I passed the judge's assistant without so much as acknowledging her. I knocked on the judge's door and immediately opened it, not waiting for a response. Judge Whelan stood behind his desk, robe on but unzipped. He looked surprised to see a lawyer barge in without invitation.

"What are you doing?" he demanded.

"Sorry, Judge. This couldn't wait." I paused, allowing D-Cal to enter the room. Then I continued, "Your Honor, I move for an immediate substitution of counsel."

"Oh, come on, Euchre. I know you're getting your ass kicked but finish out the game," D-Cal said, genuinely annoyed. But that was nothing compared to how irate I had become.

"This isn't a fucking game to me!" I said. "Gardner was my friend, and that son of a bitch killed him!"

"Lower your voice," Judge Whelan commanded. He walked to the door and closed it. "Mr. Euchre, you knew who he was accused of killing. No one forced you to defend him."

"Your Honor—"

"Furthermore," he continued, letting me know to keep my mouth shut, "this is a capital case, and if there is a conviction, it will certainly be appealed. I am not permitting defense counsel to drop his client midway through. It is in everyone's interest that this trial unfold by the book, so I am going to forget the request you've made here today. Put your faith in the system and allow it to work as it was designed to."

"How am I supposed to represent him?" I could feel tears cloud my eyes.

"That's the job, Mr. Euchre. If you want to let your second chair handle every witness from here until the end of the trial, that is your prerogative. However, you will be seated at the table with your client every single day. The jury will see that the defendant's attorney remained by his side. Now get out of my chambers."

I entered the courtroom at the last possible moment and took my seat at the table, as I'd been instructed to do. I didn't say a word to Layla or Amir. Judge Whelan brought the jury back in, and D-Cal called his next witness.

Ethyl Mayer was the court clerk who served Judge Gardner for his entire tenure on the bench. She was well into her seventies with silver hair and an old-time Texas accent that sounded as Midwestern as it did Southern. She looked like a librarian, and everyone called her Miss Ethyl.

D-Cal began by asking the witness about her relationship with Judge Gardner. She told the jury she'd served him faithfully for twenty years and that she'd never met a kinder man. Her testimony was intended to pull at the heartstrings, to remind the members of the jury about the victim in this case. She did a good job, even summoning tears that seemed entirely authentic.

Miss Ethyl's testimony made me sad but not for the reasons it was supposed to. D-Cal had handpicked her as the person who could garner the most sympathy from the jurors, the person who could talk about how much she loved Judge Gardner. In most murder trials, that witness would be a family member, a spouse, a parent, or an adult child. But Judge Gardner didn't have any of those. There were plenty of people who cared for him, but there was no one who really knew him. There was no one who was particularly close to him. There was no one who bore witness to his life.

D-Cal walked Miss Ethyl through the day she learned of Judge Gardner's death. She arrived at the federal courthouse that morning, and word had already begun to spread. The first person she saw was another clerk, who had assumed Miss Ethyl had already heard the news, so she just blurted it out. Miss Ethyl cried as she talked about cleaning out his office and having nowhere to send his personal effects. She said he was the most admired man in our community and that he was taken from us too soon.

After about an hour and fifteen minutes of testimony, D-Cal had gotten everything he needed. Judge Whelan called on me, and without rising from my seat, I replied, "No questions, Your Honor."

D-Cal rose and buttoned his jacket. "Your Honor, the prosecution rests."

It was a well-presented case by the district attorney. Concluding on Miss Ethyl's tearful testimony was smart. Even more strategic was the fact that D-Cal wrapped just before a three-day weekend. The jury would have eighty-seven hours to think about this pivotal day of testimony. From Thursday afternoon until Monday morning, the jurors would replay Amir's missing three hours, a knife that had vanished, and Miss Ethyl's tears. The defense would have to wait an eternity to begin its attempt to chip away at the prosecution's case. But none of it really mattered anyway because we had no response.

I pushed my way out of the courthouse, determined to get to my truck, buy my alcohol and cigarettes, and get back to my house to shut down. The Leg caught up to me just as I reached the parking lot.

"Euchre."

"Not now, Lisa."

"Can I do anything for you?"

"Find the missing knife," I said. "And if you do, turn it over to the police."

She looked disappointed in me. I climbed into the Dodge and sped off.

· TWENTY-SIX ·

I stopped by the dingiest liquor store in town to buy a case of Miller Lite and two packs of Marlboro Reds. I could have purchased these items at the grocery store, but clerks at those places tend to see a customer getting a lot of booze and then say something annoying like "Where's the party tonight?" The tattooed former junkie who works the night shift at G.R.'s Liquor knows better. I wanted to procure my stuff from a professional.

The bell above the store door chimed as I exited toward my truck. I'd already unwrapped one of the packs of cigarettes before I'd hit the curb. By the time I was in the driver's seat, I had one fired up and ready for the ride home.

My house felt emptier than usual. Painful memories flickered through my mind. I took a swig from a bottle of Jack, knowing that my best chance to dull the hurt was in the whiskey. I brought my first beer with me to my closet and swapped out my suit for a T-shirt and jeans. Just as I finished changing, there was a knock on the door. I opened it and saw that Layla had changed out of her suit as well.

"Are you going to invite me in?" she asked.

I opened the door wider, and she walked inside. She took note of the booze and cigarettes.

"You look like you're in for a bad night."

"Bad nights tend to follow bad days," I said.

"About Abe . . ." she said, trailing off.

"No need to apologize."

"I wasn't going to."

"You spied on me," I said indignantly.

"I wasn't *spying* on you. He's my boss, and I gave him an update on our case. I didn't tattle on you."

"You disagreed with my strategy of going after Knox."

"And I told you that. You weren't supposed to accuse him during cross."

"That was my choice to make."

"Yes, and you fucked up. It's time to face the consequences, painful as they may be." I wanted to respond, but she wasn't finished. "This isn't patent law, James, and you're not some freewheeling local hired for your folksy charm. This is criminal defense, and your duty is to represent a man on trial for his life. You don't like that you got admonished for doing a bad job? Do a better job then. But stop taking it out on me because I don't answer to you."

I was heated, and I wanted to unleash a waterfall of words to match hers. What she said stung, but she was right. And arguing wasn't going to make me feel better. I pointed to the twelve-pack and then to the Jack. Seeing that I was conceding, Layla let her guard down.

As I poured her a glass, she stepped closer to me.

"I'm sorry for running from this case," I said.

"You gonna run from me, too?" she asked.

"No."

"Good, because I don't plan on chasing you."

Layla took a big gulp, polishing off the first drink of whiskey. I quickly followed suit and then poured us another. We went from the kitchen to the living room. I carried our drinks, and she brought the bottle. Our bodies brushed up against each other as we moved.

I put a record on, an early Garth Brooks album. It reminded me of my youth. The songs told sad stories in two or three verses. The instrumentals captured the mood I was already in.

We sat on the same couch, close together. We weren't playing games; we weren't trying to feel each other out. We didn't speak about the case again. We didn't speak about much of anything. Before we could finish our next drink, we were in each other's arms. There was a feeling of desperation, as if we were hoping our salvation was inside the other person.

She wrapped her legs around me, and I stood up. We never pulled apart as I carried her down the hallway and entered the first bedroom on the right. For a brief moment, I caught Layla looking around at the room. It was sparsely decorated, with an antique dresser and two end tables that were empty, save for matching lamps. The bed was perfectly made because no one ever slept in it. She knew why I'd chosen this room. But in her grace, she left it alone, and we continued the dance.

I woke up disoriented. Once I found my pants and my phone, I realized it was late in the night. I crept out quietly, grabbed a jacket, and stepped outside onto the back porch for a smoke. The cold air helped me shake off my sluggishness, though there was still plenty of alcohol in my blood. A few moments later, the door behind me opened. Layla touched my shoulder, and I grabbed her hand. When she sat down in the chair next to me, I saw she was wearing my other coat. She lit a cigarette for herself and then looked deep into the darkness.

"That was the guest room?" she asked, without any indication of hurt or anger. I nodded. "But that's not where you usually sleep," she said.

"No," I said. I allowed myself one more big inhalation and exhalation of smoke before I began. "My wife's name was Amy. She died four years ago. I haven't gotten around to changing anything. Our bedroom was upstairs, and it still sort of feels like it's ours."

"What happened to her?"

A downside to living in a small town is that everyone knows

your business. But that can also be a good thing, particularly when something painful happens. No one has to ask about it, and you're not forced to retell it over and over. In that way, Marshall had always protected me from having to share my secrets.

I extinguished my first cigarette and lit my second as I spoke. "Amy and I lived one street apart for our whole childhoods. When my mom was working nights and her mom was out at the bars, Amy would stay over. We took care of each other. She was my best friend." I looked out at the trees that were no longer swaying because the wind had settled.

"During our senior year, something switched inside of Amy. It was like there was a monster that had been lying in wait. One day it just woke up. Suddenly, she felt like everyone in her life was letting her down. She began accusing the people who loved her the most of betrayal. She broke up with me at prom and refused to speak to me all summer. When I left for college, we didn't even say goodbye.

"We tried to give each other space, but we always found our way back. We dated other people but nothing very serious. Then one day, toward the end of my time at law school, I came home, and we both knew what we wanted. It was one of the best years. It just didn't last."

I skipped past most of the symptoms and went straight to the diagnosis. "I never became an expert on borderline personality disorder, but the way Amy explained it to me was to say that she experienced extreme emotional swings and had no ability to regulate them. She had no choice but to ride the nightmare. It was like she absorbed all the pain from the outside world, the way a tree takes in carbon dioxide, except that she had no process to filter out the poison, no way to make it breathable air. She was suffocating. Amy had to go all the way to Dallas to get the diagnosis. Treatment was even harder to find. No one in Marshall could help her.

"When her mom died, everything unraveled. My mother-in-law had been the rightful recipient of much of Amy's rage. But once she was gone, the only way for Amy to alleviate the pain was to inflict it on herself. One night, the pain was just too much to bear." I hoped Layla wouldn't press me on that point. She sensed she didn't need to.

"What did Samuel Earl mean when he said you should have listened to her?" she said delicately, without demand.

"When I was away at school, Sam and Amy dated. They'd fight, they'd break up, and then they'd make up and fight some more. They were just good sparring partners, I guess. In any event, he always carried a torch for her. When Amy died, there was a lot of talk about what could have been done. A lot of speculation that I didn't listen to her cries for help. People said I ignored the signs, that I should have been able to save her." I inhaled a deep breath of smoke and saw that I was nearly down to the filter again.

"Obviously, you wanted to help," Layla said.

"I made my share of mistakes. I started to pull away. The more I did, the worse it got. She could tell I didn't want to be near her anymore. Finally, she asked me why. I told her, '*Your misery is making me miserable.*' And that was the last thing I ever said to her."

I dropped my cigarette into an empty beer bottle. Layla and I walked back inside. The lone light that was on in the other room was enough to guide the way because our eyes had adjusted to the night. I understood why Layla said she was going to head back to the Compound. I told her I wished she'd stay, though, and to my surprise, she did. It was awkward, and neither one of us slept well, but it felt like one of those moments when you either choose to get closer or drift further apart. Her offer to leave was intended to give me space. For once, I didn't want it.

TWENTY-SEVEN

T he next day was Friday. It was also the first day of alligator hunting season and the start of a long weekend. There were so many judges and lawyers who were also hunters that, back in the 1980s, it became common for all legal businesses to take an unofficial holiday. I explained this to Layla, and for a moment she thought I was joking.

"Well, should we go catch ourselves an alligator then?" she asked as she rolled onto her stomach in bed.

"I have to go to Dallas."

Samuel Earl's final disciplinary hearing before the Texas State Bar had been scheduled for this day because everyone in Dallas knew that everyone in Marshall had the day off.

"Oh," Layla said. "What should I do today?"

"You want to come to Dallas?" I asked.

"Sure."

I got dressed while the coffee brewed. We fixed some mugs for the road and then got into the Dodge and headed to the Compound so Layla could get some fresh clothes. I stood behind her on the porch as she typed in the code that unlocked the door. She took two steps inside and stopped. Her body tensed.

"What's wrong?" I asked.

She held her hand up, indicating that we should be quiet. The place looked like it had been ransacked. The furniture was knocked over and the shelves tossed. Everything was out of place. A small noise echoed upstairs. Footsteps followed. I inched my way in front of Layla and looked around for some way to defend against an attack. I quickly remembered that D-Cal had bagged and tagged everything sharp, so my only hope was that he'd left behind a blunt object somewhere. The footsteps moved through the hallway and arrived at the top of the stairs. We took cover behind a wall in the living room. Unarmed, I braced myself for hand-to-hand combat as the intruder reached the ground floor. My instincts told me they knew we were there.

The stranger took two more steps and stopped. I tried to peek around the corner, but all I could see was an arm. I only had the element of surprise for another second, so I seized it. I grabbed the wrist that was attached to that arm and heaved the accompanying body around the corner, throwing it to the ground. The maneuver was easier than I'd expected, probably because the Leg barely weighed a hundred pounds.

"Jesus fucking Christ, Lisa," I said. Layla exhaled dramatically.

The Leg moaned in pain, grabbing her shoulder as I helped her to her feet.

"I would have kicked your ass, Euch," she said as she winced.

"We thought we'd been robbed," Layla said.

"I've been here all night. Searching for the missing knife."

"Did you find it?" I asked.

"No."

"I'm going to change," Layla said as she headed upstairs, happy we didn't have a burglar.

The Leg turned to me with a Cheshire grin on her face. "I was wondering why she didn't come home last night."

I gave her a look that suggested I didn't want to have that conversation.

"I guess you two were working late," she said, offering me an alibi we both knew was bullshit.

I didn't respond, and I hoped she would let it go.

"What's the plan today?" the Leg asked.

"We're heading to Dallas. I've got the disciplinary hearing."

"She's going with?"

"Yes."

"Pretty soon I won't be able to tear you two apart."

I didn't have a little sister, but I imagined this was what it was like when a younger sibling discovers a secret about her older brother.

"So did your all-nighter bear any fruit, or are you just here to annoy me?" I asked.

"I found something," she said cryptically.

"What is it?"

"I need to look into it. Let's wait until you get back from Dallas."

My investigator was thinking strategically. She could do anything or nothing with whatever she'd learned. But once I knew about it, and particularly if I intended to use it in court, I would be bound by the rules of discovery to disclose it. She was keeping me in the dark for my own protection.

"All right. Let's catch up this evening."

Layla came downstairs a few minutes later. She wore pants and a blouse, and I tried my best not to stare. I think the Leg caught me looking anyway because that grin came right back.

As soon as we were heading west on I-20 toward Dallas, I rolled down my window and lit up a Marlboro. I hadn't given much thought to the day's proceedings until Layla asked me about them.

The process for censuring an attorney in the state of Texas is arduous. After an initial grievance is filed against the lawyer in question, there are several steps by which judges and panels of people from the Chief Disciplinary Counsel's office review and rule on the validity of the claim. Samuel Earl had lost at every turn. He was found to have violated Rule 8.04 of the Texas Disciplinary Rules of Professional Conduct, which broadly covered a wide range of misconduct. There was one final hearing for the matter, and it was at the Dallas regional office. Its purpose was to determine his punishment.

"So this could be Sam's last day as a licensed attorney?" Layla asked.

"From your lips to God's ears," I replied.

"Deep down, he must know he's not terribly bright," she said. "It can't be easy carrying that around."

"You're not going to make me feel bad for the guy."

Layla snatched the cigarette from me and took the final drag. She rolled her window down. "You had a good run, Samuel," she said as she flicked the butt onto the highway.

I held the steering wheel with my left hand so that, with my right, I could hold hers. We drove like that for miles.

We pulled into the parking lot of a commercial office building on the north end of Dallas. It was a large, glass structure that was home to several businesses and law firms, including the one hosting us that day. As I searched for a parking spot, I noticed a matte black Mercedes-AMG GT with a yellow racing stripe at the very edge of the lot. It had been backed in, with the passenger side against the curb so no one could park on that side of it. The spot next to it, on the driver's side, was vacant. Sam probably figured no one else in their right mind would want to park that far away from the building.

"Why don't you step out?" I said to Layla. I don't think she knew why I was making the suggestion, but she complied. I drove my truck just past Sam's Mercedes and then backed into the space next to his, putting my passenger side within three inches of his car, my right mirror hanging over his driver's-side door. I was careful not to touch his car but made sure I was close enough that he wouldn't be able to get in.

"You don't feel that's a bit juvenile?" Layla asked me as I stepped out.

"He's bound to do something in there that's going to piss me off. Call it a preemptive strike."

. . .

I left Layla in the firm's reception area. An assistant escorted me to a conference room with a shiny table and a dozen chairs. I could see Samuel Earl through the glass wall before I entered. He was seated on the far end of one of the long sides of the table. I was shown to my seat at the near end of the same side. The assistant offered me water, but I declined. She said the committee would be right with us, and she left. Samuel Earl and I didn't say one word to each other.

The members were led in by Walter Quigley, a partner at the firm and the chairman of the State Bar's District 1 Grievance Committee. Quigley's once-black head of hair was graying on the sides, revealing the salt-and-pepper direction the rest was sure to go. His background was in mergers and acquisitions, so neither Sam nor I had encountered him in court. He introduced his fellow members of the committee and got down to business.

"The purpose of today's hearing is to review our findings in the case of Mr. Samuel Earl Whelan and to determine the proper sanction in this matter. Mr. Euchre, the committee thanks you for taking the time to join us today. We understand you were the victim in this case. You should know that the account of the incident, as described in the original claim, was not disputed by Mr. Whelan. That being said, in the interest of painting as full a portrait as possible, we want to afford you the opportunity to weigh in."

"Thank you to the committee," I replied, not knowing what else to say.

"Were you furnished with a copy of the complaint made by the late Judge Gerald Gardner?" Quigley asked.

"No, I never saw it," I said.

Quigley thumbed through a file and found the document in question. He began reading aloud. "'On September twenty-third, Samuel Earl Whelan, an attorney in the Eastern District, admitted by the State Bar of Texas, physically assaulted a fellow attorney, James Euchre, during the course of a patent trial in which I was the presiding judge.'" Quigley continued to read the summary of the event, a summary that defined the attack on me as "violent" and "unprovoked." As Gardner's words moved from describing the altercation to describing the people therein, I glanced in Sam's direction. " 'This is not the first time Mr. Whelan's behavior has been unbecoming of an attorney, nor is it the first time I have had to reprimand him in my courtroom. However, due to the nature of this incident and the fact that his actions threatened the safety of another attorney, I am compelled to issue this formal complaint. As far as I am concerned, there is no place in the Texas State Bar for a lawyer like Mr. Whelan.' "

As I listened to the scathing indictment of Sam's character, I glimpsed him sitting quietly, staring down at the table. As the son of a lawyer who was more respected than his offspring ever would be, I supposed I sympathized with him. I still felt that he was a miserable attorney, but he hadn't been gifted any special skills or intellect at birth, and I'm sure a part of him knew that.

"Mr. Euchre," Quigley said as he put Gardner's letter away, "is there anything you would like to add?"

"There is," I said, straightening up. "Judge Gardner and I were very close. At times, you could say he was my guardian angel. He was also, and I mean this with love, a tough old bastard. The case I'm involved in at this very moment has repeatedly referenced Judge Gardner's rigid adherence to protocol. He built the Eastern District by revamping the rules and then demanding that we all abide by them. He was never known for leniency." I paused and considered my next move, but in reality, I had already decided what to do. "The thing is, though, I knew him for his leniency. For some reason, it was a quality he reserved only for me, and he displayed it again and again. He bailed me out of trouble, he provided me with second and third chances, and he forgave me my sins. I don't dispute his account of what occurred nor would I question his intentions in drafting that complaint. However, I would like to add to it, as you said, to paint a fuller picture. Mr. Whelan and I go way back. We grew up together, and our rivalry extends well beyond the courthouse doors. While I certainly didn't appreciate being blindsided on the day in question, to characterize it as an unprovoked attack might be a bridge too far. I'd been needling him throughout that entire trial. It wasn't the first time one of us wanted to take a swing at the other. It was simply the first time one of us did so in a courtroom. I have put this minor scuffle behind me, and in the spirit of the same forgiveness that Gerald Gardner always afforded me, I ask that the same be done here for Samuel Earl. He ought to be allowed to continue the practice of law."

I never once looked over at Sam, though I suspected he was taking a peek or two at me. I felt a weight had been lifted.

Layla and I rode the elevator down. "How'd it go in there?" Layla asked.

"I'm glad to put it to rest."

We exited the building and headed toward the truck. I heard Sam call my name. We turned to find him jogging toward us. We stopped and waited for him to catch up. I could see Layla bracing for the worst.

"Thanks for what you said, Euchre."

"Don't worry about it."

"I'll probably get to keep my license."

"Good, then I can keep kicking your ass in court," I said. He smiled, knowing damn well that I meant it.

"Are you serious with this?" Sam asked as he walked toward our two vehicles parked side by side.

"Oh, is this your matte black Mercedes?" I said. He knew he had to suck it up and take it. He'd made out far better than he could have hoped for.

I climbed into the truck as Sam and Layla moved out of the way so I could pull out. I rolled the windows down and started to inch my Dodge forward.

"Be careful, please," Sam said with concern.

I cleared my truck away from the Mercedes, and Sam got into his car. "See you around, Euchre." I gave him a two-fingered wave as he drove away.

Layla's phone rang. She answered it and said, "He's right here," handing it through the window to me. "It's Lisa."

"What's up, Leg?"

"I've been trying to call you."

"I was in the hearing. My phone's off."

"You need to get back to Marshall."

"What happened?" I asked.

"I found a cell phone last night. It was dead and hidden in the Compound."

"Whose is it?"

"I think it's Amir's."

"The police took his phone," I said.

"They didn't take this one. I spent the day looking into it. There's a lot I need to tell you."

"James?" Layla was still standing outside the truck when she called to me. I looked over at her, sensing it must be important since she obviously knew I was on a call with Lisa.

"Euchre, you've got to come home. There is a shit-ton of intel we need to sift through," the Leg said.

"James," Layla called out again. She was staring at something.

I put the truck in park and stepped out. "We'll be back in a couple hours," I said to the Leg.

"Run the reds, Euchre. If I'm right about this, I think Amir might be innocent," she said.

The Leg's words hit me right as I passed the front of the truck and joined Layla on the other side. I could see what had caught her eye. She was looking at the spot where Samuel Earl's Mercedes had been. There, on the asphalt, dead in the center of the parking space, were three small circles, one on top of the other. They were fresh oil stains that formed an eerily familiar shape: the silhouette of Frosty the Snowman, minus the corncob pipe and silk hat.

"We're on our way," I said to the Leg. I hung up the phone and handed it back to Layla, who started taking photos of the parking spot.

· TWENTY-EIGHT ·

My truck never dropped below ninety miles per hour. Layla and I spent the entire drive home putting a mental puzzle together. The more we thought about it, the more the pieces fit together perfectly. By the time we pulled up to the Compound, the puzzle's image had taken form.

The Leg was waiting for us at the dining room table. The house still looked like it'd been hit by a tornado thanks to her all-night search for the knife, but the table was spotless except for a single cell phone lying on it.

"I found it late last night," she said.

"Where was it hiding?" Layla asked.

"Inside the air-conditioning vent, below the stairs, in the back."

"Did you have to unscrew anything to remove it?" I asked.

"No. I just pulled off the grate."

"So if Amir had broken the rear window, opened the door, set off the alarm—"

"He still would have had enough time to stash this phone inside the vent," the Leg said.

"How'd you think to look in there?" Layla asked.

"I got cold. It was freezing last night, and for some reason, the A/C turned on. I was trying to find the thermostat, and as I walked past this vent, it blew cold air on me. Something told me to look inside."

"Searching for a knife, but you find a phone," I said.

"It's even better than a knife," Lisa said. "There's a lot on this little phone."

The phone was dead when she found it. While waiting for it to charge, she emailed a contact of hers who was, as she described him, a tech wizard. She asked if they could meet up. It was the middle of the night, but when he woke, they set a time. She fast-forwarded to lunch, when she met her tech friend, Max, who blew past the phone's passcode.

"There's one email account set up, and it's encrypted. There's messaging on here, but that's also encrypted. And there are only a handful of apps," the Leg reported. "I looked back at the police report, and it says the officers found a cell phone in this house and took it with them when they arrested Amir."

"This was his secondary phone," Layla said.

"His secret phone," the Leg added.

"Were you able to get past the encryptions?" I asked.

"No. Maybe with more time, but the whole point of this phone is to protect secrets, so it's pretty fortified."

"How do you even know it's his?" I asked.

"Max was able to pull up all of the geotracking data from the location app. We have the time and coordinates of every movement this phone ever made. It flew from the Bay Area to Dallas on the morning of the murder, averaged eighty miles per hour along Interstate 20 into Marshall, and spent several hours in the parking lot near the Eastern District, presumably because Amir left the phone inside his bag in the car."

"Abe told us not to bring our phones into the courtroom," Layla said.

"So it remains in the vehicle through your lunch and the eligibility hearing in Gardner's court. Then, and here's how I knew it was Amir's phone, it traveled to Texarkana—"

"Where Amir was being held for contempt," Layla said.

"Right," the Leg said, looking at Layla. "You took the phone with you when you went to bail him out. Then it travels back to Marshall, to this location at the Compound."

"It must have been in his luggage the whole day," I said.

"And does it stay here, in this house, until you found it this morning?" Layla asked.

"No," the Leg said, "it makes one more journey."

Layla and I followed the Leg outside as she continued to narrate the secret phone's travel history.

"The phone leaves the house at 11:25 p.m."

"Which lines up with the last time the alarm system showed the front door opening and closing," I added.

"Right. Then it waits out here for six minutes and must get into a vehicle because it travels for ten minutes at upwards of forty-five miles per hour."

"Where does it go?" I asked

"Let's take a ride," said the Leg.

The three of us got into my truck, and I took East Houston Street away from the town square, with no idea where we were headed. The Leg gave me turn-by-turn directions but wanted to hold off on the big reveal. As I made a left onto East Travis Street, we passed Amir's current place of residence: the Harrison County Jail. I tried to imagine my client taking this same ride in the middle of the night. I tried to envision where he might have been going and what he would have been doing once he got there.

The road was four lanes, two going in either direction. As we reached the outskirts of town, we passed a couple schools and half a dozen churches. It seemed the only entities interested in this dreary land were the government and God.

"Amir didn't have a car, so who drove him?" I asked. "Medallion isn't running in Marshall."

"Did he take an Uber?" Layla asked.

"There are no rideshare apps on this phone," explained the Leg.

"But he did make one call from this number a little before eleven o'clock."

"And you're able to see the number he called?" I asked.

"The phone function itself isn't protected," the Leg said. "Care to guess who he called?"

I thought about it for a moment and then the answer came to me. "A taxi service," I said.

As we drove down Indian Springs Drive, the Leg told me to make a left up ahead. I knew exactly where we were going. Layla recognized it as well when she spotted the control tower in the distance.

We pulled into the parking lot of the Harrison County Airport, the same place Abe's private jet had departed from earlier in the week. I put the truck in park, and we got out. An old single-engine Cessna 152 was executing a touch-and-go, landing on the runway and then immediately speeding up and taking off again.

"The phone gets here at 11:41," the Leg began, "and it remains here for about two and a half hours."

"Doing what?" I asked aloud.

"Don't know. But just after 2:00 a.m., it travels by vehicle the reverse route we just took and doesn't stop until it arrives back at the Compound."

We approached the chain-link fence that separated the small airport from the forest around it. The sound of footsteps along gravel stirred on our right. Someone was walking along the fence, toward us. I saw her Wayfarers first.

Charlotte Mayhew sauntered up to us with a smile. "Hello," she said, as if it were perfectly normal that the four of us would meet this way.

"What the hell are you doing here?" I demanded. "Did you follow us?"

"Please, I was already here when you arrived. Care to tell me what brings you to this part of town?" She was so calm and confident. She had this way of asking questions while giving the impression she already had the answers. If she hadn't become a reporter, she would have made an excellent attorney.

"We were going to take my Gulfstream for a jaunt to Cancún, but the damn pilot is late," the Leg said.

Mayhew smiled at her. "You don't know why you're here, do you?"

"Why are you here?" the Leg asked.

"If you want to trade secrets, give me a call," Mayhew said as she removed a business card from her backpack. She scribbled something on it and handed it to the Leg.

"What's this?" the Leg asked, looking at the handwritten note.

"Call it a gesture of goodwill," the reporter said as she put her bag over her shoulder and walked away.

"What the fuck is going on?" I said to my team.

"Let's go speak to the taxi company," Layla suggested. "A driver is sure to remember a late-night trip out here."

"No," I said. "Our client knows everything. He's lied to us for the last time."

Amir was already meeting with Furqan Haq when a guard brought me, Layla, and the Leg inside. They stopped their conversation, and the guard left. I placed Amir's secret phone on the table between us. He stared at it for a few seconds and then looked up at me without so much as an attempt to explain himself.

"Typically, when someone who's accused of murder lies as much as you do, it's because they're guilty," I said.

I could see him trying to sort out what we knew and what we didn't.

"Haq, why don't you give us a minute?" Amir said to his friend. Haq didn't budge.

"Why'd you hide this phone, Amir?" I said. "What's on it that you didn't want anyone to find?"

"This isn't a privileged conversation," Amir said.

"Fuck your privilege!" I shouted. "Why did you hide this phone?"

"That's my business."

"We found out where you were that night. You're the only person I know who steps outside to light up a joint and then drives five miles to an airport to smoke it. What was at the airport, Amir?"

Again, he sat in silence, trying to concoct a story that might be believable.

"Tell me the goddamn truth, or I'll turn this phone over to the feds and let them figure it out," I warned.

I could tell he believed me. I could also see that whatever information was on that phone was information he didn't want getting out. Presented with the options of confessing to me or having the authorities investigate, Amir decided there was no choice.

"I had a meeting," he said.

"In the middle of the night at the Harrison County Airport?" I asked.

"It was supposed to be in Dallas." Amir looked at Layla. "We were scheduled to be back in the city that evening. Then Judge Gardner threw me in jail. This isn't the kind of person to wait in Dallas until the morning, so he flew to Marshall, and I met him at the airport."

"Who is he?" I asked.

"Doesn't matter," Amir said.

"I will decide what matters and what doesn't."

Amir glanced in Haq's direction and then sat back, crossing his arms, letting me know he had no intention of revealing this information.

"Do you know much about planes, Amir?" The best way to handle him was to push the conversation out of his areas of expertise, to make him feel uneasy. "There are these things on every plane called ADS-Bs, automatic dependent surveillance-broadcasts. They're mandatory on any plane that flies into controlled airspace. It means every plane is tracked."

I removed Charlotte Mayhew's business card from my pocket and showed him what she had scribbled on the back of it: "N517EQ."

"That's a tail number, Amir. Now, I searched it, and it's not public, so I don't know who that plane belongs to yet. Lisa, you got any contacts at the FAA?" I asked over my shoulder.

"I may know a guy," the Leg said, playing along.

"If a plane landed at the airport that night, I'll find it. And if you make me look for it, Amir, I swear to Christ I'm not keeping it a secret."

It was his last chance. He'd lied to me all along, every step of the way. I was done with it. Telling me was the only way to avoid me telling the world.

"The plane belongs to Oliver Glanzman," Amir said.

I looked at Layla and registered her surprise. But Layla's shock was nothing compared to the astonishment on Haq's face. With one name, Amir had shattered Haq's entire world.

Oliver Glanzman was a Swiss national who made his first billion dollars as the founder of a European search engine he sold before his fortieth birthday. He'd had his hands in various endeavors since, but the one he was most known for was his pledge to create and sell the first fully autonomous vehicle. Every investor in the world had placed bets one way or the other on whether or not Glanzman's new automobile company would succeed. For his part, Glanzman reveled in the spotlight and loved making bold predictions about his future accomplishments. Everything he did made headlines. I remembered one that crowned him "The King of Automation." And now we knew he had been meeting with "The Rideshare Prince."

"Why were you with Oliver Glanzman?" Haq asked. I could hear the emotion in his voice.

"We needed to have a private conservation."

"You had to keep it a secret, even from me?" Haq said.

Amir hesitated and then he looked at all of us. "You can't reveal this to anyone," Amir demanded.

"We ran into Charlotte Mayhew at the airport," I said. "She's the one who gave us that tail number."

"Fuck!" Amir reacted instinctively. His mind raced for ways to

246 · JOEY HARTSTONE

"I'm not your fucking publicist," I said.

"What was the nature of the meeting?" Layla asked, repeating Haq's last question.

Amir knew he needed our help, more than ever at that point. He also knew he had to earn it.

"Glanzman and I have agreed to a merger."

"You son of a bitch," Haq said.

"He wants to put his product to work as rideshare vehicles under Medallion's banner," Amir said.

I was angry for so many reasons. First among them was that Amir had made my job of defending him in court almost impossible because he'd been lying to me the whole time. But his reason for lying was also infuriating.

"You're telling me that Medallion, the company that's supposed to reimagine the gig economy so it works for the workers, so it benefits the drivers, may be the first to use fully autonomous vehicles?" I asked. Amir didn't respond, so I continued. "The mission statement of your company is complete bullshit?"

"We're adapting to an ever-changing world," Amir said matter-of-factly. "Medallion won't just be the future of ridesharing; we are going to lead the autonomous revolution. People won't need to own cars anymore. They'll own monthly passes, Medallion cards, that grant them unlimited access to the roads. This will change everything."

"We used the stories of our fathers to build a company that, if you're successful, would have made them unemployable," Haq said.

"Someone is going to build that company. Why shouldn't it be the sons of taxi drivers?" Amir said.

"Because that's not who we are," Haq said.

"Immigrants throughout this country, people like our fathers, are told over and over, in every way imaginable, it is their duty to assimilate. Same for their children. From the language we speak to the clothes we wear to the beliefs we hold, the most fundamental of

American values is greed. That's how we topple the power dynamics on which this country was built. We accumulate the kind of wealth that only a few in the world possess. We make so much goddamn money we become the system. I have no problem using the memory of my father for that."

It was painful to watch Amir's friend, the man he'd described as his brother, be confronted with the worst type of betrayal. Haq had been a true believer, an apostle for a movement whose founder was a fraud.

At the same time, I was struck by how similar Amir and I were. Two sons defined by their fathers yet furiously straying from their paths. Maybe he had every right to do what he was doing, but by insisting that this meeting with Glanzman remain a secret, Amir was taking his own alibi off the table.

"Amir, this meeting could be your ticket to freedom. You can't hide it."

"As you noted, part of Medallion's brand is its relationship with its drivers. I need that brand to build my empire. By the time Glanzman's vehicles are fully operational, and we're ready to roll out our partnership, Medallion will be a hundred times the size it is now. Our brand will be able to evolve. But for the moment, I need it intact."

"We need Glanzman to testify," said Layla.

"Absolutely not," Amir responded.

"He's the only alibi you've got," she said.

"If I was willing to use him, I would have told you by now."

"What good is protecting your company if you die in prison?" I asked.

"I refuse to accept that my options are binary. My life and my company as indivisible from each other. Neither exists without the other."

I had tried to drop Amir as a client when I was convinced he had killed Judge Gardner. Now I knew he was innocent, but he wouldn't let me do my job, at least not how I wanted to do it.

"Amir, the judge refused to let me off this case. There was a point last night when I thought I was going to have to sacrifice my license to practice law so I could throw you to the wolves. I didn't think it was possible, but I like you even less now than I did yesterday."

I knocked on the door to let the guard know I was ready to leave.

"What the hell does that mean?" Amir demanded.

"I'm still your lawyer, but not because the court told me I couldn't quit. We're going to see this case to the end because, despite your best efforts to sabotage yourself, I know you're innocent. And even without your help, we can prove it."

TWENTY-NINE

In a practical sense, there was no need for us to bring Amir up to speed on our strategy, particularly because he wasn't contributing anything to his own defense. We had an innocent client who refused to let us help him because it would compromise his business. I had more important things to worry about.

Having a client who is innocent and *proving* a client is innocent are two entirely different things. Perhaps Amir thought he could conceal his alibi during trial but use it on appeal if he were convicted. Once you're on death row, though, you have to move mountains simply to get a shot at a new trial. And those metaphorical mountains, just like everything else in Texas, would be much bigger. Amir's only real hope for freedom was to secure an acquittal from this jury.

I dropped Layla and the Leg off at the Compound. As I left for the Marshall police station, I thought about the last time I'd driven there, in the dead of night with no idea what I was heading toward.

I gave the desk sergeant my name, and he disappeared through a secure door. I turned around and saw only one other soul in the waiting room. He was a young man in his mid-twenties, wearing boots, jeans, and a black sleeveless shirt with a logo that looked like a neon bar sign that read: "Ladies Night." The skin on his arms was pale and covered in green tattoos. A lot of the ink indicated that he was a veteran. Given his age, I figured he'd served in some war that, one way or another, had begun on September 11, during a year in which he had still been a young child. But battle ages people. He saw I was looking at him, and he changed his posture, as if he were ready to throw down.

"Were you in the 101st?" I asked, trying to ingratiate myself to him.

"That's right," he mumbled. "You serve?"

"Had a couple friends at Fort Benning." I knew I'd failed to impress him with that information.

The guy was clearly coming down off something. My guess was heroin. If he'd had more money, he would have probably sprung for oxy.

"You a cop?" he asked with disdain.

"Lawyer."

"Oh yeah. Check this out, lawyer man." He turned his left arm so that I could see a phrase tattooed around his bicep. The words read: "The right to bear arms shall not be infringed."

I raised my eyebrows, overtly feigning interest.

"You got a problem with the Second Amendment?" he asked, apparently because I hadn't shown the proper admiration for his tattoo.

"Nope. But if I were to get one of those, it'd be the Seventh Amendment."

"Which one is that?" he asked.

"It says, 'The right of trial by jury shall be preserved.'"

In truth, there were about forty more words in that amendment, but since he had no problem abridging his, I felt it fair for me to edit mine.

The desk sergeant returned to the side door and opened it. "You can come on back," he announced.

As I moved to follow him, the strung-out veteran hollered after me, "Hey, I'm bailing out a buddy. He might need a lawyer. You got a card?"

"Did this friend of yours invent something?"

"No," he answered with confusion.

"Then you're gonna have to find him another lawyer." I followed the sergeant down the hall.

Detective Elliot was leaning against a desk and talking to the desk's owner, a younger officer who was sitting in a chair. They were chuckling about something. I was relieved to have found him here, the police station being preferable to the tiny kitchen in his trailer.

"James Euchre," Elliot proclaimed. "You must be in trouble."

"You got an office?" I asked.

"You're in my office," he said. His colleague laughed as I looked around at the main floor. It housed several desks, one of which I reasoned belonged to Elliot.

"Is there someplace we can talk?" I said, with a "please" in my tone.

"Let's go."

I followed him out a back door that led to a parking lot full of squad cars. He leaned against the side of a Ford Explorer whose body was painted with blue letters that spelled "POLICE." Elliot lit up a cigarette. I was glad I had my pack on me because conversations between smokers always seemed to go more smoothly.

"What do you need?" Elliot asked, getting down to business.

"My client's innocent."

"You've mentioned that."

"I can prove it."

"Prove it, then."

"I'm trying. But I could use a favor."

"Uh-huh," he said.

"I know who killed Judge Gardner."

He stared at me for a long moment. "You waiting for a drumroll?"

"If I tell you who it is, will you look into him?"

"It depends on how much meat is on that bone."

"Can you at least promise me you won't give the prosecution a heads-up? My trial strategy sort of depends on it."

He exhaled a lung's worth of smoke and then mimed the zipping of his lips.

"Samuel Earl Whelan," I declared.

"The judge's son?" he said with a coughing laugh.

"Yeah. And here's the thing: I'm right this time."

While Detective Elliot smoked, I did my best to chisel away at his skepticism. I told him about the oil stains in the courthouse parking lot. I mentioned that they were right next to the final drops of blood, where the killer must have stopped. I told him about the disciplinary hearing I had just attended and the scathing letter Judge Gardner had written, calling for Sam's disbarment. I assured him that Sam's career had been in jeopardy because of Gardner.

"What do you think?" I asked hopefully.

"Well, I like him for it better than the magistrate judge. But that's not saying a whole lot."

"Look, I've got my investigator on it, but she's only one person. You've got a badge. Can't you use it to cut through some red tape, maybe run some tests that we can't do on our own?"

"I'll look into it," he said.

"Thank you."

"But if I don't like what I see, I'm done. I don't work for you."

"Understood."

"Get out of here," he said as he stepped on the butt of his smoke.

I spent the next forty-eight hours at the Compound, revisiting every aspect of Judge Gardner's murder with Layla, from the timeline to the blood drops to all the evidence the prosecutor threw at us during the presentation of his case. The Leg was in and out all weekend, searching for any bit of information to support the defense we were preparing to mount. As Saturday quickly gave way to Sunday, our theory grew stronger, but I still wanted a silver bullet. I'd been hired to save Amir from lethal injection, but I also wanted justice to be done for Judge Gardner.

"I wish we had the knife," Layla said, as if reading my mind.

"Maybe Detective Elliot will find it," I said.

"By tomorrow morning?" she asked.

"Why don't I go search Samuel Earl's place?" asked the Leg.

"No," I said. "It's unlikely the murder weapon would still be there, even less likely that you'd find it. And the chances of tipping him off are too risky."

"Speaking of tipping him off," said Layla, "how do we get him into the courtroom tomorrow?"

Our new strategy required Sam to testify. Somehow, amid all the chaos of the weekend, I'd completely forgotten about the simple fact that I couldn't call a witness to the stand who wasn't actually in court and ready to go.

"You've got to talk to him," Layla said.

"I'll have to do it first thing in the morning. I can't give him all night to prepare or to leak it to D-Cal. We need the element of surprise," I concluded.

"I'm going to stake out Sam's place," said the Leg, "because if he randomly decides tomorrow's a good day to go fishing, then we're screwed."

I nodded. She was right about that.

"You two have a nice night," she said with a glint in her eye.

"Bye, Lisa," said Layla.

The door closed behind her, and the headlights passed through the window as she drove away.

"You want a drink?" Layla asked.

"Not tonight."

"Good. You're going to have to be sharp as a razor tomorrow."

I nodded.

"You abstaining from cigarettes, too?" she asked.

"God, no," I said, jumping out of my seat. She laughed as we stepped outside and fired them up.

With no alcohol inside of me, the full effect of the cold air meeting my natural adrenaline felt good.

"In the event it isn't obvious," I said, "I'm really grateful you agreed to work on this case."

"I was ordered to," she said. "But I'm glad I was." I gave her an inquisitive look, so she elaborated. "Working this case has made me like being a lawyer again."

I watched her put the cigarette to her lips.

"What does Abe think about our new approach?" I asked.

"I forgot to mention it to him," she said with a smile.

I nodded in appreciation.

"So tomorrow," Layla said, shifting subjects, "you need to hit Sam fast and hard. The prosecutor isn't going to sit back and watch. And if you thought you were on the judge's bad side before, just wait until you attack his son. It's going to take a stroke of genius to keep this trial from going off the rails."

"Well," I said while taking a drag, "I'm sure you'll think of something."

THIRTY

I rose before the sun the following morning, feeling well rested. I'm sure it helped that I'd skipped my allotted three beverages the night before, though I suspected the true reason for my reinvigorating slumber was lying in bed next to me. I tried to stand up without waking her, but Layla stirred. I kissed her on the forehead and told her I needed to run home to change. She let out a little moan, and I couldn't tell if it was in protest or just a wordless "hello" from a sleeping beauty. Either way, it was fucking adorable.

It was still dark outside, and my morning Marlboro glowed orange. I watched the ashes flicker and disappear each time I put it near my window as I drove back to my house. After a shower and shave, I decided the day called for my best suit. It was at that moment that I realized my favorite sartorial selection was dirty. It was still in a pile at the back of my closet, along with my best shirt, stained with my blood from when Amir attacked me in court three months earlier. I'd come home from the Christmas party that night and tossed more clothes on top of my favorite suit, burying it from view and apparently from my mind. I wasn't a particularly superstitious person, but it was jarring to have to wear my second-best suit to court. Things were not off to a perfect start.

I called the Leg, and she confirmed that Samuel Earl had been at home all night. He left for work early, and she was still tailing him to his office just in case. I gathered everything I needed and departed from my house.

On my drive into town, I called Detective Elliot. He said he had interviewed a server from the Christmas party. She told Elliot that Sam had been drunk and that around eleven o'clock, he had fallen and knocked over a table of cupcakes and cookies. That's when she cut him off from the bar. Sam did not take this news well. Ultimately, a few bystanders calmed him down and convinced him to leave the party several minutes later. That put him outside and agitated right around the time Gardner would have been making his way toward his vehicle.

I thanked the detective for his intel and suggested he might want to attend the trial that morning.

"We'll see," he said.

I pulled my truck into the redbrick parking lot in the center of town. As I stepped out, I spotted the Leg in her car, keeping an eye on Sam's office. She gave me a thumbs-up, and I headed that way.

Sam rented a two-room office in a building used exclusively by local patent lawyers. I had looked into a space there years earlier but felt that being stuck among a dozen other locals made it look like I was in a meat market. I liked giving the impression I wasn't simply one of many. If you wanted my services, you had to seek me out specifically. Sam, however, was lucky to be one of the pack.

I knocked on the door, and he opened it, surprised to see me.

"Are we friends now, Euchre?"

"Absolutely not," I said.

He laughed and let me in. We sat across from each other. "I was hoping you could help me out, Sam."

"With what?"

"I need a witness today, someone who was at the Christmas party. To set the scene for the jury."

I could see that he was looking for an excuse to get out of it.

"I have a clerk willing to testify, but she left the party early," I said. "And I have a server who could do it, but her strongest memories of the evening are about the appetizers and which partygoers had too much to drink. I was hoping you might pinch-hit for me." As he considered it, I pressed ahead. "You saw Judge Gardner's speech, and you know everyone in town. It's the first day of the defense, and it'd really help me out if I could start with a lawyer. I'll have you in and out in half an hour, tops."

Considering I'd just saved his career a couple days earlier, he wasn't in much of a position to say no. Still, if he had been a smarter person, he would have refused.

"Sure, what the hell."

"Thanks, Sam."

The courtroom was packed with spectators. D-Cal had done a damn fine job of making it look like Amir had killed Judge Gardner and then ditched the murder weapon. There was speculation that we might change our plea to guilty.

I spotted Detective Elliot in the back and gave him a quick nod. As I got to the front, I saw the Leg seated close to our table, where Layla was reviewing her notes.

"Did you get Sam?" Layla asked.

"Yeah. I told him I needed an attendee to testify about the Christmas party."

"That's not a particularly clever lie."

"Sam's not a particularly clever person."

D-Cal and his crew made their way to their table. Amir joined us at ours. Judge Whelan entered and took his seat. He called in the jury and then welcomed everyone back from the weekend.

"Mr. Euchre, is the defense ready with its first witness?"

"We are, Your Honor. The defense calls Samuel Earl Whelan."

D-Cal jumped out of his chair like he'd been bitten by a rattler. "Objection, Your Honor. Your son," he stopped and rephrased, "*this person* is not on the defense's witness list."

Layla stood up. "Your Honor, Mr. Whelan was on the *prosecution's*

258 · JOEY HARTSTONE

witness list." D-Cal looked to his assistants for verification. Layla continued, "Mr. Lucas included every person at the Christmas party on his list of potential witnesses. And while that may have been a ploy meant to confuse the defense, the fact remains that Mr. Whelan is at our disposal."

"Counsels," Judge Whelan said as he motioned us toward the bench.

"Your Honor, having your son testify is obviously a stunt intended to distract the jury."

"Judge, if anyone is guilty of using his witness list as a stunt, it's the district attorney," I countered. "Furthermore, I don't see how Mr. Lucas can object to a witness whose name he added to the list himself."

"What exactly is he supposed to testify about? Can we get an offer of proof, Your Honor?" D-Cal demanded, prompting Judge Whelan to look at me.

"The witness was at the Christmas party and was, therefore, not only privy to Judge Gardner's statement that night, but he was also one of the last people to see the victim alive," I replied. "His testimony is material to our defense, and there's no reason to block him from taking the stand."

The judge weighed his decision for a long beat. "Go back to your seats," he said without any indication of which way he intended to rule. I looked at D-Cal. Neither of us wanted to back away just in case we needed to plead our case again, but we obeyed.

I gave a slight shrug in Layla's direction, letting her know I was no more informed than I had been before the sidebar. I took my seat and waited for an eternity. If Sam was prohibited from testifying, I didn't have a plan B. I would have to ask for a continuance, and that was sure to start our defense off on a horrific note.

Judge Whelan looked out at all the faces eagerly awaiting his decision. "I am going to allow the witness," he said to D-Cal's dismay, "but let me caution you, Mr. Euchre: stay between the lines on this one."

"Yes, Your Honor."

We had just cleared the first hurdle.

Sam was in the back of the courtroom and was called forth to testify. He was sworn in and took a seat on the witness stand. I stepped toward the podium, but before I could speak, the judge interjected, "A point of clarification for the members of the jury. You just heard the witness's name, and I'm sure you noticed it is the same as mine. The witness is my son. That should in no way impact how you view the testimony he is about to give. Please treat it with the same consideration, and skepticism, with which you've shown every other witness. Proceed, Counselor."

"Mr. Whelan, would you please tell the jury how you knew the victim in this case?" I asked.

"Same as you, Mr. Euchre. I am a local patent attorney in the Eastern District, which was Judge Gardner's jurisdiction."

"You're a fairly successful attorney, wouldn't you say?"

"I do all right."

I walked to my table and grabbed a blown-up photograph of Sam's home that the Leg had taken over the weekend.

"Is this your house?" I asked.

"Sure is," he said with confusion, wondering why I had the photo.

"And that's your Mercedes in the driveway?"

"That's her."

"So you're being modest when you say you do all right. You're a top attorney in town, aren't you?"

"I won't argue with you," Sam said.

I went through five minutes of mundane biographical information, just to make sure my witness was relaxed. I asked him about some of his trial experience and then brought it around to the Christmas party.

"Were you in attendance that night, the night of December tenth?"

"I was."

"Did you have a good time?"

"Yeah, it was a party."

"Open bar?"

"As I recall."

"Do you recall Judge Gardner's speech that night?"

"It was short and sweet. He thanked everyone for their support and then declared his intention to reign over the Eastern District for another twenty years."

"Were you happy about that announcement?"

"Everybody liked Judge Gardner."

"Even you?"

Sam shifted in his seat. "He was an important judge, and I had the utmost respect for the man."

I changed course. The plan was for me to plant several seeds and then pray I could harvest them all at once, before my examination was inevitably halted.

"Mr. Whelan, were there any disturbances at the party? Any altercations?"

"Not that I recall."

"You weren't agitated at any point?"

"It was a celebration."

"Do you remember being cut off by the bartenders?"

"Objection, Your Honor. Relevance?" D-Cal was not going to sit on his hands during this witness's testimony.

I kept calm, my face stoic, as I turned to the bench. "Judge, I'm asking the witness to recount the night of the murder, and I would like to ascertain his level of intoxication, as that might have had an effect on his memory."

"If you didn't trust his recollection, Euchre, why call him as your witness in the first place?" D-Cal was scared, and I knew that would help me with the jury. Judge Whelan, on the other hand, I did not want to aggravate.

"Mr. Euchre, ask your questions but get to your points swiftly."

"Yes, Your Honor." I turned back toward Samuel Earl. "Did you have a lot to drink that night?"

"I may have had a few too many."

"Weren't you, in fact, asked to leave the party?"

"It was suggested I go home, and so that's what I did."

"You remember what time you called it a night?"

"Not that late. Before midnight. I had to get up early the next morning."

"Why's that?"

"I was heading out to my family's cabin to go deer hunting."

"You do that every year?"

"Since I was old enough to fire a weapon."

"Did you get anything that day?"

"Objection, relevance." D-Cal had no idea where I was going, but his instincts told him he should try to stop me.

"Your Honor, this is the defense's first witness, and I'd appreciate being able to get through a complete train of thought without being interrupted by the prosecution," I replied.

"I am going to overrule the objection, but make haste, Counsel."

I turned back to Sam. "Was the hunting trip a success?"

"Nabbed an eight-pointer."

"Did you field dress it?"

"Of course."

"You drained it of blood?"

"As quickly as possible."

"You ever shoot a deer and discover it's not yet dead?"

"It happens."

"What do you do then?"

"Finish the job."

"How?"

"You could put another bullet through its head or just take a knife to its throat."

"Hit the carotid artery?"

"Exactly."

"Do you carry a knife on you, even when you're not hunting?"

He paused. Sam had enjoyed our conversation about hunting so much that he'd let his guard down. Now he regretted it as he sensed danger.

"Sometimes," he said. Another seed planted.

"OK. Let's go back to the Christmas party for a minute. Do you remember talking to me that night?" I asked.

"I believe we spoke briefly."

"About what?"

Sam wasn't thrilled I was bringing it around to this.

"I, uh, I asked you for a favor."

"To do what exactly?"

"I had a small matter before a disciplinary committee of the Texas State Bar. It involved you."

"Because you attacked me in the middle of open court?"

"After you goaded me."

"What was the favor?" I asked.

"I was hoping you would write a letter on my behalf."

"Asking for leniency?"

"That's right," Sam said.

"Do you remember when our altercation in court occurred?"

"Late September."

"Why did you wait to discuss it until the middle of December?"

"No particular reason."

I stared at him for a few seconds to make him uncomfortable and to let everyone watching know that I didn't believe his answer. I turned back toward my table, and Layla handed me a document. I asked permission to show it to the witness and then handed it to him.

"Mr. Whelan, what is the document in your hand?"

"It's an official complaint that was sent to the disciplinary committee regarding our altercation."

"What's the date on that complaint?"

"September twenty-ninth of last year."

"Do you remember when you first became aware of the complaint?"

"Not off the top of my head."

I made the same walk back toward Layla, and she handed me another document. With permission, I handed it to Sam.

"And what is that document, Mr. Whelan?"

"This is a letter from the Chief Disciplinary Counsel informing me they had found just cause to proceed on the complaint against me."

"What's the date on that letter?"

"December eighth."

"Did that letter come to you with anything else?"

"A copy of the original complaint was attached."

"Did you receive those in the mail on December tenth, the day of the Christmas party?"

"Probably right around then."

"Who was the author of the original complaint against you?"

"It was Judge Gardner."

"And in it, did Judge Gardner recommend that you be disbarred for your actions?"

Sam glanced in his father's direction, as if looking for help. Then he realized he was on his own. "Yes, he did."

"Are you sure you liked Judge Gardner?" I asked, returning to an earlier question.

"Objection. Argumentative." D-Cal was starting to annoy me.

"Sustained," Judge Whelan said with extra authority in his voice.

The DA sat back down, and I considered my next move.

"Did you drive your Mercedes the night of the party?"

"It's the only car I own."

"Where'd you park?" I asked.

"Right out front in the main lot."

"You remember which spot?"

"It was months ago."

"I bet you like to put that Mercedes someplace special, where it's less likely to be hit."

"Your Honor," D-Cal let the exasperation spill out of him, "how much more of this do we have to sit through?"

"Mr. Euchre, I'm inclined to ask you the same question. Are we about done?"

"One more short set of questions."

"Get on with it."

I walked back to the table and picked up copies of two photos. I held them up for Sam.

"Can you tell me what you see in this first photo?"

"It looks like the brick parking lot outside this courthouse."

I walked closer so he could see the photo's details.

"Can you read the time stamp on it?"

"It says December eleventh at 7:48 a.m."

"The morning after Judge Gardner's murder. And what's this second photo?"

"It looks like a close-up in the same parking lot. It's a photo of an oil stain."

"Three oil stains, right?" I clarified.

"Yeah, three small circles."

"Here's another photo in front of your house," I said as I retrieved it. "Would you say the oil stains on your driveway match those in the parking lot photo from the morning after the murder?"

"Objection, calls for speculation." D-Cal was right, and Judge Whelan sustained it.

"Is that where you parked the night of the party?" I asked, pointing at the photo of the oil-stained spot in the brick parking lot.

"I don't remember."

"Would you agree that those oil stains in the parking lot outside, those oil stains right next to several drops of Judge Gardner's blood, look remarkably similar to the oil stains on your driveway?"

"Objection, Your Honor!"

"Sustained."

I nodded but didn't slow down. It was time to reap what I had sown.

"Mr. Whelan, forgive me, I'm trying to replay the events of the night, from your perspective. At some point that day, you receive a piece of mail informing you that Judge Gerald Gardner has filed an official complaint with the Texas State Bar in which he recommended that your license to practice law be revoked. You have several drinks, you show up at the party, you're heated, angry that Gardner might have cost you your career. You drink more, so much that you get cut off and kicked out. Then you walk outside of this very building, just before midnight, which is perfectly in the time-of-death window that the coroner's report established for the victim. Did you bump into Judge Gardner in that parking lot?"

"No, I did not."

"You didn't see him as you walked to your car?"

"Asked and answered," D-Cal objected.

"Sustained."

"You're telling this court that someone else happened upon Judge Gardner in that very same spot during the very same window of time, someone else who had reason to want Judge Gardner dead, someone else who used a knife with perfect precision, jamming it into the neck of the victim and then slicing open his carotid artery, killing him almost instantly?"

D-Cal objected, but I didn't wait for a ruling.

"You saw the judge who wanted to destroy your career, you were drunk, you were angry, you had a knife in your pocket, and you knew how to use it!"

Judge Whelan banged his gavel, but I wasn't stopping for him either.

"Come on, Sam, you're a lawyer. You know what to do. Did you kill Judge Gardner?" I asked.

All at once, everyone fell silent. The question hung out there, and regardless of whose side anyone was on, we all wanted to hear the answer. The rage in Sam's eyes was perfect because I knew it must have been the same look he had in the parking lot that night. And I knew the jury would see it, too. Finally, he said the only thing that was left to say.

"I invoke my Fifth Amendment right."

There was another long pause as I looked at the twelve jurors, their attention rapt.

"We're taking a recess. Counsel, my chambers." Judge Whelan's voice shook.

THIRTY-ONE

I told Amir to look calm and confident on his way in and out of the courtroom. As I followed Layla through the crowd and into the hall, Detective Elliot grabbed my arm and pulled me aside.

"I'm going to go find another judge and get authorization to seize that Mercedes," he said. "There's no way Sam could have committed the murder and then driven that car without getting blood all over. And I'm betting we'll still find traces on it."

"That's great, Detective."

"It's going to take some time though."

"How long?" I asked.

"A few days, minimum."

I nodded, knowing I couldn't count on it for my purposes. I thanked him and followed Layla upstairs.

We entered the outer office to Judge Whelan's chambers. His assistant must have been in the inner office with him because D-Cal and his two guys were the only ones there.

"You are one deceitful son of a bitch," D-Cal said before we were even inside.

"I told you the whole way that you had the wrong guy," I responded.

"There are ways to handle situations like this, and they all involve professional courtesy."

"You know what, D-Cal, take your professionalism and shove it up your ass."

He stepped to me, and for the first time in a while, I was prepared for someone to punch me.

"Knock it off!" Judge Whelan stood in the doorway. "Get in here, all of you!"

As we filed into the judge's chambers, I was irked by the notion that D-Cal was mad at me. He wasn't grateful I'd solved the case. He wasn't appreciative that I may have saved him from convicting an innocent man. He was pissed he was going to lose and angrier still that his failure would be public.

Judge Whelan's robe was sprawled on a chair by the bookshelves. In the silence, I could feel D-Cal dying to talk. But he waited, and so did I.

"This is an unmitigated disaster," Judge Whelan said. "I am at a loss for how to proceed."

"Your Honor, Mr. Euchre ambushed the court today," said D-Cal. "He ignored all rules of discovery and went out of his way to mislead the state. It is my recommendation that he be censured and that this jury be dismissed on the grounds that there is no way to undo the damage he has done." There was desperation in his voice.

"To hell with you and your rules of discovery," I said, having had enough of the DA's bullshit. "You buried every piece of evidence you had among a pile of irrelevant materials, you put half the town on the witness list, and now you want to accuse me of deception?"

"There's an ethical code to what we do," he said.

"Which you don't give a damn about," I said. "You sprung a murder weapon on me in open court."

"This whole case is permanently tainted now," D-Cal said to the judge. "There is no way to unring that bell. This has to end in a mistrial."

"In your dreams!" I shouted.

"You've turned this trial into a circus!" D-Cal shouted back.

"I exposed the real killer, which I could have sworn was supposed to be your job!"

"Stop it!" Judge Whelan said with a slam of his palm on the desk. Thus far, he had proven himself to be an evenhanded jurist. But at that moment, he was also a father.

"The fact of the matter is, Mr. Euchre, you have implicated a family member of mine in a case in which I am the sitting judge. I see no way to proceed."

"Your Honor—"

He raised his hand to stop me.

"I can't preside over the second half of this trial now. That must be clear to all involved. You must have realized that when you concocted this *strategy*." He said that last word through gritted teeth.

"Your Honor, if you insist on ending this trial here, then the defense requests that you dismiss all charges with prejudice so my client is free from further prosecution."

"That is not his call to make," D-Cal said.

"Mr. Lucas, I'd caution you about proclaiming what is and what is not my call. However, Mr. Euchre, I cannot render a decision that would be permanent in this case. You've removed any perception of my impartiality. We cannot proceed."

"Then let's finish the trial today," I said, putting forth the idea Layla had conceived of only hours earlier.

"What?" said D-Cal in total shock.

We had intended to call at least half a dozen witnesses. Dr. Cole was scheduled to provide blood and DNA analysis. I wanted a hunting expert to examine Sam's techniques and compare them to Gardner's injuries. We would have loved to wait for Detective Elliot's pending search of the Mercedes, submitting whatever he found into evidence, but this was no ordinary trial, and we had run out of time.

"Your Honor," I began, "the defense believes it has already presented a compelling case for the innocence of our client. You say you can't preside while the defense puts on the remainder of our witnesses. Fine. We accept that. The defense rests."

"You've called one witness, Euchre." D-Cal could feel his mistrial slipping away.

"The witness has taken the Fifth. Neither of us can ask him any additional questions. But it also means that if we had to do this trial over again, my client's defense would not have the ability to reexamine this witness. My client could not benefit from what has transpired today. He deserves to have the testimony from this witness factor into the consideration of his verdict. Our client has a right to a trial, and a verdict, by *this* jury. If neither of you is willing to drop or dismiss these charges and guarantee that Mr. Zawar will never be tried again, then my client insists on his constitutional right to have those twelve members of this community decide his fate."

Judge Whelan put his hands in his pockets and jingled his keys. The rest of us waited with bated breath while he searched the recesses of his mind for a decision.

Layla and I stepped out of the courthouse. My phone rang. Honest Abe was calling. I put it on speaker so Layla could hear.

"Hello, Abe."

"What the hell did you do, Jimmy?"

"Hopefully just exonerated our client."

"By accusing the judge's son? Is your plan to alienate everyone in the whole fucking town before this trial is over?"

"Doesn't look like I'll have enough time. Summations are this afternoon."

"Are you out of your fucking mind? I want you off this case. Put Layla on the phone!"

"Abe, there's something you always seem to forget: I don't work for you." I hung up and put the phone back in my pocket.

We only had an hour to prepare for the final round. But I lived for closing arguments.

"If you don't mind," I said, "I think I'm going to go clear my head."

"OK," Layla said. "I'll see you in a little bit."

I climbed into my Dodge Ram and headed south on Washington Avenue. It only took a couple minutes for me to reach my destination.

I parked up against the chain-link fence that separated the Marshall High School football stadium from the rest of the world. One hundred yards of green turf were surrounded by a four-hundred-meter track for sprinters. There were bleachers on either side, squared off against each other, stretching from one twenty-yard line to the other. And towering behind the bleachers, like guardians watching over everything, were the lights.

As I sat down on the home team's side, the cold from the aluminum passed through my pants and into my legs. I stared out at the fifty-yard line and the painting of the school's mascot in red. The bull's face stared back at me. I always loved that Marshall's team was the Mavericks. I liked the rebellious nature of the name. A maverick was more than just a rebel, though; what made a cow a maverick was that it remained unbranded. That was a struggle in life, to reject the definitions thrust upon us by others. It was also a battle in the courtroom. Our job as lawyers was to define the important elements in a case while resisting the other side's attempts to do the branding. If I did my job well, the jury would adopt my definitions and make them their own.

I had come to the outdoor stadium to think about the case, but my mind wandered. So many paths in my life could be traced back to my high school's football field. Whether it was the people I'd met or the person I'd become, I wondered how much of it had been determined right there.

I remembered so many little moments. A single play that changed the course of a game. The sounds that two thousand Marshall fans make when a player breaks free and scores. Most of my memories weren't highlights though. The successful events never remained in my mind for very long. The mistakes, the busted plays, those haunted me forever. If I thought hard enough, I could remember every frame of that last series, ending with D-Cal dropping back and throwing a miracle pass. I was on the other side of the field with no chance to make a play. I was relegated to being a spectator as the receiver came down with the football, and my childhood dreams shattered in front of the whole town.

I thought back to Amir, who had put his life in my hands. I'd spent my entire career avoiding such stakes. I was comfortable in a courtroom where the only thing that could be won and lost was money. A human life brought with it the possibility of true failure. Only once in my life had I been responsible for another person. I had vowed never to take that burden on again. But we don't always have a choice in the matter.

I barely listened to D-Cal's closing argument. He implored the jurors to ignore what they had seen earlier in the day. He wanted them to focus on Amir, to renew their suspicions about him as an outsider who had disappeared for three hours on the night of the murder. D-Cal talked about an angry outburst and a missing knife. Ultimately, he tried to infect every member of the jury with enough presumption of guilt so as to allow their consciences to convict.

When my time came, I knew I would do my part to cast suspicion in the direction of Samuel Earl Whelan. I believed that, at minimum, anyone trying to be objective would agree there was at least as much reason to suspect Sam as there was Amir. I could also argue reasonable doubt because I believed we had achieved it. But before I got to any of the legal qualifications for guilt or innocence, I wanted to talk to those seven men and five women about something else.

"Ladies and gentlemen of the jury, I am a patent lawyer. Usually, this is the moment when I would stand up in Judge Gardner's courtroom and try to make a complex question of intellectual property law seem simple enough for any ordinary person to find the answer. The trick is to convey confidence. If the lawyer seems confident, then the jury will believe him. It's easy to be confident in patent court. We deal with product designs and dollar amounts. The facts are all right in front of us, and the outcome is purely financial. But that's not the case here.

"A good man was murdered in our town. I know you all want to find out what really happened. Human beings crave certainty. We rarely get it. You may have your suspicions that the real killer is still out there. You may even believe he was in this courtroom earlier today. You've heard a lot of theories about what other people think. Now it all comes down to you.

"I wish I could give you certainty. I even thought I might try to fake it, but that'd be a mistake. Jurors are human lie detectors. I knew you'd see right through me. So rather than pretend I know everything, I want to talk for a moment about doubt." I walked right up to the railing that separated me and those twelve people. I didn't want any space between us.

"My favorite closing argument, the one I love to deliver in patent court, is about the first truck I ever owned and the man who stole it from me. I tell that story because it evokes emotion in me, and emotions are transferable from one person to another. I also tell it because it happens to be true. However, like a lot of stories, just because it's true doesn't mean it's complete. There's another part to the story.

"It was a 1964 Ford F100 that I bought when I was in high school. It was torn up to all hell, and other than gasoline and oil, I never put another dollar into that old beater. It was stolen from me, but I eventually got it back. I took it to college and then to law school. After my second year as an attorney, I finally had enough money to buy a brand-new truck. So I did, but I couldn't part ways with this old one. I don't even think a scrap yard would have taken it off my hands anyway. I held onto it, and every once in a while on a random weekend, I'd take it out for a drive. Amy, my wife, begged me so many times to get rid of it. She called it a nostalgic waste of space. And as was often the case with Amy, she was right."

I looked down at the floor beneath my shoes. My thoughts were running ahead of my words, and I needed them to get back in sync.

I hoped the jury would forgive me if I took a moment to myself. I'd never told the next part before.

"My wife suffered a lot in her life. There were days when her pain was so bad that she couldn't get out of bed. During the worst times, all we could do was hold on tight and try to wait it out. You never quite get used to it, but after you've weathered enough storms, you start to take for granted that every one of them will pass.

"We'd fight sometimes, especially in those days when we needed each other the most. You fight with the ones you love, that's just how it goes. One morning, I said some things I didn't mean. When I came home that evening, I knew right away that something was wrong. As the garage door went up, I could see Amy's new car parked in its spot, but my old Ford was gone. Amy never drove that truck."

I cleared my throat.

"They found my Ford at the bottom of the Brandy Branch Reservoir. Amy's body was still inside, no seatbelt on, windows rolled down so the water could consume it quickly. When someone you love takes their own life, you spend a lot of time wondering what you could have done to stop them. You replay it over and over again, pulling apart every little detail, examining every word that was spoken, wondering if you missed something, and praying for one more chance to do it over.

"Did I do everything I could to prevent it? Did she try to tell me? Did I fail to hear her? Did my mistakes cost Amy her life? I know what it is to have doubt."

I locked eyes with each of the twelve members of the jury. I wanted them to see me as the final piece of evidence, not for guilt or innocence, but as proof of what happens to a person who carries the responsibility of another's life with them forever. "We all have secrets, even from those closest to us. We keep them with us, burdens we cannot share. If you're unsure, if you have doubt in your soul, I urge you to listen to it. A man's life is in your hands. If you aren't absolutely certain, then do not cast a vote that condemns him to death. I swear to you, if you ignore that doubt, it will haunt you for the rest of your days."

· THIRTY-TWO ·

Layla and I sat with Amir in a holding room. We had no idea how long the jury would be out or, for that matter, if they'd even finish deliberating that afternoon. But we had nowhere else to be and nothing else to do, so we just kept our client company.

The Leg knocked on the door and entered. "Euch, can you come out here for a second?"

I stepped into the hall. Charlotte Mayhew was waiting for me. She removed her Wayfarers as I approached.

"You know you have that look like you should be listening to Bob Seger and sliding around your parents' house in your underwear," I said.

"It wouldn't work. I don't wear underwear," she replied.

"Knew it!" the Leg said.

I shot my investigator a look and then shifted to the reporter. "What can I do for you?" I asked.

"Like every other journalist here, my next story is going to be about the verdict. I'd love a quote."

"Sure, I'll talk to you when it's over."

"Thanks."

"Anything else?"

"After the trial, I'm going to write something bigger."

"An exposé?" I asked.

"A book. About Amir, about Medallion, all of it."

"You want his cooperation?"

"He'd never cooperate with the book I'm going to write. But maybe you and I could talk a couple of times, go over some of the events that happened here?"

"I'll give you what I can, but it won't be much," I said.

"I'll take what I can get," she said. Then she glanced down the hall toward a man who was sitting alone. He stood up and walked toward us. It was Haq. Amir mentioned that Haq had resigned from Medallion, so I was surprised he hadn't left town. Apparently, he still cared enough about his friend to remain by his side until his fate was determined.

As Haq joined our circle, he didn't even acknowledge Mayhew. They'd already become well acquainted it seemed.

"You're going to be her source?" I guessed.

"I want to tell the story of Medallion, about what it was supposed to be. Who knows, maybe someone else will be inspired to lead the revolution," Haq said.

"Why not you?" I asked.

"I'm not a leader," he replied.

"So the two of you are going to take down Amir's empire?" I asked.

"You can't destroy men like him," Mayhew said. "Too many people stand to make too much money."

"If you're right, then, Haq, you're about to forgo a lot of future profits," I warned.

"I told you," he said, "it was never about the money."

I heard a squeak of shoes on the floor, and I turned to see the jury bailiff rushing toward the judge's chambers. That could only mean one thing: the verdict was in.

It's always been strange to me, the moments when I found myself thinking about my father. He died a few months after I graduated from law school. I was clerking for Judge Gardner, so I hadn't even tried a case yet. He never got to see me in court.

The Darrow of Dallas was as much a legend as it was an accurate representation of Robert Euchre. It was true that he won many big trials, some that other lawyers would have almost certainly lost. But I heard many stories about him that couldn't possibly have been true. I heard tales of surprise witnesses and unparalleled oratory that brought courtrooms full of people to tears. There were brilliant legal maneuvers and combative cross-examinations that destroyed prosecutors' cases in one fell swoop. However real or imagined his heroics were, they remained the unreachable bar my outstretched hands could never grasp.

About eighteen months into my practice as a patent attorney, I delivered a pivotal closing argument in a case about the design of an airplane's lavatory. My client was an engineer, and he was suing all the major airlines and airplane manufacturers. It was the first nine-figure verdict ever awarded in the Eastern District. I wished that my dad had been there to see it. I used to imagine besting him, making him jealous, even envious of something I had accomplished. But that day, I just wondered if he would have been proud.

I knew the courtroom was going to be at capacity even before we stepped back inside. There was an overflow of people into the hallway. Apparently, word had gotten out that we had a verdict, and everyone within a mile of the old Harrison County Courthouse wanted to hear it for themselves.

People were vying for positions and couldn't be bothered to part ways to allow the attorneys to pass through. I had to turn sideways and use my briefcase to wedge people apart. I could feel Layla behind me as she used me like a fullback to clear the way. We made it to our table and took our seats, even though nearly everyone else was still standing. Amir was brought in and escorted to his chair next to ours. We waited for what I imagined were the longest ten minutes of his life.

When Judge Whelan entered, a murmur rippled through the courtroom. By the time he arrived at the bench, all was silent.

"Bring in the jury," he ordered. His demeanor had noticeably changed. I wasn't surprised he was angry, but I had expected him to hide it a little bit better.

The twelve members found their seats. I searched for eye contact. It's hard to look in the direction of the defendant if you're about to declare him guilty and condemn him to death. Somehow, they all managed to neither look directly at us nor entirely away.

"Has the jury reached a verdict?" Judge Whelan asked.

Juror Number Two stood up, and she declared, "We have, Your Honor." She handed the verdict form to the bailiff, who, in turn, walked it to the judge.

Whelan reviewed it carefully and showed no signs either way, save for a long blink that I swore was disappointment. Then he looked in our direction. "Mr. Zawar, please rise for the reading of the verdict."

Layla and I stood shoulder to shoulder with our client as Judge Whelan read the case number in *The State of Texas v. Zawar*. I felt a surge of fear run up my body. I inhaled and knew I wouldn't breathe again until the results were in. Then the judge read from the jury's form. "'We the jury unanimously find the defendant, Amir Zawar, not guilty of murder, as charged in the indictment.'"

Amir gasped as he dropped his forearms to the table. All of his bravado vanished, and I could see just how scared he had truly been. Layla whispered into his ear. The Leg ran up from behind me and jumped on my back, nearly tackling me to the ground. I shared her excitement. Then Layla turned and wrapped her arms around me. It was, without question, the most exhilarating moment I'd ever experienced in a courtroom.

The reactions in the crowd were varied and loud. Judge Whelan asked for silence, presumably hoping for a quick end to the matter. He went through the motions of asking the foreperson if it was her signature on the verdict form and then asking the other eleven members to declare, with a raising of their right hands, that this was indeed their verdict.

"The court thanks you for your service. You are permitted to discuss this matter if you are so inclined. The defendant will be processed and released. This court is adjourned." He banged his gavel quietly and disappeared into the bowels of the courthouse.

I looked over at the prosecution's table. D-Cal sat alone while his assistants chased after jurors, hoping to get interviews and answers to how and when they'd lost the case. I approached him and could see he was in a daze. He unconsciously fidgeted with his state championship ring. That piece of jewelry, for the first time, seemed small to me.

"D-Cal," I said, putting my hand out. He snapped out of it and slowly stood. "It was a privilege to share the courtroom with you."

He shook my hand and searched for an appropriate, if not insincere, response. "Hell of a job, Euchre."

I returned to my table and explained to Amir how he'd be processed. We promised to meet him at the county jail to welcome him back to freedom. Then the guard took him away.

"Well, Counselor," Layla said to me, "what are you thinking?"

"That I like being a lawyer."

PART V

NON OBSTANTE VEREDICTO

Notwithstanding the Verdict

· THIRTY-THREE ·

We all have blind spots. They're not defects or even short-comings. There are simply things we don't see because we weren't trained to look for them, or painful experiences taught us it was better not to look at all. The best we can do is be aware that blind spots exist and accept the reality that none of us can see the full picture, at least not right away.

I stepped out of the main entrance to the old courthouse and discovered that the media had stormed the parking lot like the beaches of Normandy. There were news vans and satellites, cameras and microphones. I still couldn't get used to the idea that the world was watching what unfolded in a Marshall courtroom. Reporters swarmed me and fired off questions quicker than I could field them. I did my best to answer the ones I heard with clichés like "We are just happy to know that justice was done" and "This was a good day for the rule of law." After several interrogatories about Amir, most of which I deflected, the reporters turned to the matter of Samuel Earl. "Let me just say this: I think we came one big step closer to finding, and hopefully convicting, the true killer of Judge Gerald Gardner."

I eventually broke away from the press and made the short walk to the Compound, where Layla and the Leg had reconvened. The jail had Layla's phone number and said they would call in a few hours when Amir was released. The Leg managed to speak to two jurors, both of whom said the deciding factor in their verdict was that they believed Samuel Earl Whelan had most likely committed the murder. Some other dude did it.

I heard a car door shut, and I looked through the living room window to see a black Escalade outside. Honest Abe climbed out of the back seat and was walking up toward the door of the Compound. Layla peered over my shoulder. "I called after Sam's testimony. Told him we might have a verdict today," she said.

Abe entered the house with a burst of energy. "Jimmy, you fucking did it!" He wrapped his arms around me and lifted me off the ground. "And Layla, impressive work! Truly."

"You got here quickly," I noted.

"If I were Amir, I'd want to get the hell out of Dodge." Abe planned on taking Amir back to San Francisco on the firm's private jet.

"I doubted you," Abe said, "and I was wrong."

"Apology accepted."

"That wasn't an apology. I just wanted it noted for the record because I've never been wrong before." My affection for Abe had returned.

"It'll be a couple hours until Amir is released," Layla reported.

"Great," Abe said. "Let's celebrate."

The sun was still up, but our work was done. Abe ordered a few hundred dollars' worth of sushi, beer, and sake for the table. When the waitress returned with the drinks, Abe rose to make a toast.

"A wise attorney once said, 'When the facts are on your side, pound the facts. When the law is on your side, pound the law. But when neither the facts nor the law is on your side, pound the table.' From what I hear, you had to pound all three of those things and in perfect harmony to create one beautiful song with a two-word chorus: *not guilty*."

We pounded the table and drank our sake. Abe told his favorite war stories from trials in New York. I shared a myth or two about my father and the legendary clients he'd had. Layla talked about the most hardened criminals she'd put away and the dumb mistakes guilty people make. The Leg told us of her own arrest south of the border and her pledge never to get busted in a foreign country again. We laughed and imbibed, and for the first time at a celebratory dinner, I wasn't merely passing through on my way to the next event. I belonged there with my team, and we enjoyed our victory together.

"Hey, Euch," the Leg said, pulling me aside. "Charlotte Mayhew gave me her number this afternoon. Said she wants to meet up. What do you think that might be about?"

"I think she's writing a book and needs as many sources as she can gather."

"You don't think maybe she just wanted to get drinks with me?"

That hadn't even occurred to me, but I could tell by the look on the Leg's face that she was hoping the reporter had been asking her out. "Oh. I don't know," I said, backtracking. "You ought to find out."

"All right," she said with a glimmer of optimism.

"But don't give her any privileged intel," I warned.

"You got it, boss."

As I returned to my seat, Layla excused herself to go to the restroom and indiscreetly squeezed my arm as she left the table.

Abe scooted his chair right up against mine. "We need to talk," he said.

"Look, Abe, Layla and I are consenting adults. It's not really your business." I maintained eye contact so he'd know I was being sincere.

"That's not what I wanted to talk about, or for that matter, what I even wanted to know about, Jimmy. But thank you for keeping me abreast of your romantic endeavors."

Suddenly, I felt pretty stupid.

"The Medallion case will be moved out of EDTX," Abe said. "Maybe the Eastern District of Virginia or hopefully the Northern District of California since I can imagine Amir would prefer sleeping in his own bed at night. You won't be working on that one, but I want to talk about our relationship moving forward."

"Being your exclusive local counsel would be nice," I said.

"It would be," he replied.

"But?"

"But Jay Knox is going to get confirmed as the next federal judge of the Eastern District of Texas. And you accused him of murder."

If Abe was concerned about how that would impact my ability to represent clients, then I was sure every other intellectual property firm would be terrified of me as well.

"I suppose that could have rubbed him the wrong way," I said.

"He'll be back in Marshall at the end of the week. Talk to him, feel him out, grovel if you must," Abe said. "Use some of that charm, Jimmy. Otherwise, you may have already tried your last patent case."

As Layla walked back toward the table, I thought about how much I'd enjoyed working with her, and how much I'd hoped it wouldn't be our last time. I figured I'd better come up with a damn fine apology for Judge Knox. But that could wait. I wanted to savor our victory just a little while longer.

We stood in the parking lot of the Harrison County Jail. My truck was parked right behind Abe's rented Escalade. Amir emerged dressed in the clothes he had been wearing when he was arrested that first night. He looked relieved to be breathing free air again. Still, there was something somber about his liberation. Ordinarily, when a defendant's life is saved, the welcoming committee would be full of family and friends, overjoyed loved ones who have come to bring him home. In Amir's case, not even Haq remained. All he had were three lawyers.

Abe gave Amir a big hug, and for the first time, I saw Amir smile. Abe explained that the Escalade was his getaway car and that a Cessna Citation was standing by at the Harrison County Airport to take him wherever he wanted to go.

"I appreciate it," Amir said. He moved to Layla. "Thank you for staying with me."

"You're welcome," she said with a sincere smile.

He glanced at Abe. "I want her on my team, a hundred percent of the time," he insisted.

"Absolutely," Abe said, trying to conceal his glee that inherent in Amir's demand was the assurance that he would retain Gordon & Greene's services for his patent litigation needs.

Amir approached me. We looked at each other for a beat without saying anything. "We're all put on this planet for a purpose," he said. "The lucky ones are those who figure out what their purpose is."

Even when he was trying to be nice, Amir irritated me. Still, he wasn't wrong. The case had changed both of us, and I was probably better for it.

"Stay out of trouble," I said. I was glad my work with him was done. We shook hands, and then he climbed into the SUV with Abe. I expected Amir would enjoy great financial success in his life. Ultimately, he'd have to decide for himself if what he'd given up was worth it.

Layla and I watched the Escalade disappear into the night; then we got in my truck and drove to the Compound.

We picked up a nice bottle of wine on our way back. Layla had the foresight to insist we buy a corkscrew as well. When I opened the bottle, she suggested we let it breathe. It was the first time we made love that night, and it wouldn't be the last. Every moment, every touch felt as if our time together was fading. I couldn't bring myself to say it out loud, but I'd hoped this wasn't going to be the end for us. I wanted to believe she felt the same.

Celebration gave way to passion, which ultimately gave way to something else. We stayed in bed, talking and laughing until night threatened to become day. When her alarm rang out in the morning, I could have sworn we had just closed our eyes.

While she showered and packed her belongings, I went out and got us coffee one last time. I had offered to drive her to Dallas, but she needed to return her rental car at the airport. It was probably better that way. The drive could have been awkward or sad, and I didn't want anything to diminish the perfect night we had just spent together.

I carried her remaining luggage out of the Compound and placed it in the trunk of her car. We met at the driver's-side door, standing face-to-face.

"This is exactly how I expected my first patent case to go," she said.

I let out a nervous laugh. I thought about all the things I could say and all the things I knew I shouldn't.

We embraced and shared our sadness for as long as we could. She wiped her eyes as she pulled away and uttered, "Bye, James," as she climbed into the car.

"Goodbye," I said. I watched her pull the car away, make a left turn, and then disappear. I reached into my pocket and pulled out my smokes. There was only one left. I fired it up and then threw the empty pack, along with my pink lighter, into a trash can on the corner. I drove away from the Compound with nowhere to go.

THIRTY- FOUR

A couple of nights later, I was back into a good routine. I was sucking on nicotine lozenges and adhering to my three-drink limit. I was excited for the unknowns that lay ahead and wanted to be prepared to embrace whatever came my way.

There was a knock on my door, and I was pleasantly surprised to discover that the Leg was stopping by to pay me a visit. She had a six-pack of Miller Lite, which we broke into immediately. We moved to the porch to chat.

"How'd it go with the journalist?" I asked.

"I thought it was going great. She seemed really into me, asked me all sorts of questions about myself. Then, about halfway through, I realized it wasn't a date."

"Ouch."

"Yeah."

"She wanted information?"

"She wanted to offer me a job," the Leg said. "Researcher. For her book."

I shifted in my seat, concerned about the potential conflict of interest.

"Relax," she said, "I told her no. I don't want to spend the next six months traveling back and forth to Silicon Valley. Those tech people

are weird. Mayhew kept using words like 'optionality' and 'abroga-
tion.' I didn't even know what the hell she was talking about."

"Did she pump you for information?" I asked.

"I didn't give her anything that was privileged. The last thing I'd
want to do is jeopardize the prosecution of Samuel Earl Whelan,
may he rot in prison."

"I wasn't worried. You're a pro, Lisa."

"Thanks, Euch." She took a drink. "You think maybe you and I
can keep working together?"

"I'd like that," I said. "I'm meeting with Judge Knox tomorrow.
That conversation may have a big impact on the direction of my
career."

"I guess you should have thought of that before you wrongly
accused him of murder."

"Maybe there's more out there than patent law."

The Leg passed me another beer.

I looked at the woods, to the point where the trees met the night.
My thoughts were running away from me.

"Are you heartbroken, Euch?"

I looked at her and thought before answering.

"Not yet."

I hadn't set foot in the federal courthouse in three months, not since
I had been summoned by Judge Knox right after the murder. Walking back in gave me an uneasy feeling. The building hadn't changed,
but the aura was completely different. I wasn't sure if I belonged
there anymore.

I entered Judge Knox's old chambers and found Tammy Tex
standing on top of her desk, removing red, white, and blue decora-
tions she'd hung from the ceiling in honor of Texas Independence
Day a few weeks back.

"Hey, Tammy," I said with a smile. She glared at me. As Knox's faithful assistant, she was going to harbor some resentment toward me for a long time. I wondered if her boss would do the same. "I'm here to see Judge Knox."

Tammy picked up her phone and pressed a button. "Your Honor, your four o'clock appointment is here." She listened for a moment and then hung up. "Have a seat, Mr. Euchre. The judge will be with you momentarily."

"Thank you, Tammy," I said with even more cheer than my original greeting. Her cold-shoulder routine was amusing, particularly because she was one of the sweetest people in town. I decided I'd kill her with kindness.

"Longhorns could be good this year," I speculated. She stared at me and then stood up and marched out of the office, apparently unable to share a room with me any longer.

My phone vibrated. Detective Elliot was calling.

"Hey, Detective, I'm about to walk into a meeting," I said.

"I just finished interviewing Brianna Lopez. Do you know her?"

"I know all the bartenders in this town," I responded.

"Right. Well, she was working the late shift the night Judge Gardner was killed."

Brianna was in her forties and had tended bar and waited tables in half the establishments in Marshall. Her current place of employment was O'Shea's, a bar that didn't have an ounce of Irish blood in it. I often went there for happy hour because it was five blocks from the courthouse.

"Ms. Lopez claimed that Samuel Earl stopped by O'Shea's the night of the murder."

"OK," I said.

"She said Sam stayed at the bar and drank through last call. They left a few minutes after 2:00 a.m. and went back to her place. He was there until the morning. He'd had so much to drink that she insisted on driving. They took her car."

I felt like I could vomit.

292 · JOEY HARTSTONE

"Maybe she's mistaken," I suggested. "Could have been a different night."

"That's why I waited to call you until now," Elliot said. "I just
reviewed the security footage from the bar. She's telling the truth. Sam
arrived shortly after getting kicked out of the Christmas party. He
was in there until close and left with Brianna. He was never alone; he
never went to his car. There's no way he killed Gardner."

Judge Knox opened his office door.

"I've got to go, Detective. I'll call you later." I hung up.

"Come on in, James."

"Thank you, Your Honor."

As I followed the judge into his office, I fired off the shortest text
message I could type: "Sam innocent."

I knew that my future in intellectual property law rested entirely on
this meeting, but my mind was flailing. Sam's drunken hookup was
an airtight alibi. I tried to put it out of my head though, just long
enough to hopefully salvage my relationship with Knox, as well as
my career.

"Thank you for agreeing to meet with me, Your Honor."

"Excuse the mess. Things have been piling up in my absence." He
cleared away some papers that comprised only a fraction of the clut-
ter on his desk. He continued to move around, straightening up the
office while we spoke.

"How is the confirmation process going?" I asked.

"I've met with nearly every senator on the Hill and attended more
luncheons than I ever thought I'd have to in one lifetime. The vetting is fairly intense."

"I can imagine."

"Everything seems to be falling into place though. There was
that small hiccup, of course, when I was accused of killing my
predecessor."

"Look, Your Honor, I've always known you to be fair, but I understand that you are human, too. If the situations were reversed, I'd be pretty pissed off. And I'm not sure I could get over it. I accept that we may not be able to put this behind us, but if that's the case, could you let me know so I can start looking for another line of work?"

He began discarding junk mail into the trash and opening other envelopes as he spoke. "Before I was a judge, I, too, was a young lawyer. And I stepped in it myself a time or two, though I never crossed a member of the court the way you did." He paused to read the opening line of a piece of mail and then decided it wasn't important and dropped it in the wastebasket.

"Given the victory you just had," he continued, "I half expected you to decide to change your practice and become a hotshot criminal lawyer. There'd be no better way to launch a new career than off of the momentum of winning the case of a lifetime. Besides, when it comes to criminal law in the state of Texas, your name means something. Your father's memory looms large. I would imagine a lot of firms would be interested in the son of Robert Euchre." He paused to skim a handwritten card, a message of congratulations for his upcoming career advancement, I figured.

"But," he continued as he set the card aside, "you're a valuable member of this community, and I know how highly Judge Gardner thought of you. That goes a long way with me. So to answer your question, no, I don't think this has to permanently taint our relationship. Assuming I do get confirmed as federal judge of the Eastern District, I trust that you and I can figure out a way to start with a clean slate."

Under normal circumstances, those words would have been music to my ears. But I barely heard them at all. Judge Knox was opening his mail, piece by piece. I had become fixated not on what he was doing but on what he was doing it with. In his hand, he held a shiny letter opener with a six-inch blade and a handle of red, white, and blue stone that looked like the Texas state flag.

"Where did you get that?" I asked.

"What?"

"The letter opener."

"It was a Christmas gift from my assistant. I don't love it, if I'm being honest, but she'd be crushed if I didn't use it."

"Your Honor," I said as I leapt to my feet, "I thank you for your time. Best of luck in Washington."

I left his office before he could even say goodbye. As I rushed past his assistant's empty desk, I yelled, "I love you, Tammy Tex!"

· THIRTY-FIVE ·

I flew home in my truck, speeding to the point of recklessness. But I had a burning question. I ran to my bedroom. I went to the back of my closet and looked at the pile of clothes that included my best suit and shirt, still bloodied from the eligibility hearing in which Amir had punched me. It was everything from the day and night of the murder. I wasn't sure I'd find anything under that pile, but as I sifted through the articles of clothing, there it was, right where I'd put it a lifetime ago. The gift-wrapped box Judge Gardner had given me after the party had been buried among my dirty clothes since December. Tammy Tex had given the same gift to all of the judges, and Gardner had passed his off to me. I'd never opened it. I'd forgotten all about it. I trembled with fear as I unwrapped the Texas flag paper and saw what was inside.

It took a couple of phone calls, but I finally got the address I needed. Dusk settled as my truck headed out on Highway 43. After big trials, people scatter. Clients return to their lives while lawyers need a break from theirs. Even judges take vacations.

I drove seventeen miles northeast toward the state line, past Karnack and into the town of Uncertain, Texas, population fewer than one hundred, and shrinking. A couple of people from Marshall and Tyler owned cabins out that way, which they used as bases of operation for hunting and fishing when they went to Caddo Lake.

I killed the headlights as I pulled up and put my truck in park. I stared down the gravel walkway at the small cabin made of lumber, likely sourced from Piney Woods. I grabbed my phone and Judge Gardner's letter opener, and I exited the vehicle.

A light was on inside. I heard the radio go quiet before I reached the door. I didn't imagine people got a lot of house calls out there, so I half-expected to be greeted by the working end of a rifle.

"Who's there?" I heard a voice holler from inside.

"It's James Euchre," I called back, trying to sound strong but nonthreatening.

I heard a few more steps inside and then Judge Whelan opened the door.

"What in the hell are you doing out here?" the old man asked.

"We need to talk, Your Honor."

He opened the door to let me enter. I could see that he did indeed own a rifle, a Remington Model Seven, which was bolt action, and I suspected he knew how to handle it. It wasn't in his hands though. He had it leaning next to the front door, and as I walked inside, I was keenly aware that he stayed between me and the gun the entire time.

"I come out here for peace and quiet. You're the last person I want to see right now."

"I'll make it quick. I spoke with Detective Elliot today and your son has an alibi." He breathed a sigh of relief, and I continued. "He went straight from the Christmas party to a bar that night and got pretty hammered."

"He does that," the judge said.

"He also went home with a bartender, spent the whole night with her."

"He does that, too."

"I figured I'd put you through enough and that you deserved to hear it immediately. I owed you that much."

"You're not a bad lawyer, Mr. Euchre; you just don't know a damn thing about criminal law. You had no business trying a murder case."

He was an ungracious prick, that much was becoming clear to me.

"It was arrogance on your part. You should have to answer for that."

I couldn't tell if he was trying to get under my skin or if it was just a natural by-product of his personality. Either way, I hadn't come there for a performance review.

"I did something right. My client was acquitted," I said.

"You may have helped a killer escape justice. Not really an accomplishment in my book."

As we stood facing each other, I took stock of my surroundings. There was a sitting area with a couch and a chair pulled up to the fireplace and a small table in a nearby corner. The walls were lined with the heads of wildlife that had once roamed the surrounding areas. I didn't have an opinion one way or the other about hunters, but I found trophies to be the sign of a fragile ego.

"I don't know how I got it so wrong," I said. "Your son had motive, he had means, and he had opportunity. He was at the party, he was a trained hunter, and Gardner was threatening to end his career. It all added up."

"Your client had motive, means, and opportunity as well, Mr. Euchre. And, unlike my boy, he has no alibi."

"Still, something is bothering me about Sam," I suggested.

"It's time to go," he said.

"Why'd he take the Fifth?" I asked.

"Any lawyer worth his salt would have done that."

"Yeah, but that's the problem; Sam's not worth his salt."

He looked surprised by my lack of respect. As Sam's father, I assume he had wrestled many times with the fact that his son wasn't the brightest bulb in the pack. Still, he didn't want to hear that from the likes of me.

"You were accusing him of murder," Judge Whelan said, defending Sam.

"But he had an alibi, and a pretty easy one to check out," I said.

"He was protecting himself," the judge said, as he put his hands in his pockets.

"I think he was protecting someone else," I said. "I actually think that, for the first time since I've known him, Sam was one step ahead of me. When I asked him about the oil stains in the parking lot, right next to the end of the trail of blood, he could have just said, 'Some woman drove me home that night. I was never even in my car.' But he didn't. He knew those oil stains had come from his vehicle. And I'm wondering if he didn't suspect that maybe someone else used his car that night to escape."

I'll never know if it was unconscious or not, but right when I mentioned someone else driving Sam's car, Judge Whelan stopped shaking the key ring in his pocket. I would have bet a million dollars that the night of the murder, the night Sam got cut off by the servers at the party, his father had confiscated his keys.

"Get off my property," the judge said, his voice low but firm.

"Don't you want to hear my new theory?" I asked.

"You've been wrong twice. You really want to go for that third strike, Mr. Euchre?"

"I'll risk it," I said. "Samuel Earl received a letter the day of the party from the Texas State Bar disciplinary committee. It came with a copy of Judge Gardner's formal complaint against him. Sam went to the party, fired up, had some drinks, and started to feel like a man who knew he was about to lose everything. That's why he asked me, of all people, to do him a favor. He probably had half a mind to confront Judge Gardner, too. But you knew that wouldn't help. I think you told him to go home and sleep it off. You told him you'd take care of it. Later that night, you left the party, and who did you happen upon in that parking lot? Judge Gardner. You asked him, judge to judge, for a professional courtesy. You wanted him to go easy on Sam. But Gerald Gardner was a stubborn old man. He refused to rescind his complaint. Your son was going to get what was coming to him. And you snapped. Maybe it was hatred for your colleague or maybe an innate desire to protect your boy. Maybe it was a combination of the two. Something in you was triggered. You stabbed Judge Gardner, stunning him with the first wound and killing him with the second. You ripped open his carotid artery just like you'd done to a hundred wild animals, just like you'd trained your son to do. Then you reached into that pocket where you're always rattling your key chain, and you remembered that you'd taken the keys to your drunk son's Mercedes. You ran to the edge of the parking lot, got into his car, and escaped. Maybe Sam put it together a while back, or maybe he was so hungover he couldn't remember how his car got home that night. But when I pointed a finger at Samuel Earl in court, he knew better than to offer an alibi because even though he hadn't killed Judge Gardner, he realized his father had."

I held Judge Whelan's stare. I never let the rifle leave my peripheral vision.

"That's a very compelling theory, Mr. Euchre. Too bad you can't prove any of it."

"Sam's car has been impounded. They're testing it for blood right now. A crime like that, in the heat of passion with no planning, it makes a mess. You may have taken a sponge and hose to it, but there's no way you scrubbed it clean. I also wonder, did you drive straight home that night? Maybe your first move was to ditch the weapon. You went out to some dump or abandoned lot where you thought you could disappear a piece of evidence. You probably didn't realize that your idiot son's ridiculous car has a tracking system. We'll be able to pinpoint its every move that night. If you did stop somewhere, the authorities are going to search every inch of that area. But even if we never find the murder weapon, rest assured that I've got the next best thing: a missing weapon."

I reached into my jacket pocket and removed the Texas flag letter opener.

"Tammy Tex is such a sweet lady. She gave every judge the same Christmas gift that night. I saw Judge Knox's earlier today. He was using it to open his mail. This one was meant for Judge Gardner, but he gave it to me. I'd forgotten all about it. Didn't even know what was inside the box until this afternoon. I know Tammy gave you one as well. You opened it at the party, probably didn't think much of it. But then, when you confronted Judge Gardner and things started to turn south, you remembered the letter opener, right there in your pocket, with its brand-new six-inch blade. You thrust it into your colleague's neck and took his life. If I'm wrong, you ought to have no problem producing the blade. And you ought to have no problem with the police testing it for DNA. What do you say, Judge?"

"I'll be goddamned," he said. "You finally got it right."

When Judge Whelan made a move for the rifle, I didn't hesitate. If my instinct had been to run away, there's no question he'd have taken me down. But I was a cornerback in high school. I was trained to charge straight at my opponent. I heard the shot ring out, but with all the adrenaline coursing through my veins, I didn't feel the twenty-two-caliber round pierce my torso. I lowered my head and drove my shoulder into the judge's gut. He fumbled the rifle as we fell to the floor.

I began swinging, landing left after right, pummeling the bastard's face. At first, it was defensive. I needed to protect myself from getting killed. But at some point, it turned into something else. He had been subdued, but I didn't let up. He was helpless, but I couldn't stop. Whatever rage drove him to commit murder was now inside my body. He had transferred it to me. I knew I was going to kill him.

But something made me stop. It might have been the sound that escaped the old man's lungs. It was weak and pathetic, a noise that inspired pity instead of wrath. Or maybe it was something else. They say your life flashes before your eyes right as you're about to die. I don't know if that's true. But I do know that my life flashed before my eyes just as I was about to end Judge Whelan's. To my surprise, there were things I saw that I wasn't ready to lose.

I let my bloodied fists fall to my side. I rolled off the judge and stood up. That's when I realized I was bleeding and that I'd been shot. As I tried to determine the extent of my injury, I didn't see Judge

Whelan locate his .357 Magnum from a duffel bag nearby. With his back on the ground, he fired upward at me, striking my left shoulder and knocking me backward onto the floor. My eyes focused on the ceiling above me, and just as quickly as I had concluded that I didn't want to die, I was sure I was about to do just that.

A lot happened in the next three seconds. I heard a bang, but this time it sounded like a more distant explosion. The noise was a combination of Detective Elliot's service weapon firing and the bullet smashing the window on its way through the cabin and into Judge Whelan's body. The judge dropped to his knees, and I lifted my head just in time to see the Leg burst through the front door, knock Whelan to the ground with the butt of his own rifle, and then use that Division I foot of hers to strike him across the face.

By the time she was helping me sit up, Detective Elliot already had Judge Whelan in handcuffs.

"How the hell did you guys get here?" I asked.

Detective Elliot nodded in the Leg's direction.

"Your text," she said.

"She reasoned that if the oil stains were from Sam's car, someone else may have driven it that night."

"Had to be a family member," the Leg said.

Elliot recited the Miranda warning to the judge and then looked at me. "Even if we can't pin Gardner's murder on him, we have him on attempted with you."

"I got him on everything," I said as I reached into my pocket and removed my cell phone. I held it up so that Whelan could see. The screen showed that it had been recording the whole time.

"Texas penal code, section 16.02. This is a one-party consent state," I said. "Hey, would you look at that: I guess I do know a little bit about criminal law." I put the phone back in my pocket and moved closer to the handcuffed judge. "As you're dying in prison, don't ever forget it was a patent lawyer who put you there."

Detective Elliot escorted Whelan out of the house while the Leg inspected my wounds. She determined they weren't life-threatening and I was going to survive. I wasn't confident she had the training to make such an assessment, but I didn't really feel like I was dying. She wanted to wait for an ambulance, but I pointed out that there was no hospital in Uncertain, Texas, and that the EMTs would be coming from Marshall anyway, so we'd get to a doctor quicker if we took my truck. The Leg agreed to drive. I considered asking her to put me in the bed of the Dodge so I wouldn't bleed on my new seats, but I knew she'd probably ignore that request. As the Leg sped down the highway, I stared out the window, a passenger in my own vehicle.

THIRTY-SIX

We all have blind spots. Mine was believing that people are selfish, that a killer's motive must have been to protect himself. I couldn't see that the true impulse was a father looking out for his son. That kind of love was outside my field of vision.

After I was released from the hospital, I drove to the town square. I parked my truck on the street and walked to the hand-laid redbrick parking lot where it all began. It was early morning, so the lot was empty and I was alone. I had never properly grieved for Judge Gardner. I had experienced the love of a father once; it just hadn't come from the man who had given me life. It had come from the man who had given my life its purpose. He was the same man who had created this little universe in the Eastern District of Texas.

I knelt by the spot where he had died. Despite the city's best efforts, the bricks were still stained with his blood. It was another town secret that would forever be etched into our collective memory, never to be forgotten. I said a prayer for him and then rose to my feet.

Behind me stood the new Harrison County Courthouse, where Judge Roy Whelan had reigned. It turned out he hadn't ditched the letter opener. He was worried that if anyone found it, it would lead right to him. He'd hidden it in his home, trusting that if anyone came looking for it, they already knew the truth. Detective Elliot sent the

304 · JOEY HARTSTONE

letter opener to the FBI in Dallas, and Agent Hull expedited the testing that night. The results came back positive for two substances: a lot of bleach and a microscopic amount of Judge Gardner's blood. Whelan would plead guilty to murder and spend the rest of his life in prison.

To my left stood the federal courthouse. I imagined one day soon Jay Knox would be confirmed by the United States Senate and would succeed Judge Gardner as the keeper of the Rocket Docket. I would be welcomed back to the world of patent law, assuming I wanted to return.

In front of me stood the old Harrison County Courthouse. It was the most beautiful building in town. It was also where my career as a criminal defense lawyer had begun. It was another universe unto itself, a place that a piece of me still yearned to explore.

Theoretical physicists believe that if two universes were to collide, the impact would cause disturbances in the space-time continuum. Nothing quite so drastic had happened here, though my existence had been disrupted permanently. My options were as varied as the buildings that surrounded me. Perhaps I would return to patent law and the world Judge Gardner had built. Or maybe I'd go forth with criminal law, in the world my father had once inhabited. Possibly there was a third option, a way for me to exist in both worlds at once. These were Texas-sized problems, but they would have to wait.

My phone vibrated in my pocket. It was the call I'd been waiting for since the moment I'd left the cabin in Uncertain.

"Hello, Kalamazoo."

"Are you OK?" Layla asked with insistence in her voice.

"I am."

"What happened?"

I thought about everything, from the evidence I had uncovered, to my confrontation with Judge Whelan, to my getting shot. There was so much to share.

"It's a really good story," I said. "Why don't I come to New York and tell you all about it?"

"Drive to Dallas," Layla said. "I'm buying your ticket right now." I told her I was on my way, and I hung up the phone.

In our final conversation, Gerald Gardner had warned me that my life was shrinking, that it was threatening to fade away. What I'd come to understand was that just because this was a small town, the life of someone in it didn't have to be small. So, with East Texas in my rearview, I headed west on I-20 to catch a flight from DFW to JFK in the hopes that my little life still had room to grow. I would return to Marshall, though. Universes have their own gravitational pulls, and sooner or later, we find our way home.

Acknowledgments

President Kennedy famously said, "Victory has a hundred fathers and defeat is an orphan." If this novel is a success by any metric, it is a credit to the many people who contributed their time and talent to it. If it falls short, the responsibility lies solely with me.

Throughout the course of writing this book, I was reminded over and over how lucky I am to have a remarkable group of friends in my life. One of the first to read an early draft was Rachael Dillon Fried. Fortunately, not only is she a close friend, she is also a world-class literary agent at Sanford J. Greenburger Associates. Her enthusiasm for this project and support for me made everything possible. It's an honor to be represented by someone so wonderful.

Jonas Brooks and Jon Cassir at Creative Artists Agency have fostered my career in television and film for many years. Their guidance keeps me focused, and their encouragement renews my optimism. Jeff Hynick at Jackoway Austen Tyerman has similarly supported me and provided me his counsel. I couldn't ask to be part of a better team.

I want to thank the group at Doubleday for their impressive work in turning a manuscript into a book. This journey begins and ends with Rob Bloom, my editor. Rob mined these chapters for every nugget of story and then polished that story so it would shine. I am tremendously grateful for his commitment to this project and the application of his craft. Likewise, this book wouldn't exist without the faith that Bill Thomas showed from the start. Nora Grubb, Nicole Pedersen, Johanna Zwirner, Cassandra Pappas, and Michael Windsor all worked incredibly hard to bring this book to life. Thank you to Carol Rutan for her attention to detail.

On September 22, 2016, this endeavor began—as many good stories do—over a few drinks with an old friend. When Nathan Speed, an intellectual property lawyer from Boston, mentioned that his work frequently took him to the unlikely town of Marshall, Texas, I knew we had stumbled into fertile territory. I'm grateful for that random Thursday night and for every moment after, when Nathan continued to humor me as I searched for this tale.

Anyone in my life who has a law degree has undoubtedly donated their time and energy to tutoring me on the finer points of the legal universe. Kathleen Cannon went above and beyond her duties as an aunt, as she has many times. I would imagine she didn't choose a career as a criminal defense attorney so that it would benefit her nephew's writing, but it most certainly has had that effect. I thank her from the bottom of my heart. Her expertise was essential in the crafting of this narrative.

Thank you to Eric Albritton, who regaled me with fascinating stories about the people of Marshall and the history of the Eastern District. Thank you to Tegan Shohet, who graciously lets me use her brilliant legal mind as my own personal LexisNexis.

I have many family members who contributed to this book. Demian Wyma, my cousin who answers all of my questions about law enforcement. Felix Borner, my brother-in-law who, thankfully, is a much better pilot than I ever was. Bryan and Cathy Ronck, my in-laws who root for me as if I were their own child. Laura Borner, my little sister who refuses to let me get away with holes in my story. Sandy Hartstone and Jamie Slee—anyone would be lucky to have a mother who is endlessly supportive; I am fortunate to have two.

I am grateful to those people who were willing to read this book in its early form. To Valerie Rosenberg, for her discerning mind.

To Beth Leedham, for her insight. To Michelle King, for her mentorship. To Liz Glotzer, whose unending generosity and friendship mean more to me than she could possibly know.

Everything begins and ends with my wife, Abby. You are present on every page of this book, just as you are in every moment of my life. Thank you for lending your knowledge, perspective, and talent to this project. You add honesty and depth to all that we do. I love looking at you, over our laptops, as we work together, often with Teddy on one of our knees. I continue to adore you, as I always have and always will.

JOEY HARTSTONE is a film and television writer. He has written two feature films, *LBJ* (2016) and *Shock and Awe* (2017), which were both directed by Rob Reiner. He wrote on the first two seasons of the legal drama *The Good Fight*. He is currently a writer on the Showtime series *Your Honor.* Joey lives in Los Angeles with his family.